INVISIBLE WEAPONS

John Rhode was a pseudonym for the author Cecil Street (1884–1964), who also wrote as Miles Burton and Cecil Waye. Having served in the British Army as an artillery officer during the First World War, rising to the rank of Major, he began writing non-fiction before turning to detective fiction, and produced four novels a year for thirty-seven years.

As his list of detective stories grew, so did the public's appetite for his particular blending of humdrum everyday life with the startling appearance of the most curious kind of crimes. It was the *Sunday Times* who said of John Rhode that 'he must hold the record for the invention of ingenious forms of murder', and the *Times Literary Supplement* described him as 'standing in the front rank of those who write detective fiction'.

Rhode's first series novel, *The Paddington Mystery* (1925), introduced Dr Lancelot Priestley, who went on to appear in 72 novels, many of them for Collins Crime Club. The Priestley books are classics of scientific detection, with the elderly Dr Priestley demonstrating how apparently impossible crimes have been carried out, and they are now highly sought after by collectors.

D1355089

915 00000178831

By the same author

Death at Breakfast
Mystery at Olympia

JOHN RHODE

Invisible Weapons

COLLINS
CRIME
CLUB

COLLINS CRIME CLUB

An imprint of HarperCollins*Publishers*
1 London Bridge Street
London SE1 9GF
www.harpercollins.co.uk

This paperback edition 2018

First published in Great Britain by Collins Crime Club 1938

Copyright © Estate of John Rhode 1938

John Rhode asserts his moral right to be identified as the author of this work

A catalogue record for this book is available from the British Library

ISBN 978-0-00-826881-7

Typeset in Sabon by Palimpsest Book Production Ltd, Falkirk, Stirlingshire

Printed and bound in Great Britain
by CPI Group (UK) Ltd, Croydon CR0 4YY

MIX
Paper from
responsible sources

FSC
www.fsc.org
FSC™ C007454

This book is produced from independently certified FSC™ paper
to ensure responsible forest management.

For more information visit: www.harpercollins.co.uk/green

Contents

PART ONE

The Adderminster Affair

CHAPTER I

It was very hot in the charge-room of Adderminster Police Station. Sergeant Cload mopped his head with one hand while he held the telephone receiver with the other.

'Yes, sir, yes, sir,' he repeated at intervals. 'Certainly, sir, I will take the necessary steps at once. I'm very sorry that you have been subjected to this annoyance. Good-morning, sir.'

He put the instrument aside and growled. 'Alfie Prince again!' he exclaimed. 'I don't know what we're going to do about that chap, Linton.'

'What's he been up to now?' asked Constable Linton, the only other occupant of the room.

'Oh, the same old game. Going round to people's houses asking for fags and cursing if he doesn't get them. This time it's Colonel Exbury. It seems that he went round there and that the colonel had the devil of a job to get rid of him. He's not a bit pleased and wants to know what we mean to do about it.'

'I can't make Alfie out,' said Linton, scratching his head.

3

'He'll do a day's job with anybody in the town when he feels like it. And then all of a sudden he'll take it into his head to go round annoying folk. And it isn't that he gets drunk, for I've never heard of anybody who's seen him the worse for liquor.'

'He's not right, that's what it is,' replied the sergeant confidently. 'I don't mean that he's out and out mad, but he comes over all batty now and then. I wonder, now!'

Again the sergeant mopped his face with that enormous pocket handkerchief. 'Damn this heat!' he exclaimed. 'It's enough to drive anyone batty. What I was wondering is whether the folk at the asylum could do Alfie any good if he went in there for a bit.'

Linton shook his head. 'He'd never go, not unless he was forced to,' he replied. 'As it is he'll never sleep within four walls if he can help it.'

'I know. That's just the difficulty. Still, something might be done if we went the right way about it. I tell you what, Dr Thornborough would help us. He'd never mind being asked to do a thing like that.'

'Like what?' Linton asked.

'I'm coming to that. It's not a bit of good our bringing Alfie before the Bench, for you know as well as I do what would happen. They'd fine him with the option. Alfie's mother would pay the fine and we shouldn't be any further forward than we were before. He'd go on pestering folk and giving us a lot of trouble.'

'We'll have to do something. It wouldn't do to upset the colonel.'

'That's just it. Now if we could get Alfie put away for a bit it wouldn't do any harm and might do a lot of good. And that's just where Dr Thornborough comes in.'

The sergeant glanced at the clock as he continued. 'It's just a quarter to one now; the doctor always gets home for lunch round about one o'clock. Jump on your bike and slip up to his place in Gunthorpe Road. I never can pronounce the name of it. Tell him what we think about Alfie and ask him if he can manage to have a quiet chat with him. And then if he thinks that Alfie ought to be put away we'll know what to do about it.'

This conversation took place on Saturday, June 12. Linton mounted his bicycle and rode through the little town until he reached Gunthorpe Road on its outskirts. He passed the public gardens and museum on his right, and a single small detached house on his left. Thus he reached a new and substantial-looking house which bore upon its drive gates the unusual name *Epidaurus*.

The gates were open and Linton turned in at the first he came to. He dismounted, left his bicycle at the end of the short semi-circular drive, and walked to the front door. It was opened by a smart and capable-looking parlourmaid who smiled as she recognised him. 'Good-morning, Mr Linton,' she said primly.

'Good-morning, miss,' Linton replied with official gravity. 'I was wondering if I could speak to the doctor for a moment.'

'He's not back from his rounds yet, though he's sure to be in before long. Mrs Thornborough is in, if you'd like to see her?'

'I'd rather wait and see the doctor, if there's no objection.'

The parlourmaid stood aside to let him enter and, as she did so a young and remarkably pretty woman appeared in the hall. 'Hullo, Linton,' she exclaimed. 'What's your business? Anything I can do for you?'

'Thank you, mam,' Linton replied. 'But I've got a message from the sergeant for the doctor.'

'Then you'd better wait for him in the consulting-room. Take Linton in there, will you, Lucy, and see that he has a glass of beer while he's waiting.'

The parlourmaid showed Linton into the consulting-room and a few moments later appeared with a glass and a jug on a tray. 'Can't stop and share it with you, as I'm busy,' she said as she frisked out again. In her haste she omitted to shut the door properly and it remained slightly ajar.

The consulting-room lay at the back of the house, and its window, which was open, commanded a view of the kitchen garden and of the garage at the end of it. Linton noticed that the garage was empty and that its doors were propped back. He poured himself out a glass of beer, sampled it and then sat down.

The door being ajar he could hear sounds of activity within the house. From the dining-room came a subdued clatter of plates and cutlery. Lucy was obviously laying the table for lunch. The kitchen premises were divided from the rest of the house by a baize door, impervious to sound or smell. The notes of a piano, strummed softly but ably, reached Linton from the drawing-room. And then as he took a second draught of beer the soft purr of an approaching car reached his ears. That must be the doctor, of course.

The car entered the drive and stopped outside the front door. Linton wiped his lips and stood up ready to greet Dr Thornborough. But, contrary to his expectations, he did not hear the front door open. An instant later, an electric bell rang insistently somewhere in the back premises.

The clattering in the dining-room came to an immediate stop. Linton heard Lucy hasten with tripping steps to the front door and open it. Next a deep voice which Linton did not recognise, and a heavy step in the hall. A visitor, obviously. Whoever it was, Lucy must have shown him into the drawing-room, for the piano stopped abruptly. Before the drawing-room door closed again, Linton heard Mrs Thornborough's voice raised in a tone of complete amazement. It seemed, then, that the visitor must be unexpected.

A minute later Linton heard the sound of a car being driven down the carriage way beside the house towards the garage. Was it the doctor's car this time? No, it wasn't. As soon as it came in sight Linton saw that. It was a very smart-looking Armstrong-Siddeley limousine, driven by an elderly and rather surly-looking chauffeur. It came to rest inside the garage. The chauffeur dismounted, and walked slowly round it. Then he produced a packet of cigarettes from an inside pocket, chose one and lighted it. Having thrown away the match, he propped himself negligently against the garage door-post.

The drawing-room door opened again and a heavy footstep crossed the hall. Linton heard the sound of another door being opened. It was shut immediately and the click of a lock followed. Somebody left the drawing-room and hurried into the dining-room. This must be Mrs Thornborough, for Linton recognised her voice as she gave instructions to Lucy. Something about it being very awkward. Cook should be asked to hold back lunch for ten minutes. And of course, another place must be laid. Oh yes, and Coates. He must be asked in to have his lunch in the kitchen. Better tell cook about it at once.

7

Linton heard her go upstairs slowly, step by step, as though upon some errand she disliked. The baize door opened and shut as Lucy went into the kitchen to break the news to cook. From somewhere on the ground floor the faint but unmistakable sound of a plug being pulled.

Followed a silence of a couple of minutes. Then an indeterminate and not very distinct sound, something between a thud and a crash. Linton supposed that cook, flustered by the arrival of this unexpected guest, had dropped something in the kitchen. He took out his watch and looked at it. Seven minutes past one. Something must have detained the doctor, for, as Linton knew, he always tried to get home by one o'clock.

A further silence of two or three minutes, then the sound of Mrs Thornborough coming downstairs again. She went into the drawing-room, leaving the door open behind her.

Then again Linton heard the sound of an approaching car. There was no doubt about it this time. It came straight in and drove rapidly down the carriage-way. Linton recognised the doctor's car with the doctor himself at the wheel. The car pulled up suddenly just short of the garage, and Dr Thornborough got out. Again Linton looked at his watch, to find that the time was now twelve minutes past one.

The surly-faced chauffeur threw away his cigarette and touched his cap. Dr Thornborough seemed to question him eagerly, to which he gave some replies. Linton could hear the sound of their voices but not what they said. Dr Thornborough hurried towards the house, which he entered by the garden door beside the consulting-room.

At the sound of this door being opened, Mrs Thornborough ran out of the drawing-room and met her husband in the hall just outside the consulting-room door. Linton could not help overhearing their conversation.

It was Mrs Thornborough who spoke first. 'Oh, Cyril, Uncle Bob's here!' she exclaimed reproachfully. 'Why on earth didn't you tell me that he was coming?'

'I know he's here, for I've spoken to Coates in the garage,' the doctor replied. 'But how could I have told you that he was coming when I didn't know myself?'

'You didn't know he was coming? But he had a letter from you this morning asking him to drive down to lunch today as you particularly wanted to see him.'

'My dear Betty! One or both of you must be suffering from delusions. I haven't written to him for weeks as you know very well. Besides, just now—'

'I know. It's absurdly thoughtless of you. I'm very much afraid that there'll be ructions.'

'Well, it can't be helped. We shall have to make the best of it. Where is Uncle Bob, by the way?'

'In the cloakroom, washing his hands. He'll be out any minute now, for he's been there quite a long time. Oh, and by the way, I almost forgot to tell you. Linton's waiting in the consulting-room to see you. He's got a message or something from the sergeant for you. You'll have time to see him before lunch because I've asked cook to put it back a few minutes.'

The door of the consulting-room opened and Dr Thornborough walked in. He was tall and slight and looked younger than his age, which was thirty-five. His normally cheerful expression was obscured by a slight frown as he greeted the constable. 'Well, Linton, what's the matter?' he inquired brusquely.

Linton started to explain the situation which had arisen

regarding Alfie Prince. But before he had got very far, the doctor, whose attention was obviously elsewhere, interrupted him.

'Alfie Prince? I saw him just now as I drove in at the gate. But look here. Excuse me a minute, there's a good fellow. I must see . . .' And he hurried out of the room, leaving the sentence unfinished.

Linton heard him go to the door of the cloakroom and rattle the handle. 'Uncle Bob!' he called. And then a second or two later, 'Uncle Bob! Unlock the door, will you? It's only me, Cyril. I want a word with you.'

Followed a pause in which every voice in the house seemed to be hushed: then Dr Thornborough battered on the door of the cloakroom with his fists. 'Uncle Bob!' he called once more.

Silence, broken only by the doctor's footsteps crossing the hall. He re-entered the consulting-room, frowning more deeply than before. 'I don't like it, Linton,' he exclaimed abruptly. 'My uncle, Mr Fransham, is in the cloakroom, and I can't get him to answer me.'

'He's been in there a good ten minutes or more, sir,' Linton replied.

'Eh!' exclaimed the doctor. 'How the devil do you know that?'

'While I was in here waiting for you, sir, I heard a gentleman go into the cloakroom and lock the door behind him.'

'Oh, I see. Well, look here. Fransham's heart is inclined to be dicky. And I'm a little bit afraid this hot weather may have upset him. I'd like to get the door open, but I don't know how to manage it.'

'Perhaps there's a window that you could climb in by, sir?' Linton suggested.

Dr Thornborough shook his head impatiently. 'No good!' he exclaimed. 'I've thought of that already. The window's barred, and, if it wasn't, it doesn't open wide enough to let anybody through. Do you think you could manage to force the door?'

Linton smiled. He was six foot two, broad in proportion and weighed seventeen stone. 'I think I might be able to manage it, sir,' he replied.

'Come along then.' They hurried across the hall and the doctor pointed to the door of the cloakroom. 'That's it,' he said. 'Now let's see what you can do.'

'I shall have to break the lock, I'm afraid, sir,' Linton replied warningly.

'Oh, damn the lock! Fire away and open the door. That's all I care about.'

Linton applied his shoulder to the door and gave an apparently effortless heave. With a sound of rending wood the door flew open. Linton entered the cloakroom, Dr Thornborough close at his heels. Just inside the doorway they came to a sudden halt. Stretched on the ground in front of them was the body of an elderly man lying flat on his back.

At that moment the deep boom of the luncheon gong rang like a knell through the house.

CHAPTER II

Before the reverberations of the gong had died away, Dr Thornborough was on his knees beside the fallen man with Linton standing close behind him. The doctor made a rapid examination.

'It's Uncle Bob, and he's dead!' he exclaimed without looking up. 'For Heaven's sake shut the door, Linton, and fix it somehow so that it won't open. We don't want the women crowding in here and seeing this.'

Linton shut the door and managed to jam the broken lock. Then he returned to his station by the doctor's side, uncertain what he should do. Even his inexperience could tell at a glance that Mr Fransham had not died of heart failure.

The body stretched on the floor was that of a man nearing sixty, grey-headed and clean-shaven. His rugged features and protruding chin proclaimed him to have been a man of strong will. In the front of his head above the middle of his forehead the skin was broken and the bone beneath it fractured. Linton felt assured that Mr Fransham had died as the result of a blow from some blunt instrument. The blood from the wound had trickled down the dead man's cheek and collected in a small pool on the rubber flooring.

The cloakroom measured about fifteen feet by twelve. Its only entrance was by the door from the hall. The wall on the left of this entrance was provided with a series of hooks, upon which hung an array of masculine coats and hats. Against the opposite wall was a water-closet and, separated from this by a thin partition running half-way across the room, a lavatory basin. In the wall behind the basin was a window, glazed with frosted glass, and between this and the basin a wide window-ledge faced with vitrolite. Only a small panel of this window, less than a foot square, was made to open. It was now open inwards and secured by a rod and pin. The window looked out upon the carriage-way running beside the house from one of the drive gates to the garage. On the outside the window was protected by stout iron bars set about six inches apart. The carriage-way was about twelve feet wide, and it was bounded on its further side by an eight-foot brick wall.

Dr Thornborough rose slowly to his feet, keeping his eyes fixed upon the dead man's face. 'This is pretty ghastly,' he muttered, more to himself than to Linton. 'Uncle Bob dead like this, and here of all places. I don't begin to understand it.' He looked up suddenly and faced the policeman. 'What are we going to do about it, Linton?' he asked helplessly.

'It's my duty to take particulars, sir,' Linton replied rather stiffly. 'To begin with, would you mind telling me this gentleman's full name and address?'

'His name is Robert Fransham,' Dr Thornborough

replied. 'His age is fifty-eight and his address is 4 Cheveley Street, London, SW1. You've heard me call him Uncle Bob, but he's not really my uncle, he's my wife's, and the devil of it is that his sister, my wife's mother, is staying with us at this very moment.'

'What in your opinion was the cause of death, sir?'

'You can see that for yourself, I should think. A depressed fracture of the anterior portion of the skull, severe enough to cause immediate death.'

'Can you suggest what could have caused such a fracture, sir?'

'I can't. That's just the puzzle. The fracture was caused by the impact of some hard body, of course. And that body must have been of a definite shape. You know what a cube is, I suppose?'

'I think so, sir. It's the shape of dice or of lumps of sugar.'

'That's right. Well, the nature of this fracture suggests that Fransham was struck by the edge of a cube an inch and a half across. And if you can suggest how that happened, you're cleverer than I am.'

'Perhaps if we were to search the room, we should find the object, sir.'

'You're at liberty to search as much as you like. In fact, it seems to me that this business is up to you. Meanwhile, I'm faced with the particularly unpleasant task of breaking the news to my wife. She and her uncle were devoted to one another, and she's going to take it pretty badly.'

Dr Thornborough walked slowly out of the room and Linton secured the door behind him. He had no wish to be interrupted at this stage of the proceedings. He was first in the field and meant to take full advantage of the fact.

The dead man was lying flat on his back at right angles to the wall on which the coat-hooks were fixed, and with his arms outstretched. His feet were towards the lavatory basin and a few inches from it in the horizontal direction. The basin itself was half full of soapy water, still warm.

Linton examined the dead man's hands and found that they were damp and soapy. This, together with the position in which the body was lying, suggested that Mr Fransham must have been actually washing his hands when he was struck. A cake of soap still moist was lying on the floor beneath the basin. Two clean towels hung on a rail nearby. Their appearance indicated that neither of them had been used.

Linton took up his position in front of the basin as though he were about to wash his hands in it. Looking straight in front of him he found that his head was on a level with the open pane of the window. Further, his view of the wall on the opposite side of the carriage-way was not obstructed by the protecting bars. From the centre of the basin to these bars was a matter of thirty inches, measured horizontally.

Linton entered these facts in his notebook and shook his head forebodingly. He didn't at all like the way in which things were shaping. But for the moment he had done everything that could be expected of him. It was time that he got into touch with his superiors.

He opened the door of the cloakroom and peeped out. There seemed to be nobody about, though he could hear the sound of voices behind the closed door of the dining-room. He went to the telephone instrument which stood on a table in the hall, and rang through to Sergeant Cload, keeping his eye on the cloakroom door meanwhile.

His report to the sergeant was very guarded, since he was not sure who might be listening to him.

'I'm speaking from Dr Thornborough's, sir. Mrs Thornborough's uncle has been found dead under rather suspicious circumstances.'

It took Cload some seconds to realise the full import of this message. 'What on earth do you mean!' he exclaimed at last. 'Let's have the particulars, man.'

'I'd rather you came and saw them for yourself, sir,' Linton replied firmly.

'Are you trying to hint that there's been a murder at Dr Thornborough's?' the sergeant asked.

'It looks very like it, sir. But least said, soonest mended.'

'I see. This is a job for the super. I'll get on to him at once and tell him what you've told me. Meanwhile you stay where you are and see that nothing's interfered with.'

Linton remained in the hall, awaiting further instructions. From the dining-room came the sound of a woman sobbing and the voice of Dr Thornborough apparently trying to comfort her. From time to time another voice—that of a woman—chimed in. The news of the tragedy had not apparently reached the kitchen, judging by the sounds of merriment which penetrated the baize door. Linton approached this on tiptoe and pushed it gently open an inch or so. He heard two women laughing, apparently at something which was being said by a man with a hoarse voice. The latter was presumably the surly-faced chauffeur and the two women were Lucy and the cook.

Linton had not long to wait for his instructions. Before many minutes had passed a car turned at high speed into the drive and pulled up with a squeaking of brakes outside the front door. Linton, recognising the sound, opened the front door and saluted. Superintendent Yateley, expectant and alert, confronted him. 'Where?' he asked.

'This way, sir,' Linton replied.

He led the superintendent into the cloakroom and secured the lock behind them. Yateley glanced at the body and then rapidly round the room. 'Who found him?' he asked.

'Dr Thornborough and I between us, sir.'

'Good. Now tell me what you know about it.'

Linton gave an account of his sojourn in the consulting-room and of the events which followed it. Yateley listened attentively.

'You've done pretty well so far, Linton,' he said. 'Now, let's get the main facts perfectly clear. You heard this Mr Fransham go into the cloakroom and lock the door behind him?'

'I heard somebody go in, sir, but of course I couldn't see who it was.'

'You did not hear the door open or shut again until you broke it down?'

'No, sir.'

'There was nobody in the room but the dead man when you broke in?'

'No, sir. I'm perfectly certain of that.'

'You have found no trace of any weapon which could have caused this wound?'

'No trace at all, sir. But I haven't moved the body to look underneath it.'

'Quite right.' The superintendent took a piece of chalk from his pocket and drew a line round the body as it lay on the floor.

'Now help me to lift him on one side,' he said.

Removal of the body disclosed nothing whatever and Yateley frowned.

'He can't have been struck by any sort of missile, or it would be still in the room,' he said. 'All right, Linton, you stay here and have another search. Look through all those coats on the pegs, in the dead man's clothing and everywhere. I'm going to get statements from everybody on the premises. Where's the doctor, to begin with?'

'In the dining-room, sir, with Mrs Thornborough and another lady.'

Yateley left the cloakroom, walked across the hall and opened the dining-room door. Dr Thornborough looked up as he did so, and the superintendent beckoned to him. With an anxious glance at his wife, who was sitting bowed in a chair with an older woman bending over her, the doctor stepped out into the hall.

'Bad business, this, doctor,' said Yateley sympathetically. 'I'd like to hear what you can tell me about it, if you don't mind. Where can we have a quiet talk?'

'Better come into the consulting-room,' Dr Thornborough replied, absently running his fingers through his hair. 'But I can't tell you anything about it, I'm afraid. It's as much as I can do to bring myself to realise that it has happened.'

Yateley made no reply until they were both in the consulting-room with the door shut behind them. 'This must have been a terrible shock to you, doctor,' he said then. 'The dead man was your wife's uncle, I understand?'

Dr Thornborough nodded. 'Yes, that's right,' he replied. 'My wife is naturally terribly upset. She has always been very fond of him.'

'You told Mr Linton that Mr Fransham lived in London. He drove down here at your invitation, I presume?'

18

'That's just what I can't understand. He told my wife when he arrived that he had a letter from me asking him to come down to lunch today. But I assure you that I had never written him any such letter. In fact, his coming here this week might have been very awkward.'

'Why was that, doctor?'

'Because my wife's mother happens to be staying with us. Fransham was her brother-in-law, but they never managed to hit it off and they've avoided one another for years.'

'What was the reason for this mutual dislike?'

'I don't think there was any real reason. Fransham didn't approve of his brother Tom's choice when he married, and that didn't tend to amicable relations. Then Tom got killed in the war while Robert, my wife's uncle, stayed at home and made a lot of money in munitions. Robert Fransham didn't take much interest in his brother's widow and it was a grievance on her part that he didn't make her a handsome allowance. Add a certain amount of mutual antipathy to all this and you'll get some idea of the situation. I may say that my mother-in-law is a woman of decided views and doesn't mince matters if anything upsets her.'

'Was Mr Robert Fransham married?'

'No, he had never been. He was what is known as a confirmed bachelor. Before and during the war he was a partner in Fransham and Innes, Brass Founders, of Birmingham. The firm was always fairly prosperous, I believe, and after war broke out it did extremely well on government contracts. In 1920 Fransham sold the business and retired. He then took over the remainder of the lease of No. 4, Cheveley Street and settled down to live there.'

'What establishment did he keep up?'

'He had a married couple, Mr and Mrs Stowell, and a chauffeur, Coates. Coates is here now with the car.'

'Mr Fransham was in affluent circumstances, of course?'

'Judging by appearances, he was. But I haven't the slightest idea what he was actually worth. He never spoke about his money and I'm bound to say that he hated parting with it.'

'You were not in the house when he arrived, were you, doctor?'

'No, I hadn't come back from my rounds. The first I knew of anybody being here was when I saw his car in the garage. I didn't recognise it, for he had bought a new car within the past few weeks and I hadn't seen him since. But I recognised Coates, his chauffeur, as soon as I set eyes on him, and I knew that the visitor must be Uncle Bob.'

'You were surprised to find him here?'

'I was, very much surprised. Uncle Bob has driven down here often enough, of course, but never without letting us know that he was coming. I asked Coates if Uncle Bob had brought anybody down with him and he said no. Then I came straight into the house where I met my wife. She told me that she had seen Uncle Bob who was then in the cloakroom.'

'What did you do next, doctor?'

'I came in here. My wife told me that Linton was waiting to see me. He began telling me something about Alfie Prince. But I'm afraid I hardly listened to him. I was worried about Uncle Bob.'

'Why were you worried, doctor?'

'For two reasons. First because my mother-in-law was here. As I told you, she and Uncle Bob have avoided one another for years. I was afraid that if they met unexpectedly in this house neither of them would believe that it was accidental. They'd think that my wife and I had arranged it between us. Family reconciliation and all that. You know what I mean. And both of them would have bitterly resented anything of the kind.'

'They didn't meet, as it happened, did they, doctor?'

'No, my mother-in-law was upstairs when Uncle Bob arrived. My idea was to see Uncle Bob before they met and explain the situation to him. I couldn't very well turn my mother-in-law out, but Uncle Bob could have gone down to the Red Lion and had his lunch there if he didn't want to see her. So I went to the cloakroom door and asked Uncle Bob to let me in.'

'You got no reply, I understand?'

'I couldn't hear a sound inside the cloakroom. And that was the second reason for my being worried. I'm not Uncle Bob's regular medical attendant, but I have looked over him once or twice when he's been staying here. His heart wasn't any too sound, though there was no reason why he shouldn't have lived for years. But I was afraid that the heat might have been too much for him and that he'd fainted. That's why I got Linton to break the door down for me.'

'You described the nature of the wound to Linton. Can you suggest what could have caused it?'

'Only a heavy blow. That blow might have been inflicted by the impact of some missile such as a stone. Or by the stroke of a weapon such as a hammer.'

'As you drove down the carriage-way towards the garage you passed the cloakroom window. Did you happen to notice whether it was open or not?'

'I didn't. By that time I had seen the car standing in the

garage and my attention was concentrated upon that, wondering whose it could be.'

'Where was Coates the chauffeur when you first saw this car?'

'I saw somebody standing beside the car but I didn't recognise him at once. The garage is dark and my eyes were accustomed to the bright sunshine. It wasn't until I got close up to the man that I saw it was Coates.'

'When Linton told you that he had come to see you about Alfie Prince, didn't you tell him that you had seen the man himself quite recently?'

'I did. I saw him in the distance just before I turned into the drive gates. You can't mistake that old army greatcoat that Alfie always wears. I don't believe there's another one so ragged in the whole county.'

'Where was he when you saw him?'

'I had come from Mark Farm. Before I turned in at the drive gate, Alfie crossed the road about two or three hundred yards in front of me. He must have come through a gap in the hedge out of that building land that lies on the other side of my wall.'

'Did you notice where he went to?'

'I can't say that I did. I wasn't at the moment particularly interested in Alfie's movements.'

'Thanks very much, doctor. That's all I want to ask you for the moment. There's just one suggestion I should like to make. Under the circumstances, wouldn't it be as well to have another opinion upon the wound? It would serve to confirm your evidence.'

'That's a very good idea,' replied Dr Thornborough readily. 'I'll ring up my partner, Dorrington. He'll come along and tell us what he thinks about it.'

'I'd be glad if you'd do that, doctor. And now, do you think Mrs Thornborough is in a fit state for me to see her?'

'I'll ask her,' replied Dr Thornborough doubtfully. 'But you'll understand that if she doesn't feel up to it, it might be better to wait.'

He went out, and a minute or two later Mrs Thornborough entered the consulting-room. She was obviously very much upset but she made a brave attempt to smile at the superintendent. 'I'm ready to answer any questions you like to ask me, Mr Yateley,' she said.

'That's extremely kind of you, Mrs Thornborough,' the superintendent replied. 'I can imagine your feelings and I won't keep you more than a minute or two. To begin with, where were you when Mr Fransham arrived?'

'In the drawing-room, waiting for my husband to come back. And when Lucy showed Uncle Bob in, I was utterly flabbergasted. He's never come down here unexpectedly like that and I was afraid that something must be wrong. And that's the first thing I asked him.'

'What was his reply, Mrs Thornborough?'

'He seemed very much surprised. He asked me why I should think anything was wrong when he'd driven down to lunch on Cyril's express invitation. This puzzled me more than ever, for Cyril had said nothing to me about it. And then Uncle Bob went on to say that he'd had a letter from Cyril this morning asking him to drive down to lunch today for he had something very particular to ask him about.

'I couldn't begin to understand this, for Cyril wouldn't do a thing like that without telling me about it. And I was afraid that mother, who'd gone up a few minutes before to get ready for lunch, would come down any moment. So I told Uncle Bob that if he wanted to wash his hands he knew where to go, and then when I'd seen Lucy I went upstairs to tell mother that Uncle Bob was here. I said that if she didn't care to meet him she could have a tray sent up to her, but she wouldn't hear of that. She said that she wasn't afraid of Uncle Bob or anyone else, and if he chose to make himself unpleasant, two could play at that game. She and Uncle Bob never got on very well, you know.'

'So the doctor has told me, Mrs Thornborough. What did you do next?'

'I came downstairs and waited for my husband. When he came in I told him about Uncle Bob and then went into the drawing-room. A minute or two later I heard him calling Uncle Bob through the cloakroom door. Then there was a crash and I wondered if I'd better go and see what was the matter. But before I'd made up my mind mother came downstairs and at the same time Mary sounded the lunch gong. So mother and I went into the dining-room, where we've been ever since. And after we'd waited for a few minutes Cyril came in and told us what had happened.'

At this moment Dr Thornborough entered the consulting-room. He went up to his wife and laid his hand on her shoulder. 'Feeling all right, Betty?' he asked.

'Not too bad,' she replied. 'I've just been telling Mr Yateley what happened.'

'Mrs Thornborough has been most kind,' said the superintendent. 'I'll leave her in your care now, doctor. I wonder if you'd mind asking Coates the chauffeur to come and see me?'

Dr and Mrs Thornborough left the room and a few minutes later Coates appeared. He was a man of about forty-five, with a hoarse voice and a rather surly expression. In reply to the superintendent's questions he said that he had been with Mr Fransham for five years, during which time he had lived in the house. Mr Fransham had always been a good master to him and very considerate. Mr Fransham never drove the car himself, but liked to go out most afternoons, either to visit friends or for a run in the country. He had very often driven Mr Fransham to Adderminster. Perhaps half a dozen times or more a year. Mrs Thornborough had frequently visited her uncle at No. 4, Cheveley Street, but Coates could not remember that Dr Thornborough had ever done so. It was fifty-three miles by mileage indicator from Cheveley Street to *Epidaurus*.

'When did Mr Fransham tell you that he wanted you to drive him down here today?' the superintendent asked.

'Just after he had his breakfast this morning, sir,' Coates replied. 'He sent for me and told me that he'd have to cancel the orders given me yesterday, for he'd had a letter from the doctor asking him to drive down to lunch very specially.'

'What orders had he given you yesterday, Coates?'

'Well, sir, I'd told him that since the new car had done nearly a thousand miles, it was time that the makers looked over her to see that everything was right. So Mr Fransham had told me to take the car round to the Armstrong-Siddeley place in Cricklewood and leave her there over the weekend. But this morning he told me that would have to wait till Monday and said that a hundred miles one way or the other wouldn't make much difference. So we started away at a quarter past eleven and were here sharp at one o'clock. Mr Fransham doesn't like being driven too fast.'

'You've heard that Mr Fransham has been killed, of course?'

'The doctor told me so just now when he sent me in here, sir. And I'm bound to say that it sounds very queer to me.'

'It is, very queer, Coates. You say that you got here at one o'clock sharp? Tell me exactly what you did when you arrived?'

'I drove in at the gates, sir, stopped outside the front door, and rang the bell. Lucy opened the door and Mr Fransham went into the house. Then I drove the car round to the garage at the back. I looked round the car, then lit a cigarette. Then I waited where I was, knowing that somebody would come out and ask me into the house. I didn't like to go in until I was invited, you understand, sir. And while I was waiting the doctor came along and spoke to me.'

'Were you in the garage the whole time that you were waiting?'

'Yes, sir, I was expecting somebody to come and call me into the house at any moment.'

'Did anyone enter the carriage-way leading to the garage during that time?'

Coates shook his head with an air of decision. 'No, sir, I'm quite sure that they didn't,' he replied.

'How can you be so sure of that? You can't have been looking down the carriage-way all the time? You told me yourself that the first thing you did after you got here was to look round the car.'

'That's quite right, sir. But all the time I was looking round the car I had an eye open for somebody coming out of the house. If there had been anybody in the carriage-way during that time I should have seen them, I'm quite certain of that. And after I'd finished looking round the car, which didn't take more than a couple of minutes, I just stood inside the garage doorway smoking a fag. And I don't see how anybody could have come into the carriage-way then, without my noticing them.'

This seemed reasonable enough. The distance from the garage door to the cloakroom window was not more than fifty yards in a direct line. It was incredible that anyone could have approached the window unknown to an observer at the door, himself on the alert for an expected summons. Yateley slightly changed the import of his questioning. 'When you found the garage empty you guessed that Dr Thornborough was out on his rounds, I suppose?'

'Well, I thought he might be, sir, but I couldn't be sure. Sometimes when Mr Fransham was down here with his car, the doctor would leave his own somewhere in the town so as to leave the garage free for Mr Fransham's car. There isn't room for both, you see, sir.'

'You saw the doctor's car turn in at the drive gate, I suppose?'

'Yes, sir, I caught sight of it as soon as it came round the corner. The doctor came straight down the carriage-way, stopped just outside the garage and then got out and spoke to me.'

'Do you remember what he said?'

'He said, "Why, Coates, I am surprised to see you! Did you drive Mr Fransham down?" I told him that Mr Fransham was indoors and he hurried into the house by the garden door.'

Yateley dismissed Coates and then joined his subordinate in the cloakroom. 'Well, Linton, have you found anything?' he asked.

'Nothing very much, I'm afraid, sir,' Linton replied. 'Nothing that could possibly account for the wound, that is. I've been right through the room and I can't find a stone or anything that could have been thrown. Nor is there anything that could have made a wound of the shape the doctor described. There are a couple of walking-sticks, but they are both round with a crooked handle. And there are a couple of lady's umbrellas, but one has a round ball at the end and the other a plain handle with a strap. I've put them out in the corner, sir, for you to look at.'

'Where did you find these things?' the superintendent asked.

'Hanging on the pegs, sir, behind the coats.'

Yateley very soon satisfied himself that the blow could not have been inflicted by any of the walking-sticks or umbrellas. 'Have you been through Mr Fransham's clothing?' he asked.

'Yes, sir, I have, but there's nothing there. Nothing that could have caused the wound, that is. But I did find something else that I think you'll like to see, sir.'

He opened his notebook and took out a folded sheet of paper. 'I found that in Mr Fransham's wallet, sir.'

Yateley took the paper and unfolded it. It was a single sheet of notepaper embossed with the address *Epidaurus*, Adderminster. Under this was typed a date, June 11, and a letter, also typewritten, followed:

'DEAR UNCLE BOB, A situation has arisen here upon which Betty and myself should very much like your advice. The matter is urgent, since a decision will have to be reached upon it by Monday afternoon at the latest. I should have come up to London to see you, but you know how difficult it is for me to leave my practice at a moment's notice. Could you possibly drive down to lunch tomorrow, Saturday, and we could discuss things afterwards? It would relieve Betty's mind enormously if you would do this. We shall expect you unless we get a wire in the morning to say that you can't come. But do try to manage it, for really it's most important. Yours affectionately,'

The letter was signed in ink, 'Cyril.'

Yateley frowned as he folded up the letter and put it in his pocket. 'Have you had your dinner yet, Linton?' he asked.

'No, sir, I haven't.'

'Well, I'll see that you're relieved as soon as it can be managed. Meanwhile, I want you to stay here. If Dr Dorrington comes let him examine the body. But see that nothing whatever is taken from this room, or brought into it, either, for that matter.'

Yateley returned to the consulting-room where he found Dr Thornborough sitting at his desk. The doctor looked up as he came in.

'Oh there you are, superintendent,' he said. 'I've been on to Dorrington and he's promised to come along here as soon as he's finished lunch.'

'Thank you, doctor,' Yateley replied. 'We may find a second opinion useful. I wonder if you could let me have a sheet of notepaper? I want to jot down a couple of notes while they're still fresh in my mind.'

Dr Thornborough stretched out his hand to a stationery rack which stood on his desk. 'Here you are,' he said. 'I thought you fellows always carried notebooks?'

'So we do, but for once I've left mine behind.' Yateley scribbled a few words on the sheet of notepaper which the doctor had given him. 'I shall have to get back to my office now,' he said curtly. 'You'll see me later in the day.' And with that he left the room.

He went out by the front door and thence by the drive to the carriage-way. It had occurred to him that some trace of the weapon might be found there. But after a few minutes' investigation he was disappointed. The surface of the carriage-way was of concrete, and smoothly swept. Upon it was no sign of a missile, or of a weapon of any description.

He returned to his car and drove to the police station. His first care was to give orders to Sergeant Cload for Linton's relief. This done he put a telephone call through to the Chief Constable of the County.

CHAPTER III

As a direct result of Yateley's telephone call, Inspector Waghorn, of the Criminal Investigation Department of the Metropolitan Police, found himself in the superintendent's room at Adderminster Police Station just before six o'clock that afternoon.

Inspector Waghorn, popularly known at the Yard as Jimmy, was a Hendon graduate who had already gained the approval of his somewhat exacting superior, Superintendent Hanslet. It was Hanslet who had suggested Jimmy as the fitting person to answer the call from the Adderminster Police.

'Go down and see what you can make of it,' he had said. 'If it's all plain sailing, you know well enough what to do by this time. If it isn't you can get on to me and I'll come down and bear a hand. Away you go.'

Yateley gave Jimmy a detailed account of what had happened.

'Those are the facts,' he concluded. 'Now, I'm going to be perfectly frank with you, inspector. We didn't call in the Yard because we wanted any help in tracing the criminal.'

Jimmy smiled. 'That's what the CID is usually called upon to do, sir,' he replied.

'Yes, I know. But now it's rather different. In this case, there isn't the slightest doubt as to the identity of the criminal. The only problem—and that's a very minor one—is precisely how he did it. To put it crudely, we've only sent for you to wash our dirty linen for us.'

'I appreciate your meaning, sir,' replied Jimmy solemnly. 'But perhaps you would be good enough to tell me exactly what you want me to do?'

'I should have thought you would have guessed that. We don't want to arrest Dr Thornborough off our own bats, so to speak. He's made himself very popular while he's been here, and if we were to take action without calling in the Yard, we should arouse local feeling against us. Whereas if the Yard applies for a warrant, the responsibility can't be thrown upon our shoulders.'

'I see, sir,' Jimmy murmured respectfully. 'There's no doubt about Dr Thornborough's guilt, I suppose?'

'There's no room for the slightest particle of doubt!' Yateley exclaimed. 'Take the motive, to begin with. Mr Fransham was a total stranger to Adderminster. By that I mean, that although he had visited his nephew and niece several times previously, they were the only people in the town he knew. Nobody else in Adderminster could have had the vestige of a motive for murdering him.

'Now, had the doctor a motive for murdering him? Most emphatically he had. I happen to know that although he's got a pretty good practice here as Dr Dorrington's partner, he's been living a bit beyond his means. Neither he nor his wife have any money of their own. He built that house of his with the help of a Building Society, and he buys his cars on the hire purchase system. I won't say that he's in actual financial difficulties, but I do know that the tradesmen who supply him sometimes have to wait a bit for their money.

'There's no doubt that Mr Fransham was a rich man. For one thing he's just bought a new car which can't have cost less than a thousand pounds. For another he lives in Cheveley Street, which, as you know better than I do, isn't exactly an impoverished neighbourhood. Mr Fransham was Mrs Thornborough's uncle, and there seems very little doubt that she'll inherit his money. In fact, the motive's so adequate that it's almost enough to hang the doctor by itself.'

Jimmy made no comment upon this. 'You told me just now, sir, that you considered the doctor's statement unsatisfactory,' he remarked.

'I did, and that was the mildest word I could think of. It was definitely misleading. To begin with, he pretended that Mr Fransham's visit was a complete surprise to him. He maintained this even to his wife, for Linton happened to overhear their conversation. But Mr Fransham told at least two people, Mrs Thornborough and his chauffeur Coates, that the doctor had written to him asking him to drive down to lunch today.

'As it happens this is one of the very rare cases in which luck plays up on the side of the policeman. By a sheer fluke Linton was sent up to interview the doctor, and was in the house at the very moment the crime was committed. If he hadn't been there the doctor would have had a chance of removing the most incriminating piece of evidence. That is the very letter of invitation, which Mr Fransham happened to have in his pocket. Here it is, and here is a sample of the doctor's notepaper which I tricked him into giving me.'

Jimmy compared the two. 'They seem to me exactly similar,' he said.

'Of course they are. There's not a shadow of doubt about that. You see that the letter is dated yesterday. If it had been posted here yesterday evening, it would have reached London by the first post this morning, and, according to Coates' statement it was by that post that Mr Fransham received it. Now, what's your opinion of the typing?'

'Pretty accurate, sir,' Jimmy replied. 'I'm not an expert, but I should guess that it had been typed on one of the smaller portable machines.'

'Oh, that's your opinion, is it?' said Yateley grimly. 'That's another nail in the coffin. I happened to notice a Smith Premier portable in the doctor's consulting-room. Now then, have a look at this.'

He picked up a printed form and threw it across to Jimmy.

'That's a medical certificate excusing one of my men from duty,' he said. 'It's signed by Dr Thornborough. Have a look at the signature and compare it with the one on the letter.'

Jimmy did so. The certificate was signed 'Cyril J. Thornborough, M.R.C.S., L.R.C.P.' The writing of the Christian name corresponded very strikingly with the signature of the letter.

'So much for the doctor's pretence that his uncle's visit was unexpected,' said Yateley. 'Now we come to another point which also proves the doctor to be a liar. He returned to his house at ten minutes past one or thereabouts. In his statement to me he said that as he turned in at his drive gate, he saw a certain Alfie Prince crossing the road some yards in front of him. The doctor's house is about three-quarters of a mile from the centre of the town in an easterly direction.

'Now this Alfie Prince is one of the thorns in our flesh. He can always earn a decent wage by getting work on one of the farms round about. Normally he does so and is perfectly well-behaved, though he won't stay more than a few weeks in the same place. But every now and then he gets fits of being an intolerable nuisance. He goes round to people's houses asking for threepence to buy half a pint, or for a handful of cigarettes, or anything that comes into his head. If he gets it, he says "Thank you" very politely. If he doesn't he uses bad language and refuses to go away.

'He seems to be in that mood just now, for Sergeant Cload had a complaint about him this morning. In fact it was because of this complaint that Linton was sent up to the doctor's house. Cload, who knows Alfie better than I do, had come to the conclusion that he's not all there. He sent Linton to see the doctor about it and ask him to have a talk with Alfie.

'Now, what I want you to understand is this. This morning's complaint came from Colonel Exbury, who lives three miles out of the town in a westerly direction. He rang up directly after he had got rid of Alfie, and the call was received here at a quarter to one. If, then, Alfie was seen in the vicinity of the doctor's house at ten minutes past one, he must have covered three and three-quarter miles in twenty-five minutes. I may as well explain that there is no bus route between the two points and that Alfie has never been known to ride a bicycle.'

'Mightn't he have got a lift on a car or lorry, sir?' Jimmy suggested.

'He might, but it isn't in the least likely. No, I'm pretty sure that we shall find that the doctor made a false statement about seeing Alfie for some purpose of his own. Alfie can be questioned, of course, but it's very difficult to get any sense out of him, when he's in these wandering moods.

'Meanwhile I've had another report upon the wound. It struck me that it might be a trifle awkward if the only medical evidence at the inquest were given by the criminal himself. So I suggested that Dr Thornborough's partner should be called in. He came to see me this afternoon and described the cause of the fracture in exactly the same terms as Dr Thornborough had done. Mr Fransham was struck a violent blow by something cubical in shape. That something may have been either the head of a weapon or a missile—it is impossible to say which on the evidence of the wound alone.

'But we know that it can't have been a missile. I'm going to remind you once more of the circumstances. Linton was in the house at the time and he is ready to swear to these facts. First, that the door of the cloakroom was not opened from the time when Mr Fransham locked it behind him until Linton himself broke it open. Second, that he and the doctor entered the cloakroom together. Third, that the doctor had no opportunity of picking up the missile unobserved. Fourth, that the room contained nothing capable of having caused the wound at the time of his search.

'The remote possibility occured to me that a missile, having struck Mr Fransham's head, might have bounced out again through the window. I therefore searched the carriage-way outside but without result.

'The possibility of a missile having been employed is thus ruled out, and we are driven back to the theory of a weapon. The doctor must have crept up to the window while Mr Fransham was washing his hands, put his arm through the opening and dealt him a heavy blow with an iron instrument of some kind. That instrument can't be very far away, and, once it is found, the evidence will be complete.

'I've seen to the usual formalities, of course. I have been in touch with the coroner and he has ordered an inquest at half-past eleven on Monday. And I've arranged for the body to be taken to the mortuary this evening. Now, is there anything else you want to know?'

'How long has Dr Thornborough been in practice in Adderminster?'

'Seven years. Dr Dorrington took him into partnership then. They've got a surgery between them in the town here, and for five years Dr and Mrs Thornborough lived in the house next door. Then a couple of years ago, he built that new house of his in Gunthorpe Road. Why he gave it a ridiculous name like *Epidaurus* I can't tell you. Anything else?'

'Not at present, thank you, sir,' Jimmy replied. 'Have you any objection to my visiting the scene of the crime?'

'Not the slightest. You can't miss the house. Turn to the right at the bottom of High Street and keep straight on till you come to it. You can't make any mistake, for you'll find the name painted on the gate. You'll find Sergeant Cload on duty up there. He'll be able to tell you anything else you want to know.'

Jimmy left the police station and walked down the busy little High Street, noticing, as he did so, the brass plate on the surgery door bearing the names of Drs Dorrington and Thornborough. Following the superintendent's instructions, he turned to the right and found himself in Middle Street, a narrow thoroughfare bordered with shops on both sides. After half a mile or so the pavements came to an end, at which point Middle Street became Gunthorpe Road.

A couple of hundred yards farther on, Jimmy came to an imposing gateway on his right. A notice board affixed to this informed him that it was the entrance to the Gunthorpe public gardens and the Adderminster and District Museum. On the opposite side of the road was a single building, a small house or cottage, apparently of considerable age, and surrounded by a succession of orchards and meadow-lands. Another couple of hundred yards beyond the gateway and on the same side of the road was the first drive gate of *Epidaurus*.

Jimmy did not turn in here, but walked on until he reached the second drive gate, from which he could see straight down the carriage-way to the garage at its farther end. Jimmy, wishing to acquaint himself fully with the local topography, did not stop here. As he proceeded he found a high but ragged hedge on his right, above which towered an enormous board bearing the words, 'Building plots for sale.' Finally, about a quarter of a mile beyond *Epidaurus*, Gunthorpe Road ended abruptly at a five-barred gate, beyond which a track led to a farmhouse in the distance.

As he turned back Jimmy wondered what sort of a man this Dr Thornborough would turn out to be. One thing was already certain, that he possessed a sense of humour.

Epidaurus, the shrine of Aesculapius! What more suitable name could have been chosen for a doctor's house? Jimmy wondered how many people in Adderminster appreciated the allusion. Certainly the superintendent didn't. But then the superintendent's mind was concerned more with material facts than with classical allusions.

This time Jimmy turned in at the gate and walked down the carriage-way. When he reached the cloakroom window he became aware of a rubicund face surveying him through the opening.

'Good-afternoon, Sergeant Cload,' he said quietly. 'My name's Waghorn, and I've been sent down from the Yard to see if I can give you a hand. I'm just going to have a look round, then I'll come in and have a chat with you. You can let me in without disturbing the household, I dare say?'

'Yes, sir, I can manage that,' Cload replied. 'You come to the window when you're ready and I'll open the garden door and let you in that way.'

Jimmy nodded, and went on towards the garage. The two cars were still standing at the end of the carriage-way—Dr Thornborough's twelve horse-power Masspro outside the garage, and Mr Frasham's big twenty-five horse-power Siddeley limousine inside. Of the doctor or Coates there was no sign.

Jimmy looked in at the open window of the doctor's car and glanced swiftly round its interior. Except for a rug folded on the back seat it was empty.

At the end of the garage was a narrow bench upon which lay a few small tools. Nails driven into the wall supported a collection of miscellaneous objects. Three or four old tyres, a suit of overalls and a turn-cock.

Jimmy felt a thrill of excitement as he caught sight of this last object. He knew at once what it was. The key to the cock on the service-pipe by which the water supply to the house could be turned on or off. It was made of three-quarter inch iron rod with a T-shaped handle at one end. At the other end was a roughly cubical box, the hollow of which was designed to fit a square on the end of the cock spindle.

The key so exactly tallied with the superintendent's description of the weapon which he had imagined, that Jimmy could hardly believe his eyes. He took out his foot-rule and measured the outside dimensions of the box. It was almost exactly an inch and a half either way. But even with a pocket lens he could find no trace of blood or hair upon it. However, that meant nothing, for there had been plenty of time and opportunity to clean it since the crime had been committed.

Jimmy carefully refrained from touching the turn-cock and after a careful inspection of the garage returned to the cloakroom window. A minute later Cload had opened the garden door for him, and the two entered the cloak-room together.

'You've found nothing fresh, I suppose, sergeant?' Jimmy asked.

'No, sir, I haven't,' Cload replied. 'I thought I might just as well have a good look round while I was here, but I haven't found anything that could have made a wound like that poor gentleman's got on his head.'

The body was still lying on the cloakroom floor and had by now been decently covered with a sheet. Jimmy drew this down and examined the wound. He could see for himself that it had been caused by the blunt edge of a cube with a side of about one and a half inches. Then he stood up and examined the position of the basin in respect to the barred window. He saw at once that no weapon of the size of the key could have been swung as a hammer is swung from outside the window. The opening was far too small for that. On the other hand, it could easily have been jabbed through the window, and the edge of the box would then have inflicted just such a wound as he had seen.

Staring out of the window Jimmy considered the implications of this theory. Whoever had wielded the weapon must have been standing close up to the protecting bars. But how could this be reconciled with Coates' statement? The chauffeur had declared that if anyone had entered the carriage-way he could not have failed to have seen them. But could this statement be accepted? Jimmy already had experience of the fact that people were apt to declare impossible things which had actually happened. Not from any wish to mislead, but simply from natural conviction. Coates probably thought quite honestly that nobody could have reached the window unobserved by him. But his attention might well have been distracted for a few seconds. While he was lighting his cigarette, for instance. Or while he was looking round the car. He presumably went to the front of it, when the body would obscure his view of the carriage-way. On the whole Jimmy decided not to allow himself to be unduly influenced by Coates' statement.

And then another idea struck him. It wasn't necessary for the attacker to have been standing in the carriage-way. He might have been sitting in a car driven close up against the bars. He could quite easily have jabbed the turn-cock through the open windows of the car and the cloakroom.

It was an established fact that Dr Thornborough had driven down the carriage-way. Had he paused for a moment outside the cloakroom window and delivered the blow?

There were obvious objections to this theory, but Jimmy thought that they might be overcome. Coates was the first of these. If the doctor's car had stopped in its progress towards him he would surely have noticed it. Perhaps he had noticed and had his own reasons for saying nothing about it.

The second objection lay in the position of the wound. This showed, beyond question, that when Mr Fransham was struck, his head was bent over the basin. But surely if he had heard a car stop outside the window he would have looked up. Expecting the doctor's return, as he was, he would have at least have glanced at the car to see whether or not its occupant was his niece's husband. It was almost unthinkable that he would have continued his ablutions without taking any notice. Unless he was deaf, or had got his eyes full of soap, or something like that.

As Jimmy stared out of the window his view was bounded by the brick wall opposite. It was a good substantial brick wall eight feet high and obviously of the same age as the house. 'What's on the other side of that wall, sergeant?' he asked.

'Several acres of grassland, sir,' the sergeant replied. 'It's been up for sale in building plots ever since Squire Gunthorpe died three years back.'

'Squire Gunthorpe? This road's called after him, I suppose?'

'That's right, sir. It was like this, you see. You may have noticed the museum and public gardens as you came along here? That used to be called the Hall when the squire was alive. He'd lived there as long as anyone could remember. There wasn't any Gunthorpe Road then. Those entrance gates you may have seen, used to stand across the end of Middle Street. What is now Gunthorpe Road was the private drive leading up to the Hall.

'When the squire died, he left the house and gardens to the town and they've been turned into what you see them now. The entrance gates were moved, and the drive was turned into a public road. You may have noticed that cottage standing on the further side a little way up. That used to be the gardener's cottage standing at the end of the park. It was only the house and garden that was left to the town. The squire left the park to his family and they sold it to a speculator for building. But the only house that's been built on it so far is the one we're in now.'

'How's that?' Jimmy asked. 'Is there no demand for houses in Adderminster?'

'There's a demand for houses of the right kind, sir. Plenty of folk want houses that they can get for fifteen shillings a week or so. But that kind of house can't be built up here. I don't rightly understand it, sir, but the council stepped in with some sort of town-planning scheme. They won't allow more than one house in every two acres, and then they've got to be built of a certain size. That sort of thing comes a bit too expensive for most folks.'

'I see. Who lives in the old gardener's cottage? It appeared to be occupied when I saw it just now.'

'It was bought by a lady and gentleman from London. They pretty well pulled the inside to pieces and rebuilt it to suit themselves. But they aren't very often there, for the gentleman has business abroad somewhere and usually takes his wife with him. They aren't there now, I know for certain, but I did hear that it had been let furnished for the summer.'

'Do you happen to know who it was let to?'

'I can't say that I do, sir. But I believe it's a gentleman from London who comes down for the weekends. I don't know that I've ever set eyes on him, sir.'

'Is the vacant building land allowed to run to waste?'

'No, sir. The farmer at the end of the road rents it for the hay. He should be cutting it any day now.'

Jimmy returned to his contemplation of the wall. Its presence definitely limited the area from which the murderer must have delivered his blow. The head of a normal man bending over the basin would be level with the opening in the window. This horizontal line, if produced, would meet the wall at a point about four feet above its base. Anything projected from or over the top of the wall through the opening would strike the ledge inside the window. It followed, therefore, that the blow, whether inflicted by a projectile or a weapon, must have been delivered from the carriage-way.

Missile or weapon, that was just the point. The theory of a missile involved obvious difficulties. It must have been hard and substantial to have inflicted such a wound. It could hardly have been thrown by hand with sufficient force and accuracy. Some means of projection would have been necessary. The shape and size of the missile precluded the idea of a pistol or gun. A catapult, perhaps. But what catapultist would choose a cubical missile in preference to a roughly spherical one?

Further, if a missile had been employed, what had become of it? After striking Mr Fransham's head it would have lost its velocity and fallen. Directly beneath the point of impact was the basin, still half-full of soapy water and now quite cold. Jimmy fished through this with his fingers, only to find that the basin contained nothing but water.

Under the faintly amused eyes of Sergeant Cload, Jimmy proceeded to make a thorough search of the room. He did not desist until he had examined everything it contained, including the water-closet. No cubical object of any kind, or, for that matter, anything that could have been employed as a missile rewarded him.

There remained the possibility that the criminal had somehow retrieved the missile. But how? Constant observation had been kept on the cloakroom since Linton had broken down the door. From that moment the police had been either in the room or within sight of the door. It was practically impossible that anyone should have had an opportunity of removing anything.

Jimmy's fertile mind reviewed other possibilities, only to reject them as impracticable. The criminal might have tied a string to the missile so as to recover it when it had done its work. Or he might have fished for it through the opening in the window with some instrument in the nature of a pair of lazy-tongs. But both these suppositions were ridiculous, for what would have remained an instant longer in the carriage-way, in full view of Coates in the garage only a few yards away, than he could help?

The missile was thus ruled out, leaving the weapon in the field. The turn-cock hanging in the garage fulfilled all the necessary conditions of such a weapon. The box at its end corresponded to the dimensions of the wound. It was so heavy and substantial that, thrust violently, it would inflict considerable damage. Finally, it was amply long enough to reach its objective if wielded by someone standing outside the window. It seemed to Jimmy that his first step must be to have the turn-cock expertly examined. He left the house, took it from its nail in the garage and returned to the police station. He explained his intentions to the superintendent, and caught the last train to London, carrying with him the turn-cock carefully wrapped up in several sheets of paper.

CHAPTER IV

During the journey Jimmy began to piece together the facts which he had learnt.

The first thing to be established was the time at which the crime had been committed. Linton's presence in the consulting-room had been very helpful here. It was reasonable to suppose that the noise which he had heard and had supposed to have originated in the kitchen had been, in fact, the sound of Mr Fransham's body falling in the cloakroom. He had looked at his watch immediately after this and had found the time to be seven minutes past one. Again, Linton's observations had fixed the time of the doctor's return at 1.12 p.m.

Next, disregarding for the moment the nature of the object with which the blow had been struck, the murderer must have stood in the carriage-way in order to commit his crime. This fact was established by the presence of the brick wall. Therefore, Coates' statement that nobody could have entered the carriage-way without his knowledge must be set aside as unreliable.

This involved the consideration of a question which Jimmy had already asked himself. Could the chauffeur himself have been the criminal? The relations which had existed between him and his master had not yet been inquired into. It might be discovered that he had some grudge against Mr Fransham. On the other hand, there was Linton's presence to be considered. He had been in the consulting-room, the window of which overlooked the garage. Could Coates have taken the turn-cock from its nail, struck his employer with it, returned to the garage and cleaned the key, all without Linton having observed him?

It seemed hardly likely, and yet the possibility remained. There was no reason to doubt Linton's good faith; only the exact accuracy of his statement. Was he looking out of the consulting-room window all the time? His attention must have been diverted at intervals. While he was listening to the sounds within the house, or drinking his beer, for instance? People were so apt to say, 'I never took my eyes off so and so for an instant.' Whereas, in fact, they had only looked at it at more or less frequent intervals.

Failing Coates, was it possible to assume the guilt of some unknown person, X? Coates' statement must in any case be discounted. Someone must have entered the carriage-way and it might as well have been X as anybody else. But X must have entered by the drive gate and departed by the same route. Was it likely that he would have risked doing so in full view of the windows in front of the house? Dr Thornborough had stated that he had seen Alfie Prince crossing the road very shortly after the crime had been committed. Jimmy decided that one of his first moves on his return to Adderminster should be to interview Alfie.

Finally, there remained the doctor himself. Jimmy had not been altogether satisfied with the superintendent's reasoning. It had seemed to him that Yateley's conclusions had been based upon insufficient data and that he had closed his mind to any other possibility. But as a result of his own observations he was bound to admit that things looked pretty black against Dr Thornborough. The most plausible theory that Jimmy could evolve pointed to him as the culprit. He had taken the turn-cock with him in the car when he started on his rounds. On his return, he had stopped outside the cloakroom window and delivered the fatal blow. He had left the turn-cock in the car and in the course of the afternoon had seized an opportunity of cleaning it and putting it back in its place.

Jimmy was still pondering the fact when his train reached London. He took a taxi to Scotland Yard, where he handed over the turn-cock for expert examination. He had half-hoped to find Hanslet in his room, but by now it was nearly ten o'clock and the superintendent, not being on duty, had gone home. Jimmy went home to his quarters and after a restless night caught the first train to Adderminster on Sunday morning.

When he got to the police station he found Sergeant Cload in charge. 'Good-morning, sergeant,' he said. 'Any fresh developments since I've been away?'

'Nothing very much, sir,' Cload replied. 'The body's been brought down to the mortuary and it's lying there now. The super's given orders that a man is to remain on duty at the doctor's house until further orders. I think that's about all, sir, except that we've got Alfie Prince locked up in the cells here. I don't know what we're going to do with that chap, I'm sure.'

'What's he been up to now?' Jimmy asked.

'Stealing an overcoat, sir. It was like this. Just after you left last night, Linton was on his way up to the doctor's house to relieve me. On his way up there he passed Alfie and noticed that he was wearing a brand-new overcoat. He thought that was a bit queer, for Alfie's never been seen in such a thing before. So he jumped off his bike and asked Alfie where the coat came from and Alfie told him that he's just found it.'

Jimmy smiled. 'Not a very likely story,' he said.

'So Linton thought, sir. So he brought Alfie back here, took off his coat and had a look at it. He found a label sewn on to it with the name of Murphy's, the outfitters in Middle Street. They usually have a row of coats hung up outside the shop in fine weather, especially on Saturday evenings. So Linton took the coat round to Murphy and asked him if he'd sold it to Alfie. He said that he hadn't but that he'd just missed one from the row. So Linton charged Alfie and the super said we'd better put him in the cells till Monday morning.'

'Did Alfie make any further statement?'

'Well yes, he did, sir, but he talks in such a rambling way that you can hardly understand him. He said it was quite true that he'd found the coat for he'd seen it hanging up in Middle Street and taken it. When he was asked why he had taken the coat, he said because he wanted a new one as he had sold his old one the night before for half a crown and a packet of fags. Of course, that was nonsense, for you never saw anything so filthy and ragged as his old coat in your life. Nobody would have given him twopence for it, let alone half a crown. But that's just like Alfie. He's not quite right, as I've said all along.'

'What's his job when he feels like doing a spot of work?'

'He'll take anything that comes along, sir. He used to work as a bricklayer's labourer at one time, and got on very well, I've been told. But he wouldn't stick to it, and since then he's picked up jobs here and there just as suited him. There are plenty in the town who are glad to give him work from time to time, for he puts his back into it while the fit's on him.'

'There's no objection to my asking him a few questions, I suppose?'

'None at all, sir. But whether you'll be able to make any sense of what he tells you is another thing. I'll bring him along in here, if you like, sir.'

Cload went off in the direction of the cells, to reappear a few minutes later with the errant Alfie. The latter was a man of middle height, apparently in the early forties, with a round and rather childlike face. Beneath a tangled shock of red hair was a pair of deep-set blue eyes which seemed to be inhabited by some demon of restlessness. Without invitation he sat down in the nearest chair and scrutinised Jimmy keenly.

'You don't come from these parts, master,' he said confidently.

'All right, let him be, sergeant,' said Jimmy. 'No, I don't, Alfie, you're quite right. But I dare say we shall manage to get on all right together in spite of that. Have a cigarette?'

Alfie took the proffered case, emptied it into his hand, and put all the cigarettes but one into the pocket of his tattered coat. 'I knew you was a gentleman as soon as I set eyes on you,' he said complacently. 'And the sergeant, who's another, will give me a match, I dare say.'

The sergeant having provided the necessary light, Jimmy began his interrogation. 'Tell us the story of your old coat, Alfie,' he said encouragingly.

Alfie chuckled as though at the memory of some pleasant interlude. 'Ah, he was a good one in his time, he was,' he said. 'For nigh on twenty years I'd worn him, wet or fine, rain or sun. But all things come to an end, as my old mother says. He was getting as full of holes as a length of rabbit netting, and that's a fact.'

'So you thought it time to get rid of him?' Jimmy suggested.

'Well, maybe I wouldn't have parted with him just yet. He'd been a good friend to me, master. But I wanted a fag that badly that I'd have given the cove the very boots off my feet for one.'

'Who was this cove and where did you meet him?'

'The night afore last it was. I was walking along down by Weaver's Bridge and it must have been after hours, because the Shant was closed and I couldn't get anybody to open the door to me.'

'Weaver's Bridge is outside the town, sir,' Cload explained. 'It's about a mile and a half round by the road but rather less if you go up Gunthorpe Road and cut through Mark Farm. There's a beerhouse there which is always known as the Shant, though its proper name is The Prince of Wales, and closing time in this division is half-past ten, at this time of year, sir.'

Jimmy nodded. 'Carry on, Alfie,' he said. 'You were taking an evening stroll round about Weaver's Bridge. Is that when you met the cove?'

'That's how it was. He comes along towards me smoking a fag, so I says to him, "Good-evening, merry chum," just like that. "Good-evening, merry chum, it'd be a fine bright night if the moon hadn't gone to bed with his wife. And perhaps you've got a fag or two to spare for a poor man who's got four little kiddies and not a crust among them."'

'And what did the cove say to that?' Jimmy asked.

Again Alfie chuckled. 'He didn't say nothing, and that was the joke of it. Maybe I'd startled him a bit, for it was main dark and he couldn't see me under the shadow of the hedge, like. He takes one of them dratted flashlamp things out of his pocket and turns it on to me. "Oh it's you, Alfie, is it?" he says.'

'He knew you, then?'

The reply displayed the pride of a famous man. 'There aren't many folk in these parts who don't know Alfie Prince.'

'And did you know him?'

'How should I know him in the dark? "I'll give you a packet of fags, Alfie," he said. "But I want that old coat of yours in exchange, and I'll give you half a crown into the bargain." And that's how it happened, as true as there are angels playing on their harps up above us. The cove went off a-humming of a tune and wearing my old coat, and that's the last I've seen of him.'

'What did you do then, Alfie?'

'Why, I got the fags, and funny-tasting things they was. So I come through Farmer Hawkworth's land and settled down for the night in that field of grass at the end of Gunthorpe Road.'

'You mean the field that's for sale in building plots, I suppose?'

'That's it. I know of a corner alongside that brick wall

at the end. But I missed my old coat, for all that I got them fags and half a crown in my pocket.'

Jimmy nodded to Cload, who thereupon escorted Alfie back to the cell. 'What did you make of him, sir?' the sergeant asked on his return.

'I agree with you that he's not quite all there. You can tell that by the way he talks. But I'm pretty certain that he didn't invent that story about his old coat. It's too circumstantial for that. I'd very much like to know who it was that he met and why he wanted Alfie's old coat. You know Colonel Exbury pretty well, I expect?'

'Oh yes, sir, I've always got on very well with the colonel.'

'Then I wish you'd ring him up and ask him if Alfie was wearing his old coat when he came to his house yesterday.'

Cload put the call through and reported the result. 'The colonel says that Alfie wasn't wearing the coat, sir. He noticed that particularly for he'd never seen him without it before.'

'Then Alfie's story may be true. If so, he spent Friday night within a few yards of the doctor's house. He said something about his mother. Is she still alive?'

'Oh yes, sir. She's a very respectable woman who keeps a little ham and beef shop in Middle Street. Alfie lodges with her when it suits him, but as often as not he sleeps out somewhere, especially in the summer.'

'She might be able to tell us something about Alfie's movements on Friday and Saturday. Better get one of your men to go and have a chat with her, sergeant. Linton was on duty last night up at the doctor's house, wasn't he?'

'That's right, sir. He was relieved by one of the other chaps this morning.'

'Then he won't come to the surface again until this

afternoon. I'm going up Gunthorpe Road to have a look round, and I'll be back here before lunch time.'

Jimmy left the police station and went to the doctor's house. But he did not enter the gate, merely glancing down the carriage-way, noticing that the garage doors were shut and that no car stood in front of them. Then he went on for a few yards until he reached a convenient gap in the hedge bordering the building plot. He passed through this to find himself in a field of standing grass. It was immediately obvious to him that he was not the first to pass that way. The tall grass was trodden down into a track which led along the inside of the hedge until it reached the wall, on the other side of of which was the doctor's carriage-way. And at the end of this track, in the corner formed by the hedge and the wall, lay a discarded garment. And at the sight of it Jimmy came to a sudden stand. It was a very old army greatcoat, easily recognisable as such, though it was stained and rent in countless places.

Very gingerly Jimmy picked it up. Beneath it lay five cigarette ends which Jimmy collected, packed in a piece of paper, and put in his pocket. Then he noticed a second track at right angles to the first, running along the inside of the wall. He followed this track to find that it ended abruptly fifty-three paces from the hedge.

He returned to the point where he had found the coat, laid it down, and left the field by the gap in the hedge. Then he walked to the drive gate of the doctor's house and paced fifty-three yards down the carriage-way. The end of this fifty-third pace brought him exactly opposite the cloakroom window.

There must be some significance in the fact that the track

in the field terminated exactly level with the window. Could the criminal have used this means of approach? Jimmy had already satisfied himself that Mr Fransham could not have been attacked from the top of the wall. But could his assailant have climbed the wall and dropped into the carriage-way? Such a feat would not have been beyond the powers of an exceptionally active man. But surely Coates, however much his attention might have been distracted at the moment, would have heard or seen something of this performance?

Jimmy began to examine the wall to see if it contained any crevices which might have afforded foothold. But the wall was comparatively new, and the pointing was still almost perfect. It was a nine inch wall, built in English bond with alternate headers and stretchers. And, as Jimmy scrutinised its surface, he noticed that round one of the headers the texture of the mortar was slightly different from elsewhere. He applied his finger to the place, and found that the surface yielded to his touch. A little further investigation proved that the joint was not made of mortar at all, but of plasticine. Jimmy pressed his hand against the header, which immediately slid back.

He left it at that, and hurried back through the gap in the hedge to the farther side of the wall. Here he found one of the bricks protruding an inch or so. It was an easy matter to grasp it and pull it right out. He bent down and looked through the hole thus formed in the wall. Its line of vision passed horizontally through the opening of the window into the cloakroom beyond. When Mr Fransham bent down over the basin, the top of his head must have been exactly in front of the hole.

Jimmy very soon satisfied himself of the way in which

the brick had been removed. The mortar round it had been patiently scraped away, probably by some instrument in the nature of a long screwdriver. A few particles of this mortar lay at the foot of the wall among the roots of the grass. The brick had then been taken out and the walls of the cavity scraped smooth. But if the brick had then been reinserted, the absence of the mortar would have left a space all round it, which would have been noticed at once. An ingenious method had been adopted to get over this. The brick had been carefully wrapped in several thicknesses of gummed paper until it exactly fitted the cavity. The ends of this paper had then been masked with plasticine, coloured so as to match the mortar exactly. Upon replacement of the brick no visible sign remained of the wall having been tampered with.

Jimmy examined the paper in which the brick had been wrapped. He saw at once that it consisted of sheets of some periodical. On removing one or two layers, he found a sheet upon which the name of the periodical appeared. It was the *British Medical Journal* of the preceding May *22*.

He put the brick back very carefully in its place. Then he picked up the army greatcoat and made his way back with it to the police station.

Sergeant Cload's face stiffened as he caught sight of his burden. 'Wherever did you find that, sir, if I may ask?' he exclaimed.

'In the very spot where Alfie says he spent last Friday night,' Jimmy replied. 'Bring him along here again for a minute, will you?'

Alfie reappeared and Jimmy held the coat up before his eyes. 'Did you ever see this before, Alfie?' he asked.

Alfie's eyes opened wide in amazement. 'Why glory

hallelujah! If it isn't my old coat come back to find me,' he exclaimed. Then he frowned suspiciously. 'You must be the cove that took it off me,' he said with an air of finality.

'Wrong this time, Alfie,' Jimmy replied. 'All right, sergeant, take him away.'

By the time that Cload returned, Jimmy was busy drawing a plan in his notebook. He looked up and grinned cheerfully at the sergeant. 'Jolly case, this,' he said. 'It's absolutely brimful of contradictions. To begin with, how did Alfie's coat find its way to the corner where its original possessor spent Friday night?'

Cload shook his head. 'You can't take any heed of what Alfie says when he's like this, sir,' he replied. 'I wouldn't go so far as to say that he was deliberately lying when he told us that story just now. He may honestly have believed that those things had really happened, whereas he had only imagined or dreamt them.'

'Wait a minute,' said Jimmy, taking the paper containing the cigarette ends from his pocket. 'I found these lying on the grass under Alfie's coat just now. Alfie can't have enjoyed them very much, for in nearly every case he's left an inch of stump. And if you look closely at them, sergeant, you can see the name of the brand printed on them. Black's Russian Blend.'

'Yes, I can see that plain enough, sir,' Cload replied. 'But I don't know that I've ever heard of them before.'

'That's very likely, for they aren't sold everywhere. You can only get them at one of Black's shops in London. It seems to me that those cigarette ends to some extent confirm Alfie's story of the cove he met.'

Cload looked a trifle dubious. 'When Alfie's in these

moods, he'll ask anybody he meets for fags. And it doesn't follow that whoever gave him these asked for his coat in exchange.'

'It doesn't follow, certainly. Your theory, I take it, is that Alfie, following his usual habit, accosted some worthy citizen of Adderminster and was given the cigarettes of which these are the ends.'

'That's about it, sir. I don't somehow believe in the man with the flashlamp who bought Alfie's coat. Whoever could want such a filthy old thing as that?'

'Ah, that's just it! But do you know anybody in Adderminster who smokes Black's Russian Blend?'

'I can't say that I do, sir, but that doesn't count for much. There are plenty of people in Adderminster who go up to London three and four times a week. There's nothing to prevent any of them from buying these cigarettes at one of the shops you speak of, sir.'

'I wonder if Dr Thornborough smokes them?'

Cload shook his head. 'The doctor only smokes a pipe, sir. I've heard him say more than once that cigarettes always make him cough.'

Jimmy glanced at the clock. 'It's a quarter to one now,' he said. 'If I walk up to *Epidaurus*, I ought to catch the doctor as he comes home to lunch.'

When Jimmy reached the house, Lucy informed him that the doctor had already returned, and showed him into the consulting-room. Here, a minute later, Dr Thornborough joined him. He looked very careworn, and it was easy to tell that the events of the last twenty-four hours had played havoc with his nerves.

'Well, inspector?' he demanded curtly. 'What's your business?'

59

'My business is concerned with Alfie Prince, doctor,' replied Jimmy quietly.

Dr Thornborough had clearly expected a very different answer. 'Alfie Prince!' he said, wearily passing his hand across his forehead. 'I'd forgotten all about him. You must excuse me, but this terrible affair has shaken me up pretty badly. What do you want me to do about Alfie Prince?'

'Nothing, just now, doctor. Alfie's out of mischief for the moment in one of the cells at the police station. You saw him yesterday on your way home to luncheon, didn't you?'

'Not to speak to. He merely happened to cross the road in front of me.'

'How far away from you was he when you saw him?'

'Oh, a couple of hundred yards, I dare say. Certainly not less.'

'Did you notice him particularly?'

'I can't say that I did. Seeing that it was Alfie, I didn't take any further notice of him.'

'Were you surprised to find him wandering about up here?'

Dr Thornborough smiled a trifle wanly. 'Nobody in Adderminster is ever very much surprised at what Alfie does. Besides, he's a sufferer from claustrophobia, and I happen to know that sometimes he spends his nights in the field adjoining this house.'

'Do you happen to know whether he spent last Friday night there?'

'I don't, for I never look to see whether he's there or not. Officially I know nothing about it, for I suppose that technically he's trespassing. But he isn't doing any harm, and from the medical point of view it's better for him to sleep out than in.'

'He was coming out of that field when you saw him, wasn't he?'

'Yes. He crossed the road into the orchard opposite, and I didn't see any more of him after that.'

'You're perfectly certain that the man you saw was Alfie?'

'Oh, anyone who knew him would recognise him a mile away. He always wears a filthy old army greatcoat, so ragged that it's literally dropping off him. And as soon as I caught sight of that coat I knew it must be Alfie.'

'Where were you coming from when you saw him, doctor?'

'I'd been to Mark Farm. Mrs Hawksworth, the farmer's wife is one of my patients. I'd been to Weaver's Bridge and I drove up to the farm from that direction. I was there about a quarter of an hour, I dare say, and then I came home through the gate at the end of the road.'

'Did you see anybody else besides Alfie?'

'Not a soul. It's a dead end, you know, unless you happen to be going to Mark Farm.'

'Do you happen to know the tenant of the cottage on the other side of the road?'

'I can't say that I know him, but he came here to see me about three weeks ago. He cut his thumb rather badly, chopping wood. I bound it up for him, and wrote him out a prescription for a salve. He told me that his name was Willingdon, and that he only came down here for the weekends. I thought he seemed quite a decent young fellow.'

'I hope I'm not taking up too much of your time, doctor,' said Jimmy. 'I'd like to ask you one or two more questions and then I've finished. By the way, do you mind if I smoke?'

'Not a bit,' replied Dr Thornborough heartily. 'I'm afraid I can't offer you a cigarette though, for I never smoke the things myself.'

'Oh that's all right, I always carry my own,' said Jimmy. He produced his cigarette case, opened it and suddenly looked blank. 'Blest if it isn't empty!' he exclaimed. 'I must have forgotten to fill it.'

'You cigarette smokers are always doing that,' the doctor replied. 'Wait a minute, there are plenty of cigarettes in the drawing-room. I'll go and get you one.'

Dr Thornborough left the room, to return a few moments later with a silver box which he held out towards Jimmy. 'Here you are,' he said. 'They're my wife's. I don't know whether you'll care about them.'

Jimmy took one of the cigarettes and lighted it. 'Black's Russian Blend, I see,' he said. 'I used to have a fancy for them myself at one time. Does Mrs Thornborough always smoke them?'

'No, she smokes Player's as a rule. But her uncle, Mr Fransham, sent her a hundred of these last week. I don't think she cares about them much, though.'

'They're an acquired taste. By the way, doctor, why did you have a brick wall built on one side of your property and not the other?'

Dr Thornborough, as well he might, looked slightly astonished at this question.

'The reason's a very simple one,' he replied. 'On one side of the house, as you may have noticed, are the public gardens. They will never be built upon. But the land on the other side is for sale in building plots. Sooner or later somebody will put up a house there. Hence the wall, which I had put up in order to avoid being overlooked.'

Jimmy smiled. 'I might have thought of that for myself,' he said. 'There's just one thing I'd like to mention, doctor.

It might be advisable for Mr Fransham's solicitor to be present at the inquest tomorrow.'

'The same thing occurred to me. I got on the telephone to him yesterday afternoon, and explained what had happened. He promised to come down by the afternoon train today, and should be here about half-past four. Have you formed any opinion as to how this terrible thing can have happened?'

'I've hardly had time for that yet, doctor. Is Coates, Mr Fransham's chauffeur, still here?'

'I sent him down with Fransham's car to the Red Lion. And told him to stay there till further orders.'

'That's just as well, for his evidence will probably be wanted at the inquest. Do you happen to take the *British Medical Journal,* doctor?'

'Yes, I do. There's this week's issue lying on the table in front of you.'

'I wonder if you could find me the issue of May 22? There's an article in that number which I'm particularly anxious to read. We policemen have to try and keep abreast of certain branches of medical knowledge, you know.'

Dr Thornborough went to a bookshelf upon which lay a pile of back numbers. He ran through these twice without finding the one which Jimmy had asked for.

'That's queer,' he said. 'That particular number must have got mislaid. But I'll have a hunt for it and send it along to you when I find it.'

'Oh, please don't trouble. I've wasted enough of your time as it is.'

Jimmy left the house, being escorted to the front door by the doctor. He then crossed the road and knocked at the door of the cottage, which stood by itself in a small garden surrounded by trees. After a few minutes the door was opened by a noticeably pale young man, wearing a tennis shirt and a pair of grey flannel trousers, who remained in the dark background of the hall, from which he peered at his visitor disapprovingly. 'This isn't my at home day, you know,' he said.

'I hoped it might have been,' Jimmy replied. 'Are you Mr Willingdon?'

'Such is my ancestral name. My godfathers and godmothers in my baptism christened me Francis. To the denizens of the low haunts which I frequent I am known as Frank. And who are you that so blithely disturb my Sabbath rest?'

'I'm Inspector James Waghorn from Scotland Yard,' Jimmy replied simply.

'Be sure your sins will find you out!' exclaimed the other in a sepulchral tone. 'Where are the minions of justice? Where are the handcuffs and the gyves? Where, in fact, is the Black Maria?'

'Sorry, I forgot to bring it. But I'd be very glad if you could spare me five minutes of your time, Mr Willingdon.'

'He calls me Mr Willingdon! Indeed, my offence must be rank. Wherein have I transgressed the King's Peace? Have I driven thirty and a half miles an hour in a thirty mile limit? Have I consumed alcohol during the hours when such indulgence is not permitted? Have I been so lost to all sense of decency as to loiter with intent? Come inside, and tell me the worst.'

He led the way into a room furnished as a lounge, with the curtains drawn across all the windows. When his eyes became accustomed to the gloom, Jimmy perceived that at one end of this room was a table covered with a newspaper, on which was laid a tin can, a loaf of bread and a bottle of beer. A faint but penetrating smell of perfume pervaded the place.

'Observe the preparations for my frugal meal,' said Willingdon. 'Care to join me? I dare say I could find another bottle of beer in the refrigerator.'

'I couldn't think of depriving you of it,' Jimmy replied. 'You've heard, of course, of what happened at the doctor's house across the road yesterday afternoon?'

Willingdon shook his head. 'While I am in this rural retreat, I am a temporary anchorite,' he said. 'That's what I come here for. Life in the giddy world is so hectic that even the most pernicious of us want a rest sometimes. Don't you find that, inspector? Nothing untoward has befallen the doctor, I hope? He seemed a very good fellow the only time I saw him.'

'His wife's uncle was found dead in his house soon after one o'clock yesterday.'

'How very annoying! I should hate any of my well-loved and respected relatives to expire in my arms. Unless, of course, their testamentary depositions compensated for the shock to my nerves. But surely you haven't come to talk to me about the deceased uncle of the doctor's wife? Sounds too terribly like a lesson in elementary French.'

'That's just what I have come to talk about. It's just possible that you may have seen or heard something which may throw light upon the man's death. To begin with, what were you doing between one and a quarter past yesterday afternoon, Mr Willingdon?'

With a gesture, Willingdon indicated the table.

'Much what I'm doing now, or should have been doing

but for the unexpected pleasure of your visit,' he replied. 'Replenishing the jaded body with its needful sustenance.'

'And what did you do when you had completed the process?'

Willingdon pointed to the sofa. 'I laid myself recumbent on yonder couch,' he replied. 'And there I still was when the summons of the door-knocker roused me from my slumbers.'

'You had a visitor?' Jimmy suggested.

'You have divined the truth, inspector. It's not the first time that people have knocked on the door while I've been down here. But, as a rule, I don't open it and after a time they go away. I had no intention of opening the door yesterday afternoon, imagining that time would abate the nuisance. So it did, but the nuisance reasserted itself. It manifested itself this time by a tapping on the window. I couldn't stand that, so I got up to see who it was.'

'What time was this?' Jimmy asked.

Willingdon frowned. 'I have always refused to be a slave to that ridiculous convention which you call time,' he replied. 'Besides, there's no such thing, as any of these modern scientific johnnies will tell you. It was sometime in the afternoon, too early for my system to demand the stimulus of tea, and not yet late enough for it to have recovered from its post-prandial somnolence.'

'Somewhere between two and three o'clock, perhaps?'

'Very likely. I opened the window, and a husky voice hailed me. "Got any fags to spare, guv'nor?"'

'What did the man look like?' Jimmy asked.

'Nothing on earth. You couldn't imagine him unless you had read *The King in Yellow*, which I don't suppose you have.'

Jimmy smiled. '"Songs that the Hyades shall sing, Where flap the tatters of the king,"' he quoted. 'Is that what you were thinking of?'

'Once more you have divined it. There was something kingly in his assurance that his request would not be denied. And the tatters—the yellow tatters! Nowhere but in Carcosa could he have found a garment like that.'

'Could you describe it?'

'Words don't often fail me, as you may have noticed. But for that purpose, I can think of none adequate. It still retained a faint suggestion of military discomfort about the collar, as though some veteran of the Peninsula war had cowered in it behind the lines of Torres Vedras. In colour it was yellow, the yellow of dank and mouldering corruption. It was probably verminous, and most certainly it stank.'

'Could you describe the man who was wearing it?'

'Red hair, wandering blue eyes and a pungent aroma of perspiration. Those were my impressions.'

'Did you give him any cigarettes?'

'I did. I gave him a handful out of that box you see over there. I thought it was the quickest way of getting rid of him. And he said, "Honourable toff, here's my best thanks." I liked that, for he's the first person who's ever thought me honourable or considered me a toff.'

'What happened after that?'

'"Erupit, evasit, as Tully would phrase it!" He hasn't troubled me since, I'm thankful to say.'

In reply to further questions Willingdon gave the following information. He had taken the cottage for a month, having seen it advertised in *The Times*. During that month he had lived in it each weekend, coming down on

Friday evening and driving back to London on Monday morning. His leave expired the following week and this was, therefore, the last occasion on which he would use the cottage. He knew nobody in Adderminster except Dr Thornborough, and had only seen him once, when he consulted him professionally.

'I'd like to know your occupation and address, Mr Willingdon, in case I want to get in touch with you again,' said Jimmy, as he rose to take his leave.

Willingdon shuddered. 'Occupation is a disaster which I have always strenuously avoided,' he replied. 'I don't mind telling you in confidence what my trouble is. I've got more money than is good for my friends. As for an address, I never stay in one place longer than I can help. But if ever you want to know where I am, ask the girl in the reception office at Harlow's Hotel. The ugly one, I mean—the one with a mouth like a vacuum cleaner. The pretty one's more fun, but I'm sorry to say that she's distressingly stupid. Sure you won't try a bit of this tongue? It's the genuine article and not synthetic rubber.'

Jimmy excused himself and left the cottage. He had observed that all the windows in the lounge faced away from the road. It was therefore highly unlikely that Willingdon would have seen any of the events of the previous day, even if he had not been in the habit of sitting with all the curtains drawn. His afternoon visitor could have been none other than Alfie, attired in his now famous greatcoat.

Alfie was becoming a nuisance in more senses than one. It was inconceivable that he should have had any connection with the death of Mr Fransham. And yet his name or presence cropped up at every turn of the investigation. As

Jimmy walked back to the police station he made a mental list of Alfie's appearances.

Between 10.30 and 11 p.m. on Friday evening, Alfie was accosted by a mysterious cove near Weaver's Bridge. This cove had relieved him of his greatcoat and rewarded him with a handful of cigarettes and half a crown. The only authority for this transaction was Alfie himself.

About a quarter to one on Saturday morning, Alfie had pestered Colonel Exbury for cigarettes. On that occasion he was not wearing his greatcoat. Colonel Exbury, presumably an impartial witness, was the authority for this. About ten minutes past one on the same day Alfie, or someone whom the doctor mistook for him, was seen crossing Gunthorpe Road. He was recognised from the fact that he was wearing the unmistakable greatcoat. But this event depended on the unconfirmed statement of Dr Thornborough, and for the present at least, Dr Thornborough's statements must be accepted with caution.

Sometime in the same afternoon Alfie had called upon Mr Willingdon and demanded cigarettes. Willingdon's description could hardly apply to anyone except Alfie and his coat. And begging cigarettes seemed to be Alfie's passion at the moment.

About seven o'clock on the same afternoon, Alfie had been seen and detained by Linton. He had by then exchanged his old coat for one taken from outside Murphy's shop.

Finally, at 10.45 on Sunday morning Jimmy himself had found the coat in the corner of the grass field. Alfie had immediately recognised it as his.

Jimmy called at the Red Lion for a hasty lunch and then went back to the police station.

Sergeant Cload was waiting for him. 'I went round to see Mrs Prince myself, sir,' he said. 'I thought she'd better know where Alfie was, in case she might be worrying about him. She was a bit upset when she heard what he'd been up to, but I persuaded her that he was best where he was, out of harm's way for the present. She said she was afraid when she last saw him that one of his fits was coming on.'

'When did she see him last?' Jimmy asked.

'On Friday evening, sir. He'd been working all the week for one of the farmers just outside the town. But when he came home on Friday, his mother could see that he was restless and not quite himself. She gave him his tea and then he said that he was going out to count the fish in Weaver's Brook. She knew it was no good crossing him when he was in that mood, so she put a few slices of beef and bread in his pocket. And she hasn't seen him since.'

'She wasn't worried when he didn't come back at night?'

'Not a bit, sir. She's used to Alfie sleeping out under a hedge somewhere most summer nights. She hoped he'd get over his trouble by Monday morning and start work again then.'

'What are you going to do about him?'

'I've had a word with the super, sir. He says that I'm to get Dr Dorrington to see him on Monday morning before he comes before the magistrate.'

'That's about the best thing you can do. Has Linton come in yet? I'd like to have a chat with him if he has.'

Linton appeared, and at Jimmy's request gave a detailed account of his experiences in the doctor's house on the previous morning. Jimmy listened attentively and then began to question him.

70

'I've been up to the house and I've got a pretty good idea of the ground floor arrangements, at all events,' he said. 'Now first of all that noise you heard like something being dropped. Could that have been the sound of Mr Fransham falling on the cloakroom floor?'

'I think it must have been that, sir,' Linton replied. 'I'm quite certain the sound came from the ground floor. And while I was up there last night I asked Lucy, that's the parlourmaid, if anything had been dropped in the kitchen before lunch. She said that it hadn't, but that she thought she'd heard something fall, too.'

'That's good. You looked at your watch directly after you heard the sound, so we can pretty well establish the time that Mr Fransham was hit at seven minutes past one. Now at that time, there were, to the best of our knowledge, four people in the house. Mrs Thornborough, her mother, the cook and the parlourmaid. I'm not counting Mr Fransham. Do you know which rooms these four people were in?'

'I heard Mrs Thornborough go upstairs just before it happened, sir. I think Mrs Thornborough's mother must have been up there already, for I could hear somebody walking about overhead when I first went into the consulting-room. The cook would have been in the kitchen getting the lunch ready, and I'm pretty certain that Lucy was there, too, for I had heard her go through the baize door.'

'Which way do the kitchen windows look?'

'Towards the garden at the back of the house, sir, the same way as the consulting-room window.'

'You saw Mr Fransham's car drive into the garage and Coates the chauffeur get out of it. What exactly did he do then?'

'He walked right round the car, sir, looking over it. I

71

saw him lift the bonnet, one side after another. I dare say that took him a couple of minutes, certainly not more. Then he took out a cigarette, lighted it and leant against one of the doorposts of the garage.'

'Now, Linton, I want you to think very carefully. Did you keep your eyes fixed on Coates the whole time until the doctor came home?'

'Well, sir, I can't say that I did that exactly. I wasn't looking out of the window the whole time.'

'Then Coates might have walked up the carriage-way to the cloakroom window and back again?'

Linton shook his head.

'No, sir, I'm perfectly certain he didn't do that,' he replied. 'I won't say that I had my eyes on him all the time, for I hadn't. But if he'd walked up the carriage-way I should have noticed it. And if I hadn't actually seen him, I should have heard his footsteps on the hard concrete. Of course, I couldn't swear to it, but I'm quite certain in my own mind that he didn't move from the doorpost until the doctor's car came in.'

'When did you first hear the doctor's car?'

'When it turned in at the gateway, sir. There's some loose grit there, and tyres make a queer sort of swishing noise. I noticed it before, when Mr Fransham's car turned into the carriage-way from the front door.'

'Would you have known by the sound if the doctor's car had stopped outside the cloakroom window?'

Linton hesitated. 'It's very difficult to say, sir. It might have stopped for a moment, but no longer, for it was only a few seconds after I'd heard it turn in that I saw it through the window.'

'Was it before or after you heard something falling that you heard the car turn in?'

'Some minutes after, sir. That was when I looked at my watch for the second time and found that it was twelve minutes past one.'

'You heard the conversation between Dr and Mrs Thornborough outside the consulting-room door. Did Mrs Thornborough seem upset?'

'Yes, she did, sir. She seemed to think that it was the doctor's fault that Mr Fransham had turned up unexpectedly like that.'

'And was the doctor surprised?'

'Well, it sounded to me as if he was, sir. But then he wasn't so surprised as he might have been, for he'd already spoken to Coates and knew what had happened.'

'What exactly happened after you'd broken down the door? Who entered the cloakroom first?'

'I did, sir. The door flew open easier than I'd expected, and I went in with it. The doctor came in just behind me.'

'Then the doctor had no opportunity whatever of picking anything up without your seeing him?'

'He couldn't have done that, sir. As soon as I recovered myself, I stood aside to let him pass. We both stood still for a second or two, just as Lucy sounded the gong. Then the doctor went straight to the body and knelt down beside it. I was watching him all the time he was there, and he couldn't possibly have picked anything up.'

'You are absolutely certain that the body was not moved until you and the superintendent did so?'

'I'm positive about that, sir. I only left the cloakroom once to use the telephone in the hall, and I was watching the cloakroom door all the time. And when I got back, the body was lying exactly as I had left it.'

'Does the doctor see many patients at his house?'

'A good few, I fancy, sir. He has his regular hours at the surgery in the town, but if people want to see him out of surgery hours they go to his house.'

Jimmy nodded. 'Thanks, Linton, that's all for the present, I think,' he said, and when the policeman had left the room, he picked up his pencil and stabbed the table in front of him thoughtfully. 'If only I could make out how the crime was committed, I might form some theory of who did it,' he muttered.

CHAPTER V

That afternoon, shortly after six o'clock, Jimmy was informed that a visitor wished to see him. 'The gentleman says that his name is Mr Redbourne, and that he is Mr Fransham's solicitor,' said Cload.

'I'll see him with pleasure,' Jimmy replied. 'Bring him in, will you, sergeant.'

Mr Redbourne was introduced. He was a short, excitable little man of sixty or thereabouts. He was nearly bald and wore a pair of pince-nez with powerful lenses. The way he looked at Jimmy suggested that he was a trifle disconcerted at the inspector's youth. 'Are you the man from Scotland Yard?' he inquired sharply.

'Inspector Waghorn, at your service, Mr Redbourne,' Jimmy replied politely. 'Do sit down, sir. I'm delighted at the opportunity of making your acquaintance.'

Mr Redbourne complied with the invitation. 'Well, what are you going to do about it?' he asked belligerently.

'About what, Mr Redbourne?'

'Why, about the murder of my old friend and client,

75

Robert Fransham, of course. What else? That's why you're here, I suppose, isn't it?'

'I propose to continue my investigations,' Jimmy replied quietly. 'Dr Thornborough has informed you of the circumstances, no doubt?'

'He has,' said Mr Redbourne grimly. 'And highly suspicious circumstances they are, even by his own account. When I had heard what he had to say, I refused to remain under his roof another instant. And I have informed him that though Robert Fransham had appointed me one of his executors, I shall refuse to act in that capacity.'

'I'm naturally interested in Mr Fransham's will. Are you disposed to enlighten me as to its terms, Mr Redbourne?'

'Under the circumstances, I am prepared to give the police all the information in my power. One of my oldest friends has been brutally murdered, and no reasonable person can entertain the slightest doubt who did it. You will admit that, I suppose?'

Jimmy smiled. 'I'd rather not admit anything until after the inquest tomorrow,' he said. 'You were going to tell me about Mr Fransham's will, I think?'

Mr Redbourne looked at Jimmy over the top of his glasses. 'You appear to be a very discreet young man,' he said. 'I trust, however, that you will not allow discretion to overrule your common sense. Robert Fransham's will is in my safe at the office. In it, Dr Thornborough and myself are named as joint executors. Apart from legacies to Fransham's dependents, his niece Mrs Thornborough is the sole legatee.'

'Mr Fransham had no children of his own?'

'He had never married, and he had no nephews or nieces but Betty, whom I have known since she was a little girl.

Under the existing will, she inherits his estate absolutely.'

'Can you give me any idea of the extent of the estate?'

'I imagine that it will prove to be in the neighbourhood of a couple of hundred thousand pounds.'

'Mrs Thornborough will become a wealthy woman,' Jimmy remarked. 'Does her mother benefit by the will directly in any way?'

'No, she does not. Robert Fransham has always disliked his brother's wife. That was one of the reasons which led him to instruct me to draw up a fresh will, which he was to have signed one day this week.'

'Did this fresh will disinherit Mrs Thornborough?' Jimmy asked quickly.

'No. Robert Fransham always intended that Betty should inherit his property. The existing will to that effect was drawn up in 1917, after his brother Thomas had been killed in the war.

'Latterly, however, Robert Fransham began to have doubts of the wisdom of leaving the estate to his niece absolutely. Knowing her generous and possibly unbusinesslike nature, he was afraid that her mother and her husband might make demands upon her which she would find it difficult to refuse. It has always been a grievance with Mrs Thomas Fransham that her brother-in-law did not make her an allowance after her husband's death. There was really no reason why he should have done so, since she always enjoyed an income of nearly five hundred a year.'

'And Dr Thornborough's habits are inclined to be extravagant?' Jimmy suggested.

'Oh, so you've found that out, have you?' Mr Redbourne replied rather grudgingly. 'I happen to know that on more than one occasion Betty has approached her uncle for sums of money on her husband's account. Naturally, this made Robert Fransham rather anxious. He became afraid that after his death Dr Thornborough would gradually appropriate all his niece's money until she became destitute. And in any case he always set his face resolutely against needless extravagance. He had therefore resolved to make a new will, leaving his estate to Betty in trust. The effect of this would have been that while she would enjoy the interest, she would not have power to dispose of the capital. This will had already been drawn up and only awaited Robert Fransham's signature.'

'Were Dr or Mrs Thornborough aware of Mr Fransham's intentions?'

'That I cannot tell you. Robert Fransham may have told his niece what he intended to do. The fact of his murder strongly suggests to me, at least, that he had done so.'

'Who are the other beneficiaries under the existing will?'

'Stowell and his wife, the married couple who had been with him for years, to the extent of an annuity of one hundred pounds. Coates, his chauffeur, who had not been with him so long, to the extent of a lump sum of two hundred pounds. These legacies were provided in codicils to the original will.'

'Do you know of anybody else who benefits financially by Mr Fransham's death?'

'There is nobody else,' replied Mr Redbourne emphatically. 'But I think I have made it quite clear that there are two persons whose prospects are greatly improved by Robert Fransham's death having occurred when it did.'

'I am bound to consider every possibility, Mr Redbourne,' said Jimmy quietly. 'Mr Fransham was an old friend of yours, you tell me. I'm bound to ask the usual question, realising how difficult it is to answer. To your knowledge, had Mr Fransham any personal enemies?'

'None!' Mr Redbourne replied, taking off his glasses and waving them at Jimmy to emphasise his words. 'None whatever. Robert Fransham was not the sort of man who arouses feelings of enmity. We were at school together, and I have known him pretty intimately ever since. He may not have contracted many sincere friendships. He was too apt to keep himself aloof from other people for that. I have always thought that the reason he never married was to be found in his innate dislike of sharing his feelings with anybody else. He was, I think, fond of me in his curiously detached way, and he was, I am sure, genuinely devoted to Betty Thornborough. But I don't know that he would have called anybody else in the world a personal friend. The fact that Dr Thornborough is an executor of the existing will is a proof of that.'

'I'm afraid that I don't exactly follow your reasoning, Mr Redbourne,' Jimmy remarked.

'It's easy enough to understand. When Robert Fransham made his original will, another very old friend of his was alive. He and I were named as executors. And when this man died shortly after Betty's marriage, I suggested to Robert Fransham that he had better appoint another executor in his place. He said at first that he knew of nobody whom he could ask to undertake the duty, but later he decided that Betty's husband would be a suitable person.'

'I see,' said Jimmy. 'In your opinion, Mr Fransham, having few friends, had even fewer enemies?'

'He had none whatever, you may set your mind at rest upon that point. Since his retirement from business sixteen

79

or seventeen years ago, he had led a very quiet life, spending the greater part of his time at his club or visiting his acquaintances. He very rarely entertained anybody at home—in fact, I am one of the two or three who ever visited him at No. 4 Cheveley Street. He would give occasional small dinner parties at a restaurant, and used to say that if he wished to entertain people, he liked to do so without disturbing his own household. A very sensible attitude, especially on the part of a bachelor.'

'Was his house in Cheveley Street his own property?'

'No, it was not. Nos. 3 and 4 belong to Sir Godfrey Branstock, who himself lives in No. 3. In 1920, Mr Fransham took over the remainder of a lease of No. 4. And that lease, as it happens, expires at Christmas this year.'

'Did Mr Fransham intend to renew it?'

'When I last spoke to him, less than a week ago, he had not made up his mind on the subject. He told me that Betty had been trying to persuade him to buy a house somewhere in this neighbourhood. But he didn't seem particularly taken with the idea. He would never have been happy out of London, away from his club and his little group of acquaintances. He told me that he had spoken to Branstock, who was quite ready to grant him a fresh lease, but he hadn't done anything definite about it, because he didn't like disappointing Betty. His final decision would, I feel pretty certain, have been to remain in Cheveley Street. Had he asked my advice it would certainly have been to this effect. I am quite sure that, had he left London, he would in a very short time have regretted doing so.'

'What sort of establishment did Mr Fransham maintain?'

'A very simple one. His household consisted of the

Stowels, the married couple who ran the house for him, and his chauffeur, who lived in the house. Actually, No. 4 Cheveley Street was far too big for him. Half the rooms were rarely, if ever, used.'

'Did he ever have people staying in the house?'

'To the best of my belief, the only person who has ever stayed there is his niece. Robert Fransham hated anything that upset the regular routine of his existence, and he considered visitors in the light of an unnecessary inconvenience.'

'Had he any hobbies?'

'None whatever, unless the reading of light fiction may be described as a hobby. He was a constant frequenter of his club, and when he was at home he occupied most of his time reading. Since his retirement he has taken no part whatever in any public or social activities. I have often thought that his undoubted abilities were wasted.'

'Mr Fransham cannot have been very old when he retired?'

'He was only forty-one. Many men of that age would have found some fresh occupation for their energy. But Robert Fransham didn't, perhaps because energy of any kind had always been distasteful to him.'

'And yet he contrived to amass a fairly respectable fortune?' Jimmy suggested.

'That wasn't his fault,' Mr Redbourne replied. 'I'll give you a sketch of his life's history, if you like. As I told you before, he was at school with me, and I remember him very well there, though he was a couple of years younger than I am. His chief characteristic then was a complete indolence both of mind and body. To any suggestion involving the slightest activity he always replied, in the language of those days, that it was too much fag. He absorbed a certain amount of knowledge, passively, as a sponge absorbs water. He played games, because he had to, with a sort of contemptuous obedience to convention.

'His father was the senior partner of Fransham & Innes, a firm of brass-founders of Birmingham. Robert, the eldest son, entered the business when he left school. His brother Thomas, who had military ambitions, was put into the army. I have always understood that Thomas became a conscientious if not very intelligent soldier. He was killed in the attack on Messines Ridge in 1917.

'The business of Fransham & Innes when Robert Fransham joined it, was not in a very flourishing condition. It rather more than paid its way, and that was the best that could be said of it. In due course, Robert succeeded his father, who died shortly before the outbreak of the war. His character had altered very little in the meanwhile. He was a man who always sought the easiest path through life. Not at all the type who was capable of converting a moribund concern into a flourishing and profit-earning business.

'Then the war came, and the firm of Fransham & Innes was caught in the whirlpool of production. As it happened, its workshops were suitably equipped for the manufacture of a certain type of fuse which was in urgent demand. Government orders poured in, to be executed at fantastic profits. Robert Fransham simply couldn't help making money. All he had to do was to sit in his office and endorse the cheques as they poured in. A really energetic man might perhaps have reaped an even more bountiful harvest. I don't know. I can only tell you that by the time the war ended, Mr Robert Fransham found himself a rich man.

'Then, in 1920, one of the big armament firms made a very advantageous offer for the purchase of the business. Robert Fransham asked my advice about its acceptance, but I could see that his mind was already made up. Business, even profitable business, bored him, for it demanded a certain amount of mental effort. And here was an opportunity of release from all responsibility. If he sold the business he could sleep in such luxurious comfort as he cared to surround himself with for the rest of his life. And that is just exactly what he did. He came to London, saw No. 4 Cheveley Street, took a fancy to it and has lived there ever since.'

'I am very grateful to you for this information, Mr Redbourne,' said Jimmy. 'Can you tell me anything about Mrs Thomas Fransham and her daughter?'

'Have you met Mrs Thomas Fransham?' Mr Redbourne inquired.

'Not yet,' Jimmy replied.

'Well, you're not likely to be very favourably impressed when you do. She's one of those narrow-minded women who live in the unalterable conviction that nobody can do anything right but themselves. And she's as stubborn as a mule, too. With a little goodwill she could easily have got over Robert Fransham's dislike of her. I don't know that she would have profited financially by that, but at all events it would have made things easier between them. As it was, they were on the worst of terms and did their best to avoid one another.'

Jimmy smiled. 'I thought you told me that Mr Fransham had no enemies,' he said.

'Oh, I'm not suggesting that she was his active enemy. She disliked him and disapproved of him wholeheartedly, that's all. I dare say she thought that his bachelor establishment was the scene of saternalia revolting to her middle-class respectability. It wasn't, by the way. Robert Fransham rather avoided women than otherwise. I dare say that he thought that the pursuit of them would involve an unnecessary expenditure of energy.

'On the other hand, as I hinted just now, Betty's mother is bound to score by Robert Fransham's death at this particular juncture. I haven't a doubt that she'll prevail upon Betty to hand her over a good fat sum in compensation for the allowance, which she always maintained that Robert Fransham should have given her. If this murder was a conspiracy, and not the work of one hand alone, you won't have very far to look for the accomplice. But you asked me to tell you what I knew about her.

'Quite candidly, I don't know very much. Thomas met her when he was a subaltern and they were married in 1906. I believe she was the daughter of a retired naval captain, but I can't be sure of that. Betty was born in 1908, so that she was nine when her father was killed. Thomas Fransham inherited on his father's death a small sum bringing in about a couple of hundred a year.

'When the war broke out, Thomas Fransham was stationed at York and had taken a small house there. Mrs Fransham kept it on while he was in France and continued to do so after his death. To the best of my belief she still lives there; I don't suppose that either Betty or her husband have encouraged the idea of her living with them permanently.'

'Do you happen to know how and when Dr Thornborough met his wife?'

'Yes, I do. Thornborough's father was a doctor with a

prosperous practice in the country somewhere. He always intended his son to succeed him, but he died before Thornborough had qualified, and the practice had to be sold. Thornborough eventually qualified in 1927 and went for three years as house surgeon to a hospital in York. That was how he met Betty. They were married in 1930, when Thornborough went into practice here as partner to Dr Dorrington. Dorrington, I believe, was an old friend of his father's.'

'What was Mr Robert Fransham's opinion of Dr Thornborough?'

'He liked him well enough. He made a point of seeing him when he and Betty became engaged, and quite approved of her choice. He has told me several times that he had every confidence in Thornborough's professional ability. But, as I said just now, he viewed his extravagant habits with growing disapproval. He thought it quite unnecessary for him to build that new house of his, and he disliked the ridiculous name he gave it. Again, Thornborough buys himself a new car every year, which Robert Fransham regarded as a foolish extravagance.'

'Mr Fransham ran to a pretty luxurious car himself,' Jimmy suggested.

'That's quite different. He had the money to pay for his own luxuries and the doctor hadn't. In my opinion Thornborough has been living ever since his marriage on his wife's expectations.'

'What is your own opinion of the doctor, Mr Redbourne?'

'I think my present attitude is a sufficient answer to that question, inspector,' Mr Redbourne replied severely. 'Apart altogether from my natural horror at this brutal murder, I am surprised and deeply shocked. You must not forget that

Mr Fransham had always been a devoted uncle to Mrs Thornborough, and I believe that she was genuinely devoted to him. Her feelings have been ruthlessly disregarded.'

'You have been extremely frank with me, Mr Redbourne, and I am deeply grateful to you. Will you tell me now, in the strictest confidence, why you are so firmly convinced that Dr Thornborough is the murderer?'

Mr Redbourne nearly leapt out of his chair. 'Why I am so firmly convinced!' he exclaimed. 'Why, good heavens, young man, I'm a solicitor of some considerable experience, and as such may claim to be a man of the world. Thornborough's guilt must surely be obvious to anyone who has even the sketchiest knowledge of the circumstances. Don't you understand that if Robert Fransham had lived only a few days longer, Thornborough's prospects would have been undermined? His wife's capital would have been placed in trust, out of his reach. I may tell you that it was Robert Fransham's intention that my partner and I should have been the trustees. And we should have been adamant in the face of any suggestion of financing Thornborough out of the trust fund. You're surely not going to suggest that it is a pure coincidence that Robert Fransham should have been murdered only two or three days before his intentions were accomplished?'

'No, I shouldn't suggest that without having obtained further evidence on the point,' Jimmy replied quietly.

'Well, I'm only a respectable family lawyer,' said Mr Redbourne, once more emphasising his words by waving his glasses in the air. 'I have very little experience of criminal practice, but I have always understood that in the investigation of crime the two principles to be established were those of motive and of opportunity.

'Now, we have already dealt at some length with the question of motive. That of opportunity remains. And in that regard I will only say that when I hear of a man being killed in a private house, my common sense prompts me to seek for the murderer among the occupants of that house.'

'And yet there is some difficulty in explaining the mechanism of the murder,' said Jimmy.

Mr Redbourne's retort was prompt. 'I have always conceived that the function of the Criminal Investigation Department was precisely to remove such difficulties. I do not propose to detain you any longer from the pursuit of your duties, inspector. For your information, I may state that I shall stay at the Red Lion in this town until after the inquest tomorrow.'

At the inquest, which took place on the following day, Monday, no fresh facts were revealed. Superintendent Yateley had agreed with Jimmy that the police would gain nothing by laying their cards on the table until their case was complete. The story was, therefore, deprived of its implications and restricted to the bare facts. With these before them, the jury had no option as to their verdict. It was quite obvious that Mr Fransham had not taken his own life, and the possibility that he had been killed accidentally was too remote to be taken seriously. The jury therefore returned a verdict of 'Murder by some person or persons unknown,' a conclusion which was endorsed by the coroner.

Superintendent Yateley's inclination had been to arrest Dr Thornborough immediately after the inquest. But Jimmy had managed to dissuade him, his argument being that there was not yet sufficient evidence to secure a conviction.

'Motive goes a long way, I know, sir, but it isn't everything,' he had said. 'And it isn't enough to prove that the doctor could have committed the crime. No jury would be satisfied unless we were able to explain exactly how he did it.'

Yateley had shrugged his shoulders. 'The doctor's guilt is perfectly obvious to any sane person,' he had replied. 'It seems to me that how he managed the job is a mere detail. But perhaps you're right. I know what extraordinary verdicts an English jury is capable of. What are you going to do next?'

'I propose to pay a visit to the Yard, sir, to discuss the technical matters with the experts.'

So it happened that on Monday afternoon Jimmy found himself once more at Scotland Yard. He had brought with him the letter found in Mr Fransham's pocket, and a specimen of Dr Thornborough's signature on a medical certificate. His first action was to call in the aid of a handwriting expert to compare these.

The expert studied them carefully before he ventured upon an opinion. 'You've got two signatures here,' he said at last. 'The one on the certificate is "Cyril J. Thornborough" which is presumably the doctor's official style. The other is merely "Cyril" which is a style one might expect him to use when writing to his wife's uncle. I have therefore only one name, "Cyril," for purposes of comparison.

'I see you've got plenty of blank forms lying on your desk. They are printed upon the inferior type of paper usually used for that purpose. Take one of those and a pen you don't often use, not a fountain-pen. Now write your official signature on one of those blank forms.'

Jimmy dipped his pen in the ink and wrote his signature,

which was by now familiar at Scotland Yard, 'James L. Waghorn.'

The expert picked this up and looked at it. 'Excellent,' he remarked. 'I don't profess to tell character from hand-writing, but I should judge from this signature that you were a man of some education and fair intelligence. Now we'll suppose that last week you met a charming lady in the cocktail bar of the Pig and Whistle. You wish to make an appointment for another meeting. So you take a piece of notepaper, indite a suitable letter, and sign it just simply "James," with your own founten-pen to which you are thoroughly accustomed. You needn't trouble to write the letter. It's only the signature I want.'

The expert compared Jimmy's two efforts and smiled. 'I thought so,' he said. 'Like very many people, including Dr Thornborough, you don't remove your pen from the paper when writing your full signature. You let the "S" of the James run on to the "L" of the Lucifer or whatever your second Christian name may be. Consequently when you write James alone, the last letter has a slightly different formation.

'Curiously enough, however, the two specimens of the doctor's signature do not show the same variation. In his full signature, the "L" of the Cyril runs on into the "J" of Jeremiah. And in the case of the single name Cyril, the "L" is formed in exactly the same way. The beginning of the stroke which should connect it with the "J" is still there.'

'What does that prove?' Jimmy asked.

'Nothing whatever,' the expert replied cheerfully. 'Like most things in this deceptive world of ours, the argument has equal force in either direction. It might be argued that the exact similarity in the formation of the two L's show that they must have been written by the same person. The doctor was so accustomed to writing his full signature that when he wrote only "Cyril," his instinct was to end the word as though he were merely cutting short his usual signature. On the other hand it might be argued that the name Cyril had been forged by someone who had only the doctor's full signature to copy and was therefore ignorant as to how he would have formed the final L when he wrote that name alone.'

'That's what I call really helpful,' said Jimmy. 'Anything else?'

'There is the undoubted fact that the full signature was written with an ordinary pen and the name Cyril with a fountain-pen and a different brand of ink. Does that help you at all?'

'Not much. Dr Thornborough signed the certificate at Adderminster Police Station. If the signature Cyril is his, he probably wrote it at home with his own fountain-pen. I'm bound to confess that to my inexpert eyes the two Cyrils look very much alike.'

'They are, but they aren't exactly alike,' replied the expert pleasantly.

'Do you mean that the name Cyril on the letter is a forgery?' Jimmy asked quickly.

The expert shook his head. 'Far from it,' he replied. 'Try this experiment for yourself some time when you have nothing better to do. Write your signature on a piece of transparent paper. Repeat it on a second piece of transparent paper and continue the process as long as you like. Take any two of these and lay them one over the other. Then see if you can get the pen strokes of the two signatures to coincide exactly. By exactly, I mean when examined under an ordinary reading glass.

'You'll find you can't. Nobody's habits of writing are so exact as to pass this test. In fact if two signatures are found which do coincide exactly, that in itself provides very good grounds for believing that one has been traced from the other and is therefore in all probability a forgery. In this case you can see for yourself with the naked eye that there are certain slight differences of formation in the two Cyrils. There are also slight differences in the character of the strokes. The tail of the "Y" shows this most distinctly. But that may be accounted for by the fact that different pens were used in each case.'

Jimmy grinned. 'It amounts to this, then,' he said. 'You can't tell me whether the signature on the letter is a forgery or not?'

'I can't,' the expert replied. 'But don't let that discourage you. You're not the first budding detective to be confronted with a problem like that,' And with that he took his leave.

Jimmy's next business was to consult the department to which he had confided the turn-cock on the previous day. Here again he met with slight satisfaction. 'There are no traces of fingermarks on the key,' the inspector in charge of the department told him. 'As I daresay you've already noticed it has been wiped over quite recently with a greasy rag. Now if it had been used since then there would have certainly been fingermarks upon it. On the other hand, if it had been wiped over just after it had been used, there wouldn't. Get me?'

'Yes, I get you all right,' replied Jimmy wearily. He returned to his own room to meditate upon the vanity of police work in general and of expert evidence in particular.

Before he had been there many minutes the door burst open and Superintendent Hanslet strode in. 'Hullo, Jimmy, my lad!' he exclaimed. 'I heard you were back, so I thought I would look in and see you. How have you got on?'

'Not too brilliantly,' Jimmy replied. 'It all seems clear enough up to a point, though I'm not at all sure that some of the appearances aren't deceptive. But the chief difficulty is that I can't find the explanation of how the job was done. Like to hear the story?'

'Not now,' said the superintendent. 'But Merefield rang up this morning with an invitation from the professor for both of us to dine with him this evening. I said I'd go in any case, and I knew you would if you were in London. What about it? The professor might be interested in this problem of yours.'

CHAPTER VI

As it happened, Hanslet and Jimmy found Dr Priestley in a particularly receptive mood that evening. Perhaps it was because that irritable scientist had lately been starved of human problems. At all events, when Hanslet remarked that Jimmy had a case on hand, Dr Priestley's interest was visibly aroused.

'If the case contains any features of interest, I should be glad to hear the inspector's account of it,' he said.

'I think it contains at least one feature of interest, sir,' replied Jimmy, upon whom Dr Priestley had fixed his gaze. 'There's no question whatever as to the cause of death, which was a fractured skull. But I can't solve the problem of how that fracture was caused. I'd very much like to tell you the facts as they appear to me, if it wouldn't bore you to listen to them, sir.'

'Boredom is a complaint from which I very rarely suffer,' Dr Priestley replied with a somewhat austere smile. 'I should be very glad to listen to anything that you may care to tell me. But I need hardly remind you that I like my facts plain, unseasoned by any sauce of conjecture.'

Thus encouraged, Jimmy recounted the circumstances surrounding the death of Mr Fransham. He was careful, however, not to give any hint of his own conclusions.

Dr Priestley, seated on the chair in front of his desk, listened in silence. His attitude was characteristic, with his hands held together in front of him, the tips of their slender fingers touching. His head was thrown back, so that his slightly-puckered eyes frowned through his glasses at the ceiling.

He remained silent for a full minute after Jimmy had finished speaking. Then he turned abruptly to Hanslet. 'Have you anything to add to what the inspector has told us, superintendent?' he asked.

Hanslet shook his head. 'I haven't, professor,' he replied. 'This is the first I've heard about the case. Jimmy has been down at this place Adderminster, working on his own, you know.'

'Indeed. And now that you have heard the facts what is your opinion?'

'Well, I don't think anyone can find fault with the verdict,' Hanslet replied cautiously. 'It sounds to me like a case of murder, right enough. And I'm bound to say that things look pretty black for Dr Thornborough.'

Dr Priestley turned to Jimmy. 'Do you agree, inspector?' he asked.

'Absolutely, sir,' Jimmy replied. 'I've never had the slightest doubt that Mr Fransham was murdered. And as for things looking black for Dr Thornborough, I had the greatest difficulty in dissuading the local superintendent from arresting him this morning.'

'And why did you dissuade him?' Dr Priestley asked.

'For two reasons, sir. First because we haven't sufficient proof of how he did it. And second, because I'm not altogether satisfied in my own mind that he is guilty.'

'Failing Dr Thornborough, can you suggest any other person as the criminal?'

'No, sir, I can't, and that's just my difficulty. This is how the affair appears to me. The only people in Adderminster who can benefit in any conceivable way by Mr Fransham's death are Dr and Mrs Thornborough, and Mrs Thornborough's mother, Mrs Fransham. I except Coates the chauffeur, who benefits to the extent of his legacy, for if Linton's evidence is to be relied upon, Coates cannot possibly have committed the crime.

'Linton's presence in the house at the time the crime was committed enables us to fix the situation of the inmates. He could not see them, of course, but he could hear their movements. We can assume, I think, that the curious noise heard by Linton was the sound of Mr Fransham's body falling in the cloakroom. At this moment Mrs Thornborough and her mother were upstairs, in a room with windows looking out at the back of the house. The two servants were in the kitchen, with windows looking out the same way. I cannot imagine how anyone of these four people could have participated in the crime.'

Hanslet nodded. 'Exactly,' he remarked. 'So far as I can see every detail points to the doctor as the criminal. Where was he when Linton heard this crash, or thud, or whatever it was?'

Jimmy smiled. 'That's just it,' he replied. 'At that moment Dr Thornborough, according to his own account, was on his way home after paying his last call, which was at Mark

Farm. His route lay along Gunthorpe Road, past the grass field which is to be sold for building land.'

'Did anyone see him there?' Hanslet asked.

'Not to my knowledge. It was partly in the hope of getting some confirmation of Dr Thornborough's statement that I went to see Willingdon in the cottage on the other side of the road. But he says that he was in the lounge at the time, the windows of which look out in the opposite direction. Then, again, Dr Thornborough says that he saw the half-witted fellow, Alfie Prince, crossing the road in front of him. In view of the fact that it seems hardly possible that Alfie could have been in that particular place at the time, I haven't thought it worth while to question him on the point. Alfie's statements are so incoherent they can hardly be relied upon.'

'I am somewhat puzzled by your attitude, inspector,' Dr Priestley intervened. 'I quite appreciate that it is expedient to leave Dr Thornborough at liberty until you have definite proof of his guilt. But what reason have you for cherishing a belief in his innocence?'

'No valid reason at all, sir, I'm afraid,' Jimmy replied. 'Simply my own personal intuition. I have talked to Dr Thornborough, and I don't believe he is the type of man to commit a murder, especially in his own interests.'

Hanslet shrugged his shoulders. 'You won't talk like that when you've been in the force for a few years longer,' he said. 'How often is it the apparently unexpected people who commit the most sensational crimes? As I understand it, you don't go so far to argue that Dr Thornborough can't have done it.'

'Far from it. I've formed a theory which explains up to

a point how he could have set about it. But that theory
fails just at the critical moment.'

'I should be interested to hear it, nevertheless,' said Dr
Priestley quietly.

Jimmy hesitated. To form a theory which hardly satisfied
himself was one thing. To expound it to Dr Priestley was
quite another. 'I'm afraid you won't think very much of
it, sir,' he replied apologetically. 'It presupposes that Dr
Thornborough had made his plans in advance.

'His first move was to bend over the basin in the cloakroom and, looking through the aperture in the window,
to study the brick wall opposite. This brick wall is the
boundary of his property, and separates the carriage-way
into the garage from the building land beyond. He noticed
that the horizontal line between his head and the window
would, if extended, strike a header in the brick wall opposite.

'His next step was to loosen the mortar surrounding this
header. He worked from the further side of the wall so
that his operations would not be visible from the house.
He dug away the mortar with some sharp tool until the
brick was loose and could be removed.

'It was necessary to his purpose that no sign should be
visible that the brick had been tampered with. If he had
merely replaced the brick at this stage it would have
rested on the course beneath, leaving a gap on the top
of it and at both sides. This fact might have been noticed
by anyone using the cloakroom or the carriage-way. So
he wrapped the brick round with sheets of paper until it
exactly fitted the aperture. Then, as a further precaution
against any irregularity being noticed, he coated the ends

of the paper with plasticine coloured to resemble mortar. The brick could then be withdrawn at any time, and when it was replaced no visible sign of its removal would remain. This process was, in fact, actually carried out by someone, whether the doctor or not. I have withdrawn the brick myself and looked through the aperture thus caused in the wall. The head of anyone bending over the basin in the cloakroom would be clearly visible to an observer on the other side of the wall.

'To continue my theory. The doctor's next step was to secure the presence of his victim. There was very little difficulty about that. He knew Mr Fransham's affection for his niece and that if he were invited to *Epidaurus* he would almost certainly come. Hence the letter signed "Cyril." It was a practical certainty that very shortly after Mr Fransham's arrival, he would go into the cloakroom to wash his hands before lunch.

'Dr Thornborough, after his visit to Mark Farm, drove to the five-barred gate at the end of Gunthorpe Road. From here he could see any car which turned into his own drive gates. He waited until he saw Mr Fransham's car do so, then entered the grass field through a gap in the hedge. He walked along inside the hedge until he reached the loose brick in the wall. He withdrew this and watched until he saw Mr Fransham's head through the window of the cloakroom. And, at that critical moment, my theory breaks down.'

'Breaks down!' Hanslet exclaimed. 'Why? It sounds pretty convincing up to now. What do you say, professor?'

'I prefer to reserve my opinion until the inspector has explained himself further,' Dr Priestley replied.

'Well, sir, the difficulty is this,' said Jimmy diffidently.

'Dr Thornborough, from behind the wall, had an excellent view of the top of his victim's head. He must have been looking at the very part of it where the wound was subsequently found. But how did he cause that wound? There are only two possible alternatives. Either he projected with considerable force some missile of cubical shape, or he employed a weapon with a cubical end.

'Now, the horizontal distance from the centre of the basin to the bars protecting the window is thirty inches. The width of the carriage-way is exactly twelve feet, and the wall is nine inches thick. The minimum distance between Dr Thornborough and his victim's head was therefore fifteen feet three inches. It seems to me inconceivable that he should have wielded a weapon of anything like that length with accuracy. If it possessed the necessary rigidity, it would be very heavy and unwieldy. It would have been impossible to swing it, and it would have been necessary to thrust it forward like a spear. And it must not be forgotten that Coates was standing in the doorway of the garage not many yards away. Surely the thrust of a weapon across the carriage-way could not have escaped his attention?'

'From your description, inspector, it sounds extremely improbable that a weapon could have been employed,' Dr Priestley remarked.

'But the other alternative seems to be equally improbable, sir. It involves the use of a missile in the shape of a cube with a side of one and a half inches, sufficiently hard and solid to inflict the wound. I imagine something in the nature of a piece cut off the end of a square bar of iron. And I've been trying to think what would happen to such a missile after it had hit its mark. It seems to me that it must have done one of three things, which I will mention in the order of their possibility. It might have fallen into the basin. It might have glanced off and fallen in some other part of the cloakroom. Finally, though this seems to me very unlikely indeed, it might have rebounded through the window and fallen into the carriage-way.'

Dr Priestley nodded approvingly. 'Your reasoning appears perfectly sound, inspector,' he said.

'Then how is it that the missile has not been found, sir? I am quite satisfied with Linton's statement that Dr Thornborough had no opportunity of picking it up. The cloakroom affords no possible place of concealment, and four people, Linton, Sergeant Cload, Superintendent Yateley and myself have examined it minutely. It is absolutely certain that the missile was not in the cloakroom at the time the crime was discovered. That was only a few minutes after Mr Fransham's death. And Linton assures me that nobody could have entered the cloakroom in the interval without his knowledge.'

'I gather that Linton has only the evidence of his ears for that,' Hanslet remarked. 'He couldn't see the cloakroom door from where he was in the consulting-room, could he?'

'No, but the cloakroom door was locked on the inside and had to be broken open. That fact seems to support Linton's statement. There remains only the extremely unlikely event of the missile having bounded back into the carriage-way. Even if this had happened, it should still have been found. Neither Dr Thornborough or any other member of the household had any opportunity of picking it up before Superintendent Yateley examined the carriage-way himself.

'That's where my theory fails. The fact that no missile has been found rules out the possibility that one has been used. We are therefore, driven back to the theory of a weapon. The turn-cock that I spoke about just now fills the bill exactly. It is quite true that there are no fingermarks upon it, but that doesn't mean very much. Dr Thornborough had plenty of opportunity for cleaning it on Saturday afternoon, before I came upon it in the garage. But, if it is actually the weapon, it must have been wielded from just outside the cloakroom window. It isn't nearly long enough to have been thrust across the carriage-way from the other side of the wall. And it couldn't have been thrown through the aperture, for the T-shaped handle is far too wide to allow it to pass.'

'All the same, I believe you're on the right track with that turn-key, Jimmy,' said Hanslet. 'You tell us that the doctor drove down the carriage-way while Mr Fransham was in the cloakroom? Why shouldn't he have had the key in the car with him and jabbed it through the cloakroom window as he passed?'

'I've thought of that possibility,' Jimmy replied. 'But I can't get away from Linton's picture of Coates standing in the doorway of the garage.'

'I'd try to find out a little more about this man Coates, if I were you,' said Hanslet. 'Perhaps he knows more about this business than he thought fit to tell you. I don't suppose for a moment that he was an accessory before the fact. It isn't a bit likely that the doctor would have taken him into his confidence. But if Coates did see anything, and if he has the mentality of a crook, it seems to me that he's on velvet. For one thing he gets his legacy and for another he's in a unique position for blackmail. From what I can make out the doctor will have plenty of money to spare now.'

'I'm going to make inquiries about Coates,' Jimmy replied, 'but he isn't the only puzzle. If the blow was to be struck from just outside the cloakroom window, why was all that trouble taken to remove the brick and to disguise its removal?'

'Oh, I think that's easily explained. Criminals often try several plans before they hit upon the right one. The doctor may have originally intended to shoot Mr Fransham from the other side of the wall. That's why he removed the brick. Then I suppose that it occurred to him that the sound of the shot would certainly be heard and might give him away. So he hit upon the plan of wielding the turn-cock from the car. Naturally he'd leave the brick as it was. If and when you found it, it would put other ideas into your head. And that, of course, would be all to his benefit. It's no good, Jimmy, the more you tell us, the more firmly you fix the rope round the doctor's neck.'

'And yet I don't know,' Jimmy replied. 'It seems to me that that letter is the whole crux of the matter. Did the doctor write it or did he not? If he did, it seems to me pretty clear proof of his guilt. It's typed on the doctor's notepaper, there's no question about that. But it would be easy enough for anyone to secure a sheet of that paper. I have noticed for myself that visitors to the doctor's house, apart from social visitors, of course, are shown into the consulting-room. On the doctor's desk in this room is a stationery rack with several sheets of his notepaper in it. And you must remember that anybody who calls upon a doctor in the guise of a patient will be admitted.'

Hanslet nodded. 'I admit that piece of notepaper isn't

much to go upon,' he said. 'But the wording of the letter seems to me to suggest pretty strongly that the doctor wrote it.'

'If he did, why does he deny the fact?' Jimmy replied. 'It would have been far less suspicious if he had admitted openly that he had wanted to see Mr Fransham on some matter connected with his private affairs, shall we say?'

'Because, I suppose, the situation was complicated by his mother-in-law's presence in the house. Why did the doctor time the murder while she was there? She was only on a short visit, and if he had waited for a few days he could have asked Mr Fransham down without any secrecy whatever. Or is it that, like most criminals, he overlooked certain details? It was careless of him to wrap up that brick in sheets of a paper which could so easily be traced to him.'

'It was, if he actually did so,' Jimmy replied. 'But there, again, you've got to remember the accessibility of the consulting-room. The current number of the *British Medical Journal* was, I gather, usually to be found lying on the table there. The very fact that the doctor's issue of May 22 is missing, seems to be a point in his favour. The fact that the brick in the wall had been tampered with was bound to be discovered sooner or later. Whoever wrapped the paper round the brick must have known that. And if the doctor had done so, I feel sure that he is astute enough to have provided himself with a duplicate copy of the *British Medical Journal* to be produced when questions were asked.'

'That's all very fine, Jimmy,' said Hanslet. 'I'm quite sure that the professor will agree that it's your business to consider all the possibilities. But we come back to the problem which appears to confront your local superintendent. If the doctor didn't do the job, who did? I'm not going into the question of motive, for you may yet find that there were other people who wanted Mr Fransham's death. But who else had the doctor's opportunities for killing him by that particular method?'

'I don't know,' Jimmy replied. 'If I could think of any way that Mr Fransham could have been killed from the other side of the wall, I'd be inclined to think that the half-witted Alfie Prince might have had some hand in the affair.'

'That is a curious suggestion, inspector,' Dr Priestley remarked. 'Do you mean to imply that this man Prince's mental derangement might have produced homicidal tendencies?'

'Not in the sense that he would commit a murder on his own initiative, sir. From what I've seen of Alfie he doesn't strike me as being a lunatic, in any sense of the word. He has periods when his brain is clouded, and then he does things which he would not think of doing in his normal state. Isn't it possible that at these times he might be impelled to crime by the suggestion of a stronger will?'

'I am not an alienist,' said Dr Priestley, 'but I imagine that such a thing might under certain circumstances be possible.'

'It sounds a bit far-fetched to me,' Hanslet remarked. 'But go ahead Jimmy, there's nothing like exploring every avenue, as the politicians say.'

'I've been wondering tentatively whether Alfie can have been inspired by Dr Thornborough to commit the crime,' Jimmy replied.

Hanslet laughed derisively. 'Never!' he exclaimed. 'We've got to give the doctor credit for some intelligence, at least. Do you suppose he'd put his neck at the mercy of a man like this Alfie Prince of yours? Why, the moment Alfie felt he was suspected, he'd give the doctor away at once.'

'One of the curious features of Alfie's erratic periods is that they make no impression on his memory,' Jimmy replied. 'I am assured that when he becomes normal again, he has completely forgotten everything that happened while his brain was clouded. By his own admission, Dr Thornborough was aware of some of Alfie's peculiarities. It seems to me that he may have been well aware of this particular one.'

Hanslet whistled softly. 'By jove, that's a marvellous idea!' he exclaimed. 'The doctor gets hold of Alfie in one of his moods and puts him up to murder Mr Fransham. Alfie does the job and promptly forgets all about it. The doctor is perfectly safe, for no proof exists of his incitement. And when the painstaking Inspector James Waghorn at last completes his case against Alfie, that unfortunate individual is found guilty and committed to Broadmoor during His Majesty's pleasure. But can you work it out?'

'I'm not sure,' Jimmy replied doubtfully. 'Alfie's movements during Friday evening and Saturday are wrapped in mystery. His story of the man who accosted him at Weaver's Bridge and offered him half a crown and a handful of cigarettes for his old coat sounds fantastic. And yet there are two things which in a way support it. Alfie's reason for stealing a new coat was that he had parted with his old one. And then those cigarette ends that I found in the corner of the field. Where did Alfie get hold of that particular brand?'

'I understand that the principal symptom of Alfie's complaint is that he cadges cigarettes from everybody when he's suffering from it.'

'So it is, apparently. But very few people, comparatively speaking, smoke Black's Russian Blend. You can't go into the ordinary tobacconist's shop and buy them. And it seems to me rather remarkable that I found a box of them in the doctor's house. It suggests to me the possibility that Alfie's fantastic story is true and that the man who accosted him was the doctor.'

'But what on earth did the doctor want with Alfie's old coat?' Hanslet demanded.

'Quite frankly, I don't know. Nor do I know if it was in the course of that interview that the doctor inspired Alfie with the idea of murder. But I think there's very little doubt that Alfie spent Friday night in the corner of the field.

'Alfie's next appearance is at Colonel Exbury's house about a quarter to one on Saturday without his old coat, which is so well-known locally that it could not possibly be mistaken. I think we can accept that as a fact, for there is no reason whatever to doubt Colonel Exbury's statement. Now this appearance would, on the face of it, appear to provide Alfie with an unshakable alibi. Mr Fransham was killed at seven minutes past one and Alfie could not have covered the distance between the two points in the time. Unless, of course, he had a car at his disposal. But perhaps he had. Perhaps the doctor gave him a lift from somewhere outside Colonel Exbury's house to Gunthorpe Road. The doctor would still have had time to make his call at Mark Farm.'

Jimmy addressed Dr Priestley. 'I'm afraid you'll accuse me of indulging too lavishly in conjecture, sir,' he said.

'Not at all,' Dr Priestley replied. 'You are, I understand, merely trying to formulate a theory in accordance with the facts. In such a case conjecture is admissible as long as it is verified before the theory is accepted.'

'Thank you, sir. I won't try to guess the doctor's motives in taking Alfie's coat on Friday night. But if he actually did so, this I imagine is what he did with it. He put it in the corner of the field on Saturday morning after Alfie had gone. Alfie on his return there after his visit to Colonel Exbury, found the coat and put it on.

'This may explain Alfie's next recorded appearance. Dr Thornborough says that he saw him cross the road in front of his car as he was returning home. Superintendent Yateley dismisses that as a fable, owing to the apparent impossibility of Alfie having been there at the time. But if he had been driven there in a car this appearance becomes not only possible but also inevitable. He had done the job and was leaving the scene before the investigations began.'

'But hang it all, Jimmy!' Hanslet exclaimed. 'Would the doctor deliberately have drawn attention to his accomplice like that? Surely, he would have held his tongue and said nothing about Alfie.'

'I thought about that, and it seems to me that there are two possible reasons for the doctor's statement. The first is that somebody else might have seen Alfie crossing Gunthorpe Road and the doctor's car in the distance. If the doctor had denied seeing Alfie, suspicions might have been aroused. The second reason is that the doctor might have intended all along that Alfie should be arrested for the crime, trusting on the hiatus in his memory for his own immunity.'

'You said just now that the doctor didn't strike you as a likely murderer,' Hanslet remarked. 'Yet now you're making him out to be the dirtiest scoundrel unhung.'

'I know. But I'm not trying to prove his guilt. I'm only putting forward theories of what might have happened. And you must remember that all the time it remains a mystery how Alfie, or anyone else for that matter, can have killed Mr Fransham from behind the wall. If Alfie is guilty, he must have done the job from the carriage-way outside the cloakroom window. And I can't imagine how he could have got there without being seen by Coates.'

'As I have already suggested, Coates may have his own reasons for keeping quiet,' Hanslet remarked.

'In which case there are three of them in it,' replied Jimmy wearily. 'However, let's try and follow Alfie's movements. I don't think that there can be any doubt that it was Alfie who called upon Mr Willingdon later in the afternoon and cadged cigarettes. Willingdon's picturesque description of the coat could not possibly apply to any other garment. Besides, Alfie is the only inhabitant of Adderminster who indulges in that particular practice. So we are confronted with the fact that if Alfie ever parted with his coat he had recovered it by two or three o'clock on Saturday afternoon. But he seems to have discarded it later and left it in the corner of the field. When Linton overtook him that evening he was wearing the coat which he had taken from the hook outside Murphy's shop. Alfie's Odyssey terminated a few minutes later in a cell at the police station. And it was on Sunday morning that I found the coat.'

There was silence for a few moments before Dr Priestley spoke. 'Has it occurred to you, inspector, that someone may have acquired this man Prince's coat in order to be able to impersonate him?' he asked.

'I'm bound to confess that it hasn't, sir,' Jimmy replied, somewhat nonplussed.

'The suggestion occurred to me when you repeated Prince's account of his meeting with the man at Weaver's Bridge. The very fact that Prince's coat was notorious in Adderminster would make it an excellent disguise. People catching sight of it would assume that its wearer was Prince, and would not trouble to make any closer inspection. If you accept Dr Thornborough's statement as true, the man he saw crossing the road may not have been Prince but somebody impersonating him'

'But how about Mr Willingdon's visitor, sir?' Jimmy asked.

Dr Priestley smiled. 'He was no doubt the impersonator,' he replied. 'He wished to make it appear that Prince was in the neighbourhood of Gunthorpe Road on Saturday afternoon. Being anxious to secure evidence to this affect, he called upon Mr Willingdon. In my opinion he could not have chosen a more suitable witness. Mr Willingdon, I understand, is a stranger to Adderminster. It was extremely unlikely that he would know the genuine Prince by sight. But his attention would inevitably be drawn to the coat, which would figure prominently in his subsequent description. You yourself, inspector, have no doubt that it was actually Prince who called upon him.'

'I haven't sir, for the idea of an impersonator had never occurred to me. But who can that impersonator have been? Certainly not the doctor, for his appearance is entirely different from that of Alfie Prince. Even the wearing of Alfie's coat would not produce the slightest resemblance. Besides, Willingdon had consulted the doctor and knew him by sight. And at the time when Willingdon was interviewing his visitor the doctor was in his own house talking to Superintendent Yateley.'

'You have yourself expressed doubts of the doctor's guilt,' Dr Priestley remarked drily.

'I have, sir, but I can't suggest any alternative,' Jimmy replied. 'The difficulty is this. Mr Fransham's association with Adderminster was confined to an occasional visit to his niece and her husband. It is reasonable to suppose, therefore, that nobody in the town or district had the slightest motive for wishing for his death. It is of course, possible that Mr Fransham had enemies elsewhere and that his murder was based on revenge. The murderer may have followed Mr Fransham to Adderminster. But in that case he must have made a careful study of the place in advance.

'It occurred to wonder whether young Willingdon could have played any part in the affair. It seemed to me a bit odd that he should have taken that cottage by himself and actually been in residence there at the time of the crime. And his manner suggested that he had something to hide. So this afternoon, before I came here, I went to Harlow's Hotel in Kensington and made a few inquiries about him.

'Willingdon had mentioned to me a girl in the reception office there. She happened to be on duty and I recognised her at once from his description. With the manager's permission I had quite a long chat with her. As soon as I mentioned Willingdon's name, she laughed and told me that she knew him quite well. She referred to him as Frank, I noticed. And, as it happened, she had seen him as recently as this morning. He had looked in on his return from Adderminster and told the girl, whose name, by the way, is Miss Bayne, that he was just going to catch a train home.

'Miss Bayne was quite ready to talk about her friend Frank, as she called him. She had first met him a couple of months ago when he had stayed at the hotel for a few days. She's a thoroughly sensible girl, and Willingdon seems to have adopted her as his confidante. He told her that his father was a manufacturer in Leeds and that he himself was a junior partner in the business. But he said that at present he was rather at a loose end, for he had found it convenient to leave home and lie low till a certain unpleasantness had blown over.'

Hanslet looked up at this. 'Something fishy?' he inquired.

'Fishy, perhaps, but not criminal,' Jimmy replied. 'Miss Bayne tells me it was something to do with a girl in Leeds. Rather an involved story, I gather. Anyhow, Willingdon had thought it better to clear out and amuse himself in London for two or three months.

'According to Miss Bayne he had no lack of funds and found little difficulty in obtaining the amusement he wanted. He found his way into a set of young people of his own age and, according to Miss Bayne, had a pretty hectic time. The usual sort of thing, bottle parties, night clubs and all the rest of it.

'It was about six weeks ago that he asked Miss Bayne if she had ever heard of a place called Adderminster. As it happened she had, for a friend of hers lived somewhere down that way. She told Willingdon that it was a quiet little market town which wouldn't suit his tastes at all. To her astonishment, he replied that quiet was the very thing he was looking for. He explained that he was beginning to find weekends in London too much of a strain upon his system. Then he produced a newspaper cutting with an advertisement of the cottage in Gunthorpe Road to let furnished.

'After this Miss Bayne seems to have taken charge of his

weekend catering. Willingdon used to ask her to put up a hamper of food for him, telling her to put in enough for two in case he took a friend down with him. And it was that request which first aroused her suspicions that it was not only quiet which Willingdon sought in the weekends. These suspicions were confirmed when Willingdon called at the hotel for the hamper, in a car which he had hired to drive down to Adderminster. Miss Bayne, from her point of vantage in the reception office, saw a highly-decorative young lady sitting in the car. And then I remembered that unmistakable aroma of scent which I had noticed when I called at the cottage yesterday.'

Hanslet laughed. 'That seems to account for Willingdon,' he said.

'That's what I thought. Whether there was a lady hidden away somewhere in the cottage yesterday, I don't know. Anyway, the reason which caused Willingdon's exile from Leeds appears to be at an end. When he called at Harlow's Hotel this morning, Miss Bayne gave him a letter with a Leeds postmark addressed to him. He opened it, read it, and seemed greatly relieved. He told her that it was from his father, that everything was all right and there was nothing to prevent him going back home. He gave her a card with his Leeds address on it and told her that he'd look in and see her whenever he came back to London.'

'She showed you the card?' Hanslet asked.

'She did. I copied the address and looked it up in a Leeds directory. The occupier of the house is there given as Ernest Willingdon, Esq. Frank's father, no doubt. But, unless in the course of my investigations I can find any connection between him and Mr Fransham, he seems to be out of the picture.'

Dr Priestley had listened to this account of Willingdon's adventures without any very great display of interest. And when he spoke it was to introduce an entirely different subject.

'You have spoken of a key used for turning a water-cock, inspector,' he said. 'You have satisfied yourself, I suppose, that there is actually a water-main serving the houses in Gunthorpe Road?'

'Yes sir, Sergeant Cload told me that the mains were laid there when the road was made.'

'Is there a supply of gas and electricity as well?'

'Electricity, certainly, sir. The doctor's house is lighted by electricity and so, I noticed, is the cottage on the other side of the road. And, now that I come to think of it, there was a gas stove in the doctor's consulting-room.'

'And what are you going to do next?' Dr Priestley asked.

'I'm going round to No. 4 Cheveley Street tomorrow morning, sir, to interview the married couple employed by Mr Fransham. Then I shall go back to Adderminster in the hope of picking up some definite line on which to work.'

'You have a busy day before you,' said Dr Priestley, glancing at the clock.

Hanslet and Jimmy took the hint.

CHAPTER VII

Next morning Jimmy set out to explore Cheveley Street. He found it to be a short thoroughfare, joining two longer streets at right angles. It was bordered on one side by the railings of a square, and on the other by the fronts of six houses, numbered one to six. Numbers one to four formed a solid block. Then came a narrow entrance leading into mews at the back. This again was flanked by No. 5 which with No. 6 formed a second block.

As Jimmy rang the bell of No. 4 he noticed that all the blinds were drawn. The door was opened by an elderly man, dressed in a black suit, who looked worried and downcast. Jimmy explained who he was and was taken into the dining-room on the ground floor, a gloomy apartment furnished in heavy Victorian style.

The elderly man informed Jimmy that his name was Stowell and that he and his wife had been employed by Mr Fransham for the last seventeen years. 'Ever since Mr Fransham took this house, sir,' he explained. 'My wife and I have been in service together before, in the country. But we wanted to come to London because all her relations are here. So we put our names down at a registry office, and that's how we came to hear of this, sir.'

'I see,' Jimmy replied. 'Since you've been here all that time you can't have had much to complain of?'

'We couldn't have had a better place, sir. Mr Fransham was always very considerate and took care that we should not be overworked. It's terrible to think that he should have been killed like that. My wife's hardly stopped crying since we first heard about it, sir.'

'How did you first hear about it, Stowell?'

'Dr Thornborough rang up on Saturday evening and told us what had happened, sir.'

'What exactly did he tell you?'

'He said that we must be prepared for a shock as he had some very bad news for us. It was I who answered the telephone and I asked him what had happened. And then he said that Mr Fransham had been found dead in the doctor's house at Adderminster. I thought at first that it must have been his heart, but the doctor said that it was much worse than that. Somebody had hit him on the head and had killed him.'

'Do you know Dr Thornborough?'

'I've only set eyes on him once, sir, when he came here to lunch. That was long ago, just before he married Miss Betty, as she was then. Miss Betty was staying here at the time and the doctor came up to see her.'

'Mrs Thornborough has been here fairly often since her marriage, hasn't she?'

'Yes, sir. Sometimes she has stayed here for a night or two and sometimes she has only come in for lunch, when she has been spending a day in London shopping. She was

115

Mr Fransham's niece, as I expect you know, sir, and he was very fond of her.'

'Have you ever met her mother, Mrs Thomas Fransham?'

Stowell shook his head. 'No, sir,' he replied, then added confidentially, 'I have always understood that there was something between Mr Fransham and his sister-in-law, sir.'

'You mean that they didn't get on very well together?'

'That's about it, sir. When Miss Betty used to come and stay here before she was married, her mother never came with her, sir.'

'When did Mr Fransham tell you that he was going down to Adderminster on Saturday?'

'Not until breakfast time that very day, sir. There was only one letter for Mr Fransham that morning and I put it by his plate, as I always do. And when I was pouring out his coffee, he said to me, "It's a nuisance, Stowell, but I shall have to go down to Adderminster today. Send Coates to me when I have finished my breakfast and I'll give him his orders. And tell Mrs Stowell that I shall be out for lunch but shall be home in time for dinner."'

'Coates? Oh yes,' said Jimmy. 'That's the chauffeur, of course. I met him at Dr Thornborough's house. How long had he been with Mr Fransham?'

'It'll be a matter of five years or more, sir,' Stowell replied. 'Yes, it must be five years last April when he first came. That was when Mr Fransham first owned a car of his own. Before then he always used to hire when he wanted one.'

'How did Coates get the job? Through a registry office?'

'No, sir, it was a matter of personal recommendation. Sir Godfrey Branstock spoke to Mr Fransham about him. He's told me since that he was second chauffeur to one of

Sir Godfrey's friends in the country. He had very good references, I understand, sir.'

'Was Mr Fransham satisfied with him?'

'Perfectly satified, so far as I am aware, Stowell replied rather stiffly. 'Mr Fransham would not have kept him in his service for five years if he had had anything against him.'

Jimmy fancied that he detected a note of resentment in Stowell's voice. 'Coates lives in the house here, doesn't he?' he remarked casually. 'How do you and Mrs Stowell get on with him?'

'It's not my place to say anything against him, sir,' Stowell replied.

Jimmy smiled. 'Of course it isn't,' he said. 'I shouldn't expect you to tell tales against your fellow-servant. But the position has changed since last Saturday. Neither you nor Coates are any longer employed by Mr Fransham. I hope he has remembered you in his will, by the way?'

'I understand that he has, sir. In fact, he told me once some time ago that if my wife and I stayed with him until he died we shouldn't be the losers by it. And he told Coates the same thing at the beginning of this year.'

'I'm glad to hear that. Now, won't you tell me in confidence why you don't like Coates?'

'I never said I disliked him, sir,' replied Stowell firmly.

'I know you didn't. But you weren't exactly enthusiastic just now when I asked you how you got on with him. He struck me as being rather a surly sort of chap, if that's any encouragement to you.'

'Surly's just the word, sir. He's one of those chaps who are never content, but must always be finding something to grouse about. He makes us tired with his constant grumbling, and my wife and I have often told him so. But he always complained behind Mr Fransham's back, and took care not to say anything in front of him. And all the time it was Mr Fransham who should have done the grumbling, if he'd only known.'

'What do you mean, Stowell?' Jimmy asked quietly.

'Well, sir, I wouldn't have said a word while Mr Fransham was alive. For one thing, I couldn't prove it. But now that he's dead, it doesn't seem to matter so much. It was like this, sir: Coates used to buy everything for the car—petrol, oil, spare parts, and so forth. Mr Fransham used to give him money from time to time, and Coates would show him an account of how he'd spent it. And I know for a fact that Coates used to put in things he'd never had. I faced him with it once, sir, but he only laughed at me. He said it was a recognised perquisite. Those are the very words he used. And he had the impudence to tell me that I was a fool if I didn't do the same thing with the house-keeping money.'

'Mr Fransham had no suspicion that this sort of thing was going on, I suppose?'

'He'd have been very much upset if he had, sir. Nobody could have wanted a better master than Mr Fransham, but he was always very careful where spending money was concerned.'

'However Coates may have grumbled, he was really perfectly satisfied with his place, I suppose?'

Stowell shook his head. 'No, sir, he wasn't,' replied he. 'Mr Fransham treated him with every consideration, but Coates is one of those men who doesn't like working for a master.'

'What else could he hope to do?' Jimmy asked.

'He has a plan for starting a little business of his own, sir. From what he tells me, his brother has got a small holding on a main road in the country somewhere. Coates has always said that if he could get hold of a little capital, say a couple of hundred pounds or so, he would put up a filling station in the corner of his brother's land and make a lot of money selling petrol and so forth to passing cars. He went so far as to speak to Mr Fransham about it not more than a week or so ago.'

'What did he say to Mr Fransham?'

'He asked him to advance him the money by way of a loan, sir.'

'And Mr Fransham didn't see his way to doing that?'

'No, sir, he didn't. It wasn't likely that he would. From what Coates said to me, Mr Fransham told him not to be a fool. He'd got a sure and comfortable job where he was, and the best thing he could do was to stick to it.'

Jimmy did not think it wise just then to pursue the subject of Coates any further. 'Had Mr Fransham many visitors?' he asked.

'Very few, sir, and they were all gentlemen except Miss Betty. Now and then one or two of his friends might drop in to see him of an evening, but there weren't more than a dozen altogether that came here. And if Mr Fransham wanted to ask anybody to lunch or dinner, he always invited them to a club or to a restaurant. It has always seemed to me that he didn't like people about the house more than he could help, sir.'

'How was that? He had nothing to hide, I suppose?'

'Oh, no, sir, it wasn't that. He liked to feel that he could do what he liked without having to consider other people. For instance, in the hot weather he liked to come down to dinner in a dressing-gown and a pair of bedroom slippers. And he couldn't very well have done that if he'd had guests in the house.'

Jimmy smiled. 'No, I suppose he couldn't,' he replied. 'Do you know all Mr Fransham's friends by name?'

'I ought to, sir, after all the years I've been with him.'

'Then I'll get you to write out a list of them before I go. Meanwhile, have you ever heard the name of Willingdon— in connection with Mr Fransham, I mean?'

'I'm quite sure I haven't, sir. Mr Fransham didn't know anybody of that name. Could you tell me anything more about the gentleman, sir?'

'There appear to be two of them. Mr Ernest Willingdon is a manufacturer in Leeds, and his son Francis has been knocking round London lately. It's the son I'm particularly interested in. He's a tall, languid youth, somewhere between twenty-five and thirty.'

Stowell shook his head. 'Mr Ernest Willingdon may have been a friend of Mr Fransham's at one time, sir,' he said. 'Though I've never heard his name mentioned. But I'm quite sure that Mr Fransham didn't know Mr Francis Willingdon. All his friends were about of his own age, and the only young people he ever spoke to were Dr and Mrs Thornborough.'

'You have spoken of Sir Godfrey Branstock? He and Mr Fransham were on friendly terms, I gather?'

'Oh, yes, quite friendly, though their tastes were altogether different. Mr Fransham liked peace and quiet, but Sir Godfrey's all the other way. He lives next door, at No. 3, and the house is always full of people. Both Nos. 3 and 4 belong to him, sir.'

'Sir Godfrey has a large family, perhaps?' Jimmy suggested.

'Oh, no, sir, he's a widower with only one son. At least Mr Mayland isn't really his son, but his stepson. He's an architect, and I believe he's got rooms of his own somewhere. At all events he isn't often at home. I used to see him some three or four years back when he was modernising No. 3 for Sir Godfrey. But I don't believe I've set eyes on him since.'

'He doesn't get on with his stepfather?' Jimmy suggested.

'I don't think it's that, sir. We hear a lot of what goes on at No. 3, for my wife is very friendly with Mrs Quinton, Sir Godfrey's cook—and you know what women are. I've always understood that Mr Mayland's father died when he was so young that he hardly remembered him, and he always looked upon Sir Godfrey as his father. But his profession keeps him so busy that latterly he hadn't had much time to spend at home.'

'What sort of company does Sir Godfrey keep?'

Stowell looked down his nose. 'Not quite the sort that you'd expect of a gentleman of his standing, sir,' he replied. 'But it's not for me to criticise, though often I've been kept awake until after midnight by their goings on.'

'Does Sir Godfrey share Mr Fransham's dislike of having ladies in the house?'

Stowell permitted himself a respectful smile. 'I can't say that he does, sir. From what I've seen, as many ladies as gentlemen come to Sir Godfrey's parties. Artists and writers, and people like that they are, for the most part, I've been told.' He dropped his voice. 'And that's why Mr Mayland doesn't come to the house more,' he added confidentially. 'He's got his business to attend to and doesn't want to get mixed up with people of that sort.'

'He wouldn't be likely to get commissions from them, I

suppose?' said Jimmy. 'But so long as they keep Sir Godfrey amused, there's no particular harm done.'

'I'm not so sure about that, sir,' replied Stowell darkly.

'What do you mean? You're not suggesting that anything wrong goes on at No. 3, are you?'

'Oh, no, sir, I shouldn't think of such a thing!' Stowell exclaimed. 'Mrs Quinton told my wife that she'd got an idea that Sir Godfrey's going to get married again. And if it's to be the lady she thinks it is, she says she won't stay in the house a week after the engagement's announced.'

Jimmy laughed. Sir Godfrey Branstock's matrimonial affairs were no concern of his, but the company which frequented No. 3 was a different matter. Its members might not appeal to the industrious Mayland, but they were just the kind of people with whom Francis Willingdon consorted. Was it possible that he had been among Sir Godfrey's visitors?

Having secured from Stowell a list of Mr Fransham's friends, Jimmy called next door and asked to see Sir Godfrey. A smart and rather supercilious parlourmaid showed him into the dining-room, where a few minutes later Sir Godfrey joined him. He was a big, heavy man somewhere on the wrong side of fifty, with a jovial, florid face and a hearty manner.

'Well, inspector, this is the first time I've had the police in my house,' he boomed. 'What can I do for you?'

'I have called in connection with the death of your neighbour, Mr Fransham,' Jimmy replied quietly.

'Why, you don't suppose I know anything about it, do you?' Branstock replied. 'I didn't know he was dead until I saw the report of the inquest in the paper this morning. Bad business, eh?'

'It's a very bad business indeed, Sir Godfrey. May I ask when you last saw Mr Fransham?'

'When I last saw him? Why, on Saturday morning. I happened to be passing his door when he was getting into that new car of his. I asked him if he was going off for the weekend, and he told me that he was going down to Adderminster to lunch with his niece. And it was there that he was done in, according to the papers.'

'He was found with a fractured skull in Dr Thornborough's cloakroom,' said Jimmy. 'Do you happen to know the doctor, Sir Godfrey?'

'I can't say that I do. I don't remember that I've ever met him. But I knew his wife well enough at one time— Betty Fransham that used to be. Namby-pamby sort of a girl I always thought, with no sense of fun in her. Just like her uncle that way. I don't believe Fransham ever let himself go in his life. He was the quietest old stick you'd meet in a day's march through London.'

'Not the sort of person to make enemies?' Jimmy suggested.

'Enemies? No, nor friends either. He was one of those bloodless sort of people who just jog on from day to day without trying to get anything out of life.'

'You knew him pretty intimately, I suppose, Sir Godfrey?'

'No, that I didn't. Although he was my tenant, and we'd been next-door neighbours for seventeen years, I don't suppose I've exchanged half a dozen words a week with him on the average. I don't believe anyone could claim to know him at all intimately unless perhaps that niece of his.'

'His lease of No. 4 expired at Christmas, did it not?'

'That's so. He talked to me about renewing it for another twenty-one years, but he hadn't come to any definite decision. I told him that I was quite ready to renew the lease, and he said he'd let me know later on. I have an idea that he had an alternative scheme in his head, but what it was I can't tell you.'

'You know his chauffeur Coates, don't you, Sir Godfrey?'

'Oh, yes, I know the fellow. At one time he was second chauffeur to my cousin, who's got a place in Norfolk. My cousin, who thought quite a lot of him, told me that he wanted to get a better place in London, and asked me to put in a word for him if I happened to hear of anybody who wanted a chauffeur. It wasn't long after that, that Fransham happened to say that he thought of buying a car. I told him that he'd want a chauffeur, and that I happened to know of a chap who might suit him. Coates came along, Fransham interviewed him, and that was that.'

'You don't know anything about Coates personally?'

'Only what my cousin told me at the time. He said he was a steady enough chap and a safe and reliable driver. But he thought he was a fool for wanting to go to London.'

'Most ambitious young men are anxious to get to London.'

'Yes, I know. But my cousin used to say that Coates was cut out for a job in the country. As well as being second chauffeur, he was by way of being a sort of handy man about my cousin's place. He'd turn to and help any of the chaps on the estate. The gamekeeper especially, for I've heard that he was a very fine shot.'

'Well, Sir Godfrey, I mustn't take up any more of your time,' said Jimmy. 'There's just one more question I'd like to ask you. Do you happen to know a young man of the name of Francis Willingdon, whose father is a manufacturer in Leeds?'

Branstock shook his head. 'Never heard of him,' he replied. 'Quite a lot of young folk come to this house one way and the other, and I'm the first to encourage them. But your friend Willingdon isn't among the number.'

Jimmy left Cheveley Street and, knowing that Mr Redbourne had come back to London after the inquest, he made his way to the lawyer's office in Bedford Row. Mr Redbourne received him at once. 'Well, inspector, you have something definite to tell me, I hope,' he said.

'Not yet, I'm afraid, sir,' Jimmy replied. 'You'll understand my position. I'm bound to examine all the possibilities before I come to a final decision.'

'Of course, of course!' said Mr Redbourne a trifle impatiently. 'That's the sort of phrase we lawyers use when we want to gain time. So you haven't made up your mind that only one possibility exists?'

'I have been trying to compile a list of people who had anything to gain by Mr Fransham's death.'

The lawyer's lips curled slightly. 'I thought I'd compiled that list for you already,' he replied. 'Have you discovered any names to add to it?'

'Only one, sir. It seems that Coates the chauffeur will now be able to realise a private ambition of his own.'

'Then you suspect Coates of having murdered his employer for the sake of his paltry legacy? I don't think there are many juries who would swallow that story, if you will forgive my saying so, inspector. Besides, I understand that the evidence of a member of the police is to the effect that Coates was standing at the door of the garage when Mr Robert Fransham was murdered. Perhaps you are able to explain how, in that case, he can have been the criminal.'

'Part of my trouble is, sir, that I can't explain how anybody can have been the criminal. There is nothing whatever to show how Mr Fransham was killed.'

'Except the shocking and not inconspicuous wound on the top of his head,' Mr Redbourne remarked acidly.

'Yes, I know, sir. But I've got to prove exactly how that wound was inflicted. And so far I am utterly unable to do so.'

'I should have thought it was obvious enough, even to a policeman. While Robert Fransham was washing at the basin, Thornborough hit him through the cloakroom window.'

Jimmy smiled at the ease with which he had led the lawyer into the trap. 'Just now, sir, you drew my attention to the fact that Coates was standing at the garage door at the time,' he said respectfully.

Mr Redbourne stared at him for a moment and then laughed shortly. 'Got me there,' he said a trifle ruefully. 'But that doesn't let Thornborough out, you know. Coates may have seen more than he cares to repeat to the police.'

'I've thought of that, sir. I'm going to interview Coates again and see if I can get an admission from him. Meanwhile I'd like you to look at this list. I saw Stowell this morning, and at my request he wrote down the names of all Mr Fransham's friends that he knew. I wonder if you could add to it?'

Mr Redbourne took the list and read it through carefully. 'No, I don't think that I can,' he said. 'Stowell seems to have put down everyone who knew Robert Fransham at all well. What are you going to do with these names? I see that my own is included.'

Jimmy smiled. 'I'm going to find out where each of these

126

people were when Mr Fransham was killed,' he replied. 'It's merely a matter of routine, of course.'

'Is it indeed? Well, you'd better begin with me. I was lunching at my club, the Inns of Court, in Pall Mall. Dozens of people must have seen me there. And it was there that I got Thornborough's telephone message.'

'Thank you, Mr Redbourne. Did you ever hear Mr Fransham mention the name of Willingdon?'

'Not that I can remember. He certainly had no personal friend of that name, or I should have heard it. Is there anything else you want to know?'

'Not at the moment, thank you, Mr Redbourne,' Jimmy replied.

He left the lawyer's office and returned to Scotland Yard, where he found the answer to a message which he had sent the previous evening. The Leeds Police confirmed the fact that Mr Ernest Willingdon lived at The Howdahs, Prospect Road. Mr Willingdon was a well-known and highly-respected manufacturer. His family consisted of his wife, one son and two daughters. The son Francis was employed in his father's business, and had been absent from Leeds for about three months, but had now returned. Mr Willingdon had told people that his son's absence was connected with the affairs of the firm. But local rumour had it that a young lady was in some way involved in the matter.

Jimmy handed over the list which Stowell had given him to one of his colleagues and then caught the next train to Adderminster. His first concern on reaching the police station was to ask for news of Alfie Prince.

Alfie had appeared before the Bench and had been remanded for a medical opinion. Dr Dorrington had seen him and had reported that he had been subject to temporary derangements during which he could hardly be held responsible for his actions. This had been on the previous day— Monday. On Tuesday morning Alfie had woken up in full possession of his senses. He had no recollection whatever of anything that had happened since the previous Friday evening. He remembered coming home from work and having his tea. He also remembered that after his meal he had felt suddenly oppressed indoors and had gone out to take the air. But of where he went or of what had happened to him since then, he had not the slightest idea. Dr Dorrington, upon being consulted a second time, had said that this lapse of memory was typical of the form of mental derangement to which Alfie was liable.

Jimmy next secured the services of Linton and sent him to fetch Coates, who was still at the Red Lion. The three of them then drove up to *Epidaurus* in Mr Fransham's Armstrong-Siddeley. They found that Dr Thornborough was out on his afternoon round and that the garage was therefore empty. Jimmy told Coates to drive the car into the garage and stationed Linton at the garden door of the house.

'Now, then, Coates, I want you to carry on exactly as you did on Saturday,' he said.

Coates got out of the car and walked slowly all round it, examining the tyres and lifting each side of the bonnet in turn. This process took him three minutes by Jimmy's watch. When he had finished he took up his position in the doorway of the garage leaning against the post nearest the brick wall. Here he took out a cigarette and lighted it.

'How long did you stand like that, Coates?' Jimmy asked.

'About ten minutes or so, I should think, sir,' Coates

replied. 'Until I saw the doctor's car turn in at the gate. Then I threw away the fag and stood up ready to meet him.'

'All right, that'll do for the present. Take the car back, then wait for me at the police station. I shall want a word with you later on.'

Coates drove off and Jimmy beckoned to Linton. 'Well, was that all right?' he asked.

'It was just what I saw him do on Saturday, sir,' Linton replied.

'Very well, come with me and I'll show you something.' Jimmy led the way to the road, then through the gap in the hedge into the grass field, and so to the back of the brick wall. He found the loose brick and pointed it out to Linton. 'Someone has contrived a very neat little peephole for himself,' he said. 'Now, this is what I want you to do. Give me two or three minutes to get back to the garage. Then take out this brick as gently and quietly as you can, wait a few seconds and put it back again. When you've done that come back and join me.'

Jimmy went back to the garage and leant against the gatepost. In this position his head was within six inches of the wall and his line of vision ran straight along its surface. It was impossible for him to distinguish separate bricks at more than five yards distance. He waited, straining his eyes and ears, but neither saw nor heard anything. A minute or two later Linton appeared, walked down the carriage-way and saluted. 'I did what you told me, sir,' he said.

'Good man,' Jimmy replied. 'Now walk back to the cloakroom window and put your arm through the opening.'

Linton did so, and Jimmy, still in the same position,

watched him. From where he stood he had a perfectly clear and unobstructed view of the whole length and width of the carriage-way. It ran straight from the entrance gate to the garage, without any projection behind which a man could hide. Jimmy could plainly see the cloakroom window, and Linton's burly form as he put his arm through it. He frowned as he realised that the problem was as insoluble as ever. Then he walked down the carriage-way and joined Linton.

'All right, that experiment's over,' he said. 'Now we'll go back to the police station and I'll have another shot at that chap Coates.'

The interview took place in the room which Superintendent Yateley had put at his disposal. Jimmy put Coates in a chair, where the light fell on his face, and sat down facing him. 'Well, Coates, you'll be able to start work on that filling station of yours now, won't you?' he said cheerfully.

Coates' expression showed the surprise he felt at this opening. 'I don't know about that, sir,' he replied after a moment's hesitation. 'I haven't given it a thought since Mr Fransham's death. And Dr Thornborough asked me if I'd care to stop with him for a bit. He said that he'd probably sell his own car and take over Mr Fransham's.'

'It's a much more impressive looking car, certainly,' said Jimmy. 'And doctors have to think of appearances, I suppose. But surely you're not going to abandon that pet scheme of yours, are you?'

'I don't know how you came to hear of it, sir, I'm sure.'

'It's my job to find things out. But never mind about that. You'll have a little money to play with now, won't you? You've been with Mr Fransham five years, and surely he's left you something in his will?'

Coates' eyes narrowed. 'I don't know anything about that, sir,' he replied cautiously. 'Mr Fransham did say to me once that if I stayed with him I shouldn't have cause to regret it when he died. But what he meant by that is more than I can tell. It might be a matter of twenty pounds or so, and that wouldn't be much good to start what I was thinking of.'

'Possibly not. But you must have saved a bit while you were with Mr Fransham?'

'You can't save much in London on thirty-five bob a week, sir. Mr Fransham wasn't one to pay a higher wage than he could help.'

'Oh, but you got your board and lodging? To say nothing of the chance of making an extra few shillings a week by monkeying with the petrol bill.'

Coates started visibly at this. 'I don't know what you mean, sir,' he exclaimed virtuously. 'Mr Fransham never had any cause to find fault with my accounts.'

'Hadn't he? Well, that's perhaps lucky for you. If he'd found out that you'd been cheating him, he might have struck you out of his will altogether. But those accounts of yours are still in existence, I expect, and it may occur to Mr Fransham's executors to have a look at them. I'd bear that possibility in mind if I were you. Now, let's get back to last Saturday. You stood leaning against that door-post from shortly after you arrived until the doctor's car drove in at the gate. You still stick to that story, do you? Just think it over for a bit before you answer me.'

'There's no need to think it over, sir. It's just the plain truth, and I'm ready to swear to it.'

'Then you admit that you had an uninterrupted view of the carriage-way and of anybody who came into it?'

'Yes, sir, that's just what I've said all along.'

Jimmy shook his head. 'Then it seems to me that you're in a very awkward position, Coates,' he said sternly. 'There's not a shadow of doubt that Mr Fransham was killed through the cloakroom window. By your own admission, then, you must have seen the person who committed the crime. By withholding information from the police, you become an accessory after the fact, and in the eyes of the law, equally guilty as the criminal himself.'

Coates looked so startled that it was obvious that this aspect of the matter had not occurred to him before. 'But I didn't see anybody, sir,' he insisted.

'Perhaps because you deliberately looked the other way,' Jimmy suggested.

Coates shook his head violently. 'No, sir, once I'd leant against that doorpost I never looked round,' he replied. 'You see, sir, I was looking out for the doctor to come home or for one of the girls to come out of the house and call me in. I was watching, as you might say, all the time that I was smoking my fag.'

'Then you are prepared to swear that nobody entered the carriage-way during that period? Be careful, now. This may turn out to be a very serious matter for you.'

Coates' face remained perfectly calm. 'I'm ready to swear that I never saw anybody there until the doctor's car drove in, sir,' he replied.

'Are you equally ready to swear that if anybody had been there you would have seen them?' Jimmy asked quickly.

'Yes, sir, I'll go as far as that. I'm ready to take my dying oath that no one came into that carriage-way the whole time I was standing against the doorpost.'

'You say that you threw your cigarette away when you saw the doctor's car turn in at the gateway? What did you do then?'

'I waited for the car to come up to me, sir.'

'Did you keep your eyes on it all the time?'

'Yes, sir, because I wasn't quite sure at first whether it was the doctor or not. I didn't recognise him for certain until he was half-way down the carriage-way. It's not always easy to make out a driver sitting behind a wind-screen.'

'You are perfectly certain that you were watching the car as it passed the cloakroom window?'

'Quite certain, sir. The car must have been just about there when I recognised the doctor driving it.'

'If the car had stopped for an instant, you would have noticed it?'

'I'm perfectly certain that I should, sir.'

'And if the doctor had put his right arm out of the window of the car you would have noticed that, too?'

'I couldn't have failed to see him do that, sir.'

'And you are ready to swear that you saw neither of these things happen?'

'I'm ready to take my oath upon it, sir.'

'Have you done any shooting lately, Coates?'

Coates' face betrayed nothing beyond a certain bewilderment at this sudden change of topic. 'Shooting, sir?' he replied. 'I haven't touched a gun since I've been with Mr Fransham. In the place I was in before I went to him, the gamekeeper used to lend me a gun sometimes and take me out with him after vermin. That's all the shooting I've ever done, sir.'

Jimmy dismissed Coates, and as soon as he was alone,

lighted a cigarette and frowned thoughtfully. His cross-examination had failed to shake Coates' statement in any material detail. Jimmy, experienced by now in the demeanour of people under interrogation, felt pretty certain that the chauffeur's statements were true. In which case Mr Fransham must have been killed by a missile projected from behind the brick wall. This, on the other hand, was impossible, for no trace of any such missile had been found.

To rid his mind of such idle fancies, Jimmy left the police station and walked through the town until he reached Gunthorpe Road. He noticed in front of him a man on a bicycle, who dismounted at the gate of the cottage lately occupied by Frank Willingdon. Jimmy hurried after him and caught him up as he was unlocking the front door. 'Excuse me,' he said. 'I'm Inspector Waghorn from Scotland Yard. This cottage is unoccupied now, isn't it?'

'That's right,' the other replied. 'It's been let furnished for a month, but the lease expired yesterday morning. The owner won't be back for another week or two, and I'm just going in to see that everything's been left in proper order. My name's Didcot, by the way. I'm in business in High Street as a house agent. Care to come inside with me?'

Jimmy accepted the invitation and they entered the lounge together. Willingdon had tidied the place up after a fashion, but there was still a certain amount of litter lying about. Ash-trays with stubs of cigarettes in them, and so forth. Didcot glanced round the room appraisingly.

'Not so bad as it might have been,' he said. 'Willingdon left a quid with me to pay for a charwoman to clean the place up. She'll soon set it to rights. I'll see about that at once. Hallo, what's this?'

He put his hand into the crevice of one of the chairs and pulled out a square of white linen.

'Lady's handkerchief embroidered at the corners and scented,' he continued. 'I thought as much.'

Jimmy had been examining the cigarette ends, to find that they were all Player's or Gold Flake. He looked up at the house agent's words. 'Was the tenant married, then?' he asked innocently.

Didcot laughed. 'Anything but, if you ask my opinion. He told me when I first saw him that he was a student and wanted a quiet place where he could read during the weekends. That was when he came down to see about taking the place, which he'd seen advertised. He seemed a decent sort of chap, but he talked in a queer way that I couldn't quite understand. I came up here with him and showed him the place, and he told me that it would suit him perfectly.'

'When was this?' Jimmy asked.

'One day towards the end of April or the beginning of May. He arranged to take this place for a month from the 14th May. He said that he would only be able to use it at weekends from Friday evening till Monday morning, for he was attending lectures during the rest of the week. Before I had the chance of asking him for a reference, he told me that he didn't want to give one, because he was anxious that nobody should know where he was. He said that he was sure that his friends would come and interrupt him if they heard that he'd taken a cottage in the country. And as he forked out the month's rent then and there I didn't press the matter.'

'What was the tenant's name?'

'Willingdon. He told me that his father was a

manufacturer in a pretty big way in Leeds. He gave me his own address in London. Some address in Kensington it was. The name's slipped my memory for the moment, but I've got it down at the office.'

'Harlows Hotel, perhaps?'

'That's it. You seem to know something about this chap, inspector. He was all square and above board, wasn't he?'

Jimmy smiled. 'Up to a point, I fancy,' he replied. 'But I've reason to suppose that he's not in the habit of over-working himself with study.'

'That doesn't altogether surprise me. I had my doubts the first weekend he was here. I came up on the Saturday morning just to see that he was all right. I rang the bell, but nobody answered it for quite a long time, though I could hear somebody scuffling about inside. But at last Willingdon opened the door an inch or two and peeped out. I asked him if he'd found everything all right, and he told me that he had, but that he didn't want to be disturbed, as he was frightfully busy. And with that he shut the door in my face. I happened to look up at one of the top windows and caught sight for an instant of a woman's face peeping from behind the curtains. And a pretty decorative sort of girl she was, too, from what I saw of her.'

'You didn't see her again, I suppose?'

'I haven't been near the place again till now. It wasn't really my business if Willingdon chose to take the cottage for the entertainment of his lady friends. The less I knew about it the better, in case people started asking questions. But Willingdon was pretty discreet, I'll say that for him. He didn't parade his friends through the town, or anything like that.'

'Do you suppose that he brought a girl down every weekend with him?'

'That I don't know. All I can tell you is that last Friday, on his way here, he stopped at the garage at the far end of High Street to fill up with petrol. I happened to be walking along the opposite pavement, so he didn't see me. And there was certainly a girl in the car with him then. Whether it was the same one that I saw at the window is more than I can say.'

'Bit of a lad, in his way. Does he happen to have any friends or acquaintances in these parts, do you know?'

'I don't know,' Didcot said, winking knowingly. 'But I'll bet a good deal he hasn't. His game was to take a cottage in a place where nobody knew him, then there wouldn't be any risk of anybody recognising him and passing the word to his papa. I'll send this handkerchief on to him without comment. Would you care to come with me and look round the rest of the house?'

They went upstairs and Didcot opened a door. 'This is the best bedroom,' he said. 'There are only two, as a matter of fact, and the other's a lot smaller. Um! Fairly tidy. Only wants dusting out and the bed making. Is that what you call incriminating evidence, inspector?'

He pointed to the bed—a large double one. It was laid with two pillows, both of which had obviously been slept upon. And protruding from under one of them was a corner of a pink nightdress.

Jimmy pulled it out and held it up. 'Hardly the garment to suggest an elderly spinster of prudish disposition,' he replied. 'Willingdon's ladies seem remarkably careless with their personal possessions. You'd better enclose that in the parcel with the handkerchief. Anything else to see?'

'We'd better look into the other bedroom, I suppose,' said Didcot, suiting the action to the words. 'This one hasn't been used, by the look of it. The bed hasn't even been made up, you'll notice. I can't see any dilapidations, that's one comfort. I'll just have a look round the back premises and then I'm through.'

The search of the kitchen and scullery revealed nothing new, but Jimmy could not help noticing the completeness of the domestic arrangements. He remarked upon this to Didcot.

'Oh, yes, everything here's absolutely up to date,' the house agent replied. 'The cottage wasn't anything like this in Squire Gunthorpe's time, of course. The gardener and his wife lived here, and they didn't trouble much about appearances. But when the estate was sold Mr Whiteway bought the place. And the first thing he did was to pull it about to suit himself. Spent quite a lot of money on it, too, one way and the other. Put in all the latest gadgets— tiled bathroom, latest type of gas cooker, electric refrigerator, coke boiler for constant hot water, pretty well everything else you can think of. It's what Mrs Whiteway calls a labour-saving house, and she's about right. But it wouldn't suit me, for there isn't a coal fire in the house. That doesn't matter at this time of the year, I'll allow, but of a winter's evening I like to draw my chair up in front of a good blaze. Coal, with a nice ash log on top of it. That's what I call comfort.'

Jimmy suddenly remembered Dr Priestley's question. 'Has Dr Thornborough over the way got water, gas and electricity laid on?'

'Oh, yes. When this road was made after the estate was sold all main services were laid along it as far as the gate that leads to Mark Farm. Perhaps you've noticed that grass field beyond the doctor's? Well, that's for sale in building plots, and sooner or later it will be developed. The Council even brought the sewer up here in readiness. There'll be quite a lot of good-class houses up this way before many years. Talking of the doctor, that was a bad business at his place last Saturday. I dare say it wouldn't be a bad guess that it's because of that you're here?'

'A pretty good one,' Jimmy agreed. 'I'd like to know in strict confidence, of course, what people in the town are saying about that affair?'

Didcot shrugged his shoulders. 'There's only one thing to be said, so far as I can see,' he replied. 'There aren't many folk in Adderminster who'll care to have Dr Thornborough in their houses after this. I wouldn't myself, for one. I'd rather call in Dr Dorrington, though people do say that he's getting a bit past his work.'

'Do you know Dr Thornborough personally?'

'As well as one ever does a doctor who attends one's family. He came to see my wife a lot at the latter end of last year when she had arthritis pretty bad. I liked the doctor, I must say. It seemed to me that he was pretty good at his job. I certainly shouldn't have expected anything like this to happen.'

'Then it's a pretty general opinion that he killed Mr Fransham?'

'Well, inspector, it's like this,' replied Didcot confidentially. 'I don't pretend to know the ins and outs of the business. That's your affair, not mine. But what I say is this: If the doctor didn't do it, who did? I don't suppose there was anybody else besides him and his family in Adderminster so much as knew this Mr Fransham by sight.

And as for that poor daft chap Alfie Prince, why, he wouldn't hurt a fly, even when he's in one of those moods of his. They may say he's balmy, but he's perfectly harmless, I'll swear to that.'

The two left the cottage and Jimmy walked across the road to *Epidaurus*. He spent the rest of the evening examining the house, the garage and the building land behind the brick wall. He had hoped against hope that he would find some clue which had hitherto been overlooked, but in this he was utterly disappointed. No fresh evidence of any kind rewarded his search. At last, utterly dispirited, he returned to the police station.

Next morning, after a decidedly uncomfortable interview with Superintendent Yateley, he returned to Scotland Yard and poured out his troubles to Hanslet.

'I'm beaten, and it's no use pretending I'm not,' he said despondently. 'And the worst of it is that the local people—Yateley, for instance—obviously think that I've let them down. Yateley as good as told me that if he'd kept things in his own hands instead of calling in the Yard he would have arrested Dr Thornborough and had a statement out of him long ago.'

'Well, there's nothing to prevent him doing that now,' said Hanslet. 'Why doesn't he get on with it?'

'Because although he's convinced that the man's guilty, he isn't certain of getting an incriminating statement from him. And without that the case isn't good enough to ensure a conviction. The prosecution would have to prove how the crime was committed, and that's exactly what I haven't been able to find out. In Yateley's eyes it's all my fault. But he's not going to risk the acquittal of a man arrested by him on his own responsibility. And it makes me feel that I've made a hopeless mess of things.'

Hanslet slapped his dejected subordinate on the back. 'Don't you take it to heart, Jimmy, my boy,' he said. 'There isn't a soul in the Yard who hasn't failed in much the same way at one time or another. Besides, it's far too early to give up hope. The Yard never forgets, you know. And something may crop up one of these days to put you on the right track. Have all the usual routine inquiries made and keep the case in mind, but don't brood over it. And by way of a change, I've got another little job for you to look into: Somebody's passing dud half-crowns in the Tooting district. I'll give you the particulars as they have been reported to us, and then you can get along and see what about it.'

PART TWO

Death Visits Cheveley Street

CHAPTER I

Christopher Portslade completed the shaking of a third cocktail, and with a not over-steady hand poured a generous portion of the concoction into his glass. He was a weedy youth of twenty-two or thereabouts, with carefully-waved hair and an unpleasantly cunning expression. His evening dress, though immaculate, was cut with vulgar exaggeration. His tailor, no doubt, believed in the adage that the clothes should suit the man.

The time was ten minutes past eight on Wednesday, August 4, of the same year that had witnessed Mr Fransham's murder, the mystery of which was still unsolved. The scene was the lounge of Sir Godfrey Branstock's house, No. 3 Cheveley Street. The other two occupants of the room were girls, sitting side by side on a sofa, each with a half-empty cocktail glass in her hand. The eldest of these was Nancy Lanchester, who was to become Lady Branstock three weeks hence. Her age was thirty-six, but it was impossible to guess this under her elaborate make-up. She was of medium height, with a well-thought-out figure and a shrewd, rather cruel expression. The other girl was her cousin, Violet Portslade, Christopher's sister. She was twenty-four, willowy, innocent looking and even more sophisticated than most girls of her age. She was to be one of Nancy's bridesmaids, and the two were discussing, not very affably, some detail of the forthcoming ceremony.

Christopher turned round glass in hand, and for a few moments listened contemptuously to the conversation.

'Damn it all, what does it matter what the hell you wear?' he burst out suddenly. 'That isn't what the old boy is interested in, as you know well enough. All you've got to do, Nan, is to take care that the fish doesn't wriggle off the hook before the twenty-fifth.'

'Oh, shut up, Chris!' exclaimed his sister angrily. 'Nan knows perfectly well what she's about. Godfrey's much too keen to back out at the last moment like that. It makes me feel quite sick to think of such a thing.'

'You'd feel sicker about it if you were as broke as I am,' Christopher replied. 'As it is, I don't know how I'm going to survive the next three weeks. I say, Nan, don't you think you could touch the devout lover for a nice fat cheque in advance? A deposit on account of favours to be rendered later, so to speak?'

Nancy Lanchester drained her glass and held it out to be replenished. 'I'm not such a fool as to try that on, Chris,' she replied quietly. 'Ours is a love match, you must remember. The mutual passion of the virgin and the world-weary knight. You will have to manage as best you can for a bit. Just you leave Godfrey to me. I know perfectly well how to manage him.'

'Well, don't waste any more time than you can help,' Christopher grumbled. 'Talking about time, what's come over the old boy this evening? It isn't like him to keep his guests waiting for dinner.' He glanced in Nancy's direction. 'Especially when his fiancée is one of the party,' he added sneeringly.

Violet sniggered. 'You mustn't forget that it's his birthday,' she replied. 'He's probably dyeing his hair or something like that to make himself appear more youthful in Nan's eyes. Give me another cocktail, Chris, you beast.'

Behind the baize door leading to the kitchen premises on the ground floor Mrs Quinton, Branstock's cook, was becoming impatient.

'Nearly a quarter past eight,' she exclaimed irritably. 'I thank my stars I'm not stopping in this house much longer. Everything's gone topsy-turvy since the master took up with that Lanchester woman. I can't keep my dinner spoiling here all night. Just you go and sound the gong, Grace. Perhaps that will bring them to their senses.'

'Can't be done, old dear,' replied the parlour-maid pertly. 'The old chap hasn't come downstairs yet. And you ought to know by this time that he won't have the gong sounded until he's ready.'

'Well, he won't like his dinner spoilt, let me tell you. You run up and tap on his door, and tell him what time it is. Maybe his watch has stopped, or he's fallen asleep or something. Now, don't make a face like that, but do as you're told. I'm mistress in my own kitchen, I'll have you know.'

Grace flounced out of the room, to return a couple of minutes later with wide-open eyes. 'He's not there!' she exclaimed dramatically.

'Not there!' Mrs Quinton replied. 'What on earth are you talking about? Where is he, then?'

'How can I tell? All I know is that he isn't in his dressing-room. The door's open, and there are his evening clothes laid out just as I left them an hour ago.'

Mrs Quinton looked aghast. 'What, do you mean to say that he hasn't started changing yet, then?' she demanded.

'Looks like it. And he's not in his bedroom, either, for I peeped in there, too.'

'Drat the man!' exclaimed Mrs Quinton. 'It's my belief that he's gone clean off his crumpet lately. He'd never have fallen for that painted Jezebel else.' She made a motion of her head towards the lounge. 'Who's up there?' she asked.

'Her and the Portslade couple,' Grace replied. 'They're not worrying much. I heard the cocktail shaker going as I passed the door. You'll just have to hang on and keep the dinner hot as best you can.'

But Mrs Quinton was not so easily pacified. 'I'm not going to stand being messed about like this,' she exclaimed. 'For two pins I'd walk out of the house and leave these folks to get their own dinner. He hasn't gone to his club and forgotten all about the party, has he?'

'He was in the house soon after seven,' Grace replied. 'I saw him then, going down to the cellar to fetch up the wine, like he always does.'

'He can't be down there all this time. Perhaps he's in the dining-room uncorking the bottles.'

'I was in there just now seeing to the table, and he wasn't there then. And, now I come to think of it, he hadn't put the wine on the sideboard like he always does.'

'You're quite sure you saw him going down to the cellar?'

'Well, he was going down the steps to the basement, and they don't lead to anywhere but the cellar, as you know well enough.'

Mrs Quinton took off her apron with great deliberation. 'I'm not going to stand it,' she said. 'I'm going to find him and I'm going to tell him that if he likes to keep his dinner spoiling for half an hour he can find someone else to cook it for him.' And with a dignified air she marched out of the kitchen.

All the houses in Cheveley Street had originally been built upon the same plan. In the basement were the domestic offices, and below them again, an extensive wine cellar. On the ground floor was the hall, the dining-room and a smaller room known as the smoking-room. On the first floor were the drawing-room and morning-room. On the second floor were the three principal bedrooms, and on the third the servants' quarters.

No. 3, however, had been modernised some years earlier. New kitchen premises had been built out on the ground floor, and separated from the rest of the house by a baize door. The disused basement had eventually accumulated a collection of empty boxes and such-like rubbish. The wine cellar below it remained in use.

Apart from the addition of the kitchen premises the ground floor remained as before. On the first floor the drawing-room had been converted into a lounge and the morning-room divided into two to form Branstock's bed and dressing-room. No structural alterations had been made on the second and third floors.

Mrs Quinton began her pilgrimage by mounting to the first floor. The door of the lounge was shut, and through it she could hear the voices of its three occupants. She listened long enough to assure herself that Branstock was not in the lounge, then, seeing that his dressing-room door was ajar, she pushed it open and walked in. Branstock was not there, and a moment's survey convinced her that he had not dressed for dinner. She looked through the connecting door into the bedroom, to find it unoccupied. Even the lavatory on the half-landing yielded a negative result.

Puzzled, but by no means discouraged, Mrs Quinton returned to the ground floor. She looked into the dining-room and the smoking-room, now called the study, but in neither did she find any trace of her master. It was now an hour or more since Grace had seen him on his way to the cellar. It was ridiculous to suppose that he could be down there all this time. But Mrs Quinton was determined to find him and, as she told herself, to give him a piece of her mind.

Beside the baize door leading to the servants' quarters and on the hall side of it was a second door. Mrs Quinton opened this and found herself at the head of the flight of stairs leading to the basement. She descended this and looked about her. The first thing she noticed was that the cellar door was open and that the electric light within was on. She approached the cellar door. 'Are you down there, sir?' she called.

As she listened for the reply, she became aware of a faint and apparently distant humming noise. She could not account for this until she remembered the refrigerator in the larder on the floor above. She had not realised that its motor could be heard so clearly from the basement. And since the light was on in the cellar, Sir Godfrey must be there. Why couldn't he have the politeness to answer her? 'Are you down there, sir?' she repeated loudly.

Still no reply, and, now she came to think about it, no sound of anybody moving about. A flight of a dozen stone steps led down to the cellar floor. She descended the first three or four of these and then stopped suddenly with an involuntary gasp of dismay.

But Mrs Quinton was not the woman to lose her head in an emergency. It was no good going into hysterics because Sir Godfrey had fainted and was lying doubled up on the floor in front of the champagne bin. Resolutely she descended the remainder of the steps and laid her fingers on her master's pulse. She couldn't feel anything, and she noticed that he wasn't breathing, but that his face was more florid than ever. She made an attempt to raise him into a sitting position, but found this beyond her strength. As she desisted from her efforts, it struck her that the humming noise was even more distinct in the cellar than it had been in the basement. It seemed to get right into her head and to make her feel giddy. She couldn't do anything by herself, that was quite obvious. She must summon help.

She hurried back to the kitchen, where she arrived breathless. 'Master's fainted in the cellar,' she panted at the astonished Grace. 'Don't tell them upstairs. They'll only potter about and get in the way. Nip out and fetch the policeman. He's always somewhere round the corner at this time. And then between us we'll get the master up here.'

Grace nodded and ran out. Mrs Quinton followed her into the hall, where the telephone stood. Above the instrument hung a card upon which a list of numbers was written. Having consulted this, Mrs Quinton dialled a number.

Dr Oldland, whose dinner the call had interrupted, listened to Mrs Quinton's voluble story. 'Right,' he said curtly. 'I'll come along at once.'

The policeman, an old acquaintance of Mrs Quinton's,

was the first to arrive. 'Good-evening, mum,' he said. 'Miss Grace tells me that Sir Godfrey's been taken bad in the cellar. But it's a doctor you want, surely?'

'He's on his way,' Mrs Quinton replied briskly. 'I want you to lend a hand to get the master out. I can't move him by myself.'

They descended to the cellar, where the policeman bent over Sir Godfrey's prostrate body. 'Looks pretty bad, don't he?' he said. 'Now, then, mum, if you and Miss Grace will take one of his legs each I'll get hold of his shoulders. We'll manage to get him up these steps between us, I don't doubt. Now then, all together, and gently does it.'

They struggled up the steps with their burden, which they deposited in a sitting position on the basement floor. They had hardly accomplished this when the front door bell rang.

'That'll be the doctor,' Mrs Quinton exclaimed. 'Run up and let him in, Grace, and bring him down here.'

Dr Oldland appeared and glanced round the assembled group. Then, without speaking, he knelt down beside the man and made a swift examination. This done, he rose slowly to his feet. 'Anybody staying in the house, Mrs Quinton?' he asked.

'Not actually staying, sir,' Mrs Quinton replied. 'But there are two ladies and a gentleman come to dinner. And one of them's Miss Lanchester.'

'Miss Lanchester? She's the woman Branstock was to have married, isn't she? Where is Mr Mayland?'

'I don't rightly know, sir. He was here one day last week, but I understand that he's gone away over the holiday.'

'Oh, yes, of course. Monday was Bank Holiday. Well, you'd better get these other people out of the house as quietly as you can.' He turned to Grace. 'You're the parlour-maid, aren't you? Go and tell the guests that Sir Godfrey has been taken ill, and that his own doctor is attending him. Has that door at the top of the basement stairs got a lock to it?'

'Yes, sir,' Grace replied. 'It's locked every night.'

'Well, then, turn the key behind you and put it in your pocket. And don't unlock the door again until these people have left the house. We don't want them dithering down here.'

Grace departed, and nobody spoke until the key had turned in the lock. Then Mrs Quinton could restrain herself no longer. 'Oh, sir, is he very bad?' she asked.

'Bad or good, who can say?' replied Dr Oldland thoughtfully. 'He's dead, that's what's the matter with him. And, what's more, he's been dead for half an hour at least.'

He turned to the policeman. 'What are you doing here?' he asked sharply.

'Mrs Quinton sent for me, sir. She couldn't shift Sir Godfrey by herself.'

'Show me exactly where you found him,' said Dr Oldland.

They descended to the cellar, and the policeman indicated the position in which he had first seen Branstock's body. He had been lying doubled up on the cellar floor, with one hand extended towards the bin containing a couple of dozen bottles of champagne. Oldland nodded. 'Do you think you could find me a candle, Mrs Quinton?' he asked.

'Yes, sir, I think so,' the cook replied. 'I always keep a package in the kitchen in case anything should go wrong with the electric light. And, now I come to think of it, there are some stowed away in what used to be the old larder in the basement. I can get at them easily enough.'

Mrs Quinton returned with a candle stuck in a flat enamelled candlestick. Oldland set a match to the wick and held the candlestick on a level with his face. After a preliminary spluttering the flame burnt clearly and steadily. Then Oldland began to lower the candlestick slowly towards the floor. As he did so, the flame flickered and became less luminous. Finally, as he placed the candlestick on the ground, the flame floated for an instant above the wick and then expired.

'I thought so,' Oldland muttered. 'We'd better get out of this.'

They returned to the basement, where Oldland proceeded to interrogate Mrs Quinton. 'Was the cellar door open when you came down here to look for Sir Godfrey?' he asked.

'Yes, sir, wide open with the light on. That's how I knew he must be there. He always kept the key himself and wouldn't let anyone go inside. This evening's the first time I've set foot in the cellar, for all the years that I've been with him.'

'You don't know what time he unlocked the door this evening, I suppose?'

'Well, sir, Grace said she saw the master coming down this way about a quarter past seven. I expect that's right, for he nearly always used to fetch the wine before he dressed for dinner.'

'What time was it when you found him here?'

'It must have been twenty-past eight or more, sir. I didn't leave the kitchen till a quarter past. Then I looked for him upstairs first.'

'You tried to move him, you say? Did you feel any sensation of giddiness as you bent down over him?'

'Well, now that you mention it, I did, sir. But it may have been the shock of seeing him like that.'

'When did Sir Godfrey last have the occasion to enter the cellar?'

'He used to go down every evening when he dined at home, sir, to choose the wine he wanted. Let me see, now. Today's Wednesday. The master wasn't at home to dinner yesterday, no, nor yet the day before. He must have been down here last on Sunday, when there was a party of six to dinner.'

'And you're pretty certain that the door wasn't open between then and this evening?'

'I'd go so far as to say I was quite certain, sir. Nobody but the master could have opened it, and he hadn't had occasion to go into the cellar.'

A sound of departing footsteps followed by the slamming of the front door came to them from above. A moment later Grace unlocked the basement door and joined them.

'They've gone, sir,' she said. 'Miss Lanchester wanted to know if she couldn't stop and nurse the master, but I told her there was no occasion for that. I said that if she was wanted, the doctor would ring her up later.'

'Well done!' the doctor exclaimed approvingly. 'You've got your head screwed on straight, I can see that. Now run upstairs again and clear the dining-room table, there's a good girl. We'll lay him on that for the present.'

CHAPTER II

On Friday, two evenings later, Oldland was sitting in Dr Priestley's study with a glass of whisky and soda beside him. He had invited himself to dinner with the professor, and had suggested that Hanslet should be present. Now, to an audience consisting of the professor, his secretary Harold Merefield and the superintendent, he was recounting the circumstances of Branstock's death.

'He was a big, heavy man, weighing fifteen stone or more,' he continued. 'We had a devil of a job getting him out of that basement into the dining-room. If the policeman hadn't happened to be a bit of a Hercules we should never have done it. However, we got him on to the table at last, and I set to work to make a proper examination.

'There wasn't a shadow of doubt that asphyxia was the cause of death. Branstock had been suffocated, and the circumstances made it pretty clear how this had happened. As I've already told you, I was his regular medical attendant, but had not seen him for fourteen days before his death. I had attended him six months ago when he was suffering from high blood pressure and a few weeks ago I was called to the house to see Mrs Quinton, who was suffering from influenza. That being so, I couldn't issue a certificate, although the cause of death was obvious enough.

'I ought to explain, I suppose, that Branstock is a widower with no near relations alive. His establishment consisted of a cook—the extremely capable Mrs Quinton—a parlourmaid who, although inclined to pertness, is bright enough, a housemaid and a scullerymaid. The two latter I didn't see on Wednesday evening. I expect they were loafing about the back premises somewhere. Branstock, who I imagine had plenty of money, was an exponent of the gay life. He did himself far too well, as I've had occasion to tell him more than once. I managed to frighten him when he had that blood pressure trouble, and he eased up for a bit, but it didn't last very long. It was his fifty-fourth birthday on Wednesday, and he wasn't what the insurance companies call a very good life. However, if he had consented to follow the treatment which I had prescribed for him, he was good for another ten or fifteen years at least.

'His principal amusement was entertaining—not always, in my opinion, the most desirable people. He liked to collect bright young people about him, and never seemed to worry his head about their antecedents. He may have prided himself upon his Bohemian outlook—I don't know. I went to one of his parties once and thought myself lucky to get away without having been seduced.

'Whether things would have been different if he had lived for another three weeks, again I don't know. He was going to be married to a certain Miss Nancy Lanchester. I don't know anything about her, for I only saw her once, and at that very party I mentioned. She may conceal an angel's heart under her enamelled exterior, for all I can tell. But I didn't like her; I can't explain why. There was something about her that would have shocked a respectable prostitute.

'As it happened, this Miss Lanchester and her two cousins, male and female, had been invited to dinner on Wednesday. I managed to get them out of the house at once. I mistrust the behaviour of that type of person when faced with sudden tragedy. And these three, I gather, had been regaling themselves with unlimited cocktails. The person I wanted to get hold of was young Anthony Mayland, who is a thoroughly steady, reliable sort of chap. But they told me he had gone out of London over the holidays.'

'Who is Anthony Mayland, doctor?' Hanslet asked.

'Oh, haven't I told you? Branstock, as I said just now, was a widower. Just after the war he married a widow, Mrs Mayland, who had one son, Anthony. She died within a couple of years of her marriage, and Branstock took his stepson under his care. Anthony is now twenty-eight and in practice in an architect's office. From what Branstock once told me, I believe he's doing very well.

'Well, I'd hardly finished my examination when Anthony turned up. It was what the newspapers would call a dramatic return. Anthony had left London on the previous Friday to spend a few days with some friends in the country. I should explain that Anthony didn't live with his stepfather, though he saw a good deal of him. He has rooms of his own somewhere. I rather fancy that the atmosphere of No. 3 Cheveley Street doesn't exactly appeal to him. And I doubt that he altogether approved of Nancy Lanchester as the prospective second Lady Branstock.

'Anthony turned up soon after ten o'clock with a box of cigars for his stepfather's birthday. He knew nothing of what had happened, of course, and fortunately Mrs Quinton met him in the hall and broke the news to him. And when he came into the dining-room he was pretty badly shaken up. He and Branstock had always got on very well, in spite of their differences of taste. He told me that Branstock had always treated him as his own son, and he had always thought of him as his own father. I prescribed him a stiff brandy, and that seemed to pull him together a bit. But even then he didn't seem able to realise what had happened. He told me that when he had last seen Branstock on the previous Friday he had been in the very best of health and spirits. He had talked of nothing but his approaching marriage and the fun he was going to have at Monte Carlo on his honeymoon. I explained to Anthony why I couldn't issue a certificate, and went home leaving him in charge of the household.

'Next morning I rang up the coroner, who happens to be a personal friend of mine, and explained matters to him. He agreed with me that there was no necessity to hold a post-mortem, but directed that an inquest should be held this morning. It wasn't a very lengthy affair, as you may suppose. Anthony identified the body and gave the necessary particulars. I stated that in my opinion death was due to asphyxia, caused by inhaling a non-respirable gas, probably carbon dioxide. I mentioned Mrs Quinton's feeling of giddiness when she bent down over the body, and also my experiment with the candle later. Mrs Quinton and the constable described the position in which the body was lying when found. Mrs Quinton and Grace explained Branstock's habits regarding the cellar and his visits to it.

'I didn't mention, did I, that when we got the body upstairs I locked the cellar and put the key in my pocket? I didn't want any more cases of suffocation on my hands. Next day, at my suggestion the coroner sent an analyst to the house. He then unlocked the cellar door and lowered a candle into the place. There was still some of the gas about, for the candle went out when it reached the floor. At the inquest this morning he reported that his analysis showed the air to contain twenty per cent of carbon dioxide.

'The coroner, in his summing-up, suggested to the jury what had happened. When the deceased entered the cellar on Wednesday evening the door had not been opened for three days. During that time carbon dioxide had accumulated in the cellar, which was unventilated. It was well known that carbon dioxide, being a heavy gas, would sink to the lowest level it could find, in this case, the cellar of the house. By Wednesday evening a highly concentrated layer of the gas covered the floor, possibly to a depth of three feet or more. Deceased, bending down to reach the wine bin which stood on the floor, would have inhaled the concentrated gas. It was known that a concentrated atmosphere of carbon dioxide could produce immediate loss of consciousness and muscular power. Deceased would then have fallen to the floor, and death would have ensued within a very few minutes. It was very fortunate that the deceased had left the cellar door wide open behind him. This caused a current of ventilation which no doubt dispersed the gas. Had it not been for this, Mrs Quinton would almost certainly have been overcome in her turn when she bent over the body. As it was, she had felt the preliminary symptoms without knowing what they indicated.

'At this point the foreman of the jury asked a question. He wanted to know whether it was not most unusual for such an accumulation of carbon dioxide to take place. The coroner told him that carbon dioxide always tended to accumulate at the bottom of pits, wells, the holds of ships, and such places. In this case, however, the accumulation appeared to have been comparatively rapid. There was no evidence to show the source of the carbon dioxide, but it might possibly have escaped from an adjacent sewer. The jury returned a verdict of death by misadventure, and added a rider to the effect that the public health authority should be asked to investigate the origin of the gas.'

Oldland emptied his glass of whisky. 'So that's that,' he concluded.

Hanslet looked at him shrewdly. 'Do you agree with the verdict, doctor?' he asked.

'Absolutely. I know what's in your mind, of course; but there's no room for any suggestion of foul play.'

'Then why did you suggest that the superintendent would be interested in the circumstances?' Dr Priestley asked.

Oldland chuckled. 'Haven't you guessed?' he replied. 'I wanted to prove to him the utter fallacy of taking any notice of what people call coincidence. It might appear to be a coincidence that two men living next door to one another should have met with sudden deaths within a couple of months. The occupant of No. 4 Cheveley Street, Mr Fransham, was, as I understand, murdered early in June. Branstock was suffocated on his birthday, the 4th August. Many people would fly to the conjecture that there must necessarily be some connection between the two events. I know nothing of Fransham's murder beyond what I read in the papers at the time. But I'm perfectly convinced that Branstock's death was accidental. There is absolutely nothing in common between the two events, except the accident that Fransham and Branstock happened to live next door to one another.'

Hanslet's professional pride was hurt by Oldland's reference to Mr Fransham. 'I'm duly grateful to you, I'm sure, doctor,' he said with some asperity. 'There's been no arrest in the Adderminster affair so far, I'll admit. But it doesn't necessarily follow that the police don't know all about it. There's insufficient evidence at present to justify an arrest, that's all.'

'It's not one of your cases, is it, superintendent?' Oldland asked.

'Well, it is and it isn't. It was Jimmy's originally, but he came to a dead end. I thought there was just a chance that I might succeed where he had failed, so I took him off the job and had a look into it myself. But I immediately found myself up against the same difficulty that had bowled Jimmy out. You remember the case, I dare say, professor. It's perfectly obvious who killed Mr Fransham. Our difficulty is that we can't prove how he did it.'

'I remember the case perfectly well,' said Dr Priestley. 'Have there been any developments during the past two months?'

'We've been keeping our eyes on everybody concerned, of course. Dr and Mrs Thornborough have had to clear out of Adderminster. Not more than have a dozen of the doctor's patients would have any more to do with him. And one evening a gang of roughs went up to his house and threw stones through his window. He's taken a flat in Mayfair, and Dr Dorrington has found himself a new partner. I interviewed the doctor myself and, after warning him, tried to trip him up, but I couldn't. He stuck to his story that he didn't know anything about the affair, and didn't write the letter which brought Mr Fransham down to Adderminster that day.'

'It struck me that that letter was the crux of the whole affair. If we could prove that he had written it, after he had strenuously denied doing so, it would be a very strong point against him. The experts wouldn't give a definite opinion upon the signature; they said that it might be a forgery, or might not. So I took possession of the doctor's typewriter and handed it over to them to experiment with. But that didn't lead to anything more definite. They all agree that the letter was typed upon a nearly new Smith Premier portable. The doctor's instrument is a Smith Premier portable only a few months old. The experts say that the letter was typed on an instrument of which none of the letters were damaged or deformed. All the letters in the doctor's typewriter are perfect, but so they would be on any new machine. So we get no further in that direction. The letter may have been typed on the doctor's machine or it may not.

'The doctor himself raised a point. He declared that he never signed letters with his Christian name only. He certainly varied his signature in accordance with his intimacy with his correspondents. When he had occasion to write to Mr Fransham he always signed the letter with his initials alone—C.J.T. In the course of our investigations, we looked through such correspondence of Mr Fransham's as we could find at No. 4 Cheveley Street. We came across a letter from Dr Thornborough written, not typed, upon a sheet of paper exactly similar to the one found in Mr Fransham's pocket. It was in reply to a letter from Mr

Fransham, who had apparently written to the doctor asking him if he knew what Mrs Thornborough would like for a birthday present. And that letter was certainly signed C.J.T. But to my mind that doesn't prove anything. If the doctor had written a letter which he meant to repudiate later, one of his obvious dodges would be to employ an unusual signature.

'Of course we went very carefully into the question of his whereabouts at the time the crime was committed. I don't think there's any doubt that Linton heard Mr Fransham fall, which established the time of his death at seven minutes past one. I went to Mark Farm myself and interviewed Farmer Hawksworth and his wife. They remembered the doctor's visit that day, and are agreed that he left the house just about one o'clock. Mrs Hawksworth declares that she heard the grandfather clock strike one just after he went. It is Hawksworth's habit to listen to the time signal at half-past ten every Sunday morning. He did so on the day after the doctor's visit and found that the grandfather clock was four minutes slow. We may suppose, then, that the doctor left Mark Farm about three minutes past one. Linton says that he got home about ten minutes past one. This allows him seven minutes for the journey. Not an unreasonable time when one considers that he had to get out of the car to open the gate at the end of Gunthorpe Road, drive through and shut it again after him. On the other hand, if he had been quick about it, he would have had time to jump out, run along beside the wall and back again.'

'In other words, the possibility exists that Dr Thornborough was behind the wall opposite the cloakroom window at seven minutes past one,' Dr Priestley suggested.

'That's it, professor. The possibility exists, but we can't prove it. The doctor swears that he never left his car after he had shut the five-barred gate behind him until he got out of it at his own garage. It was just as he drove away from the gate that he saw the man cross the road in front of him. He recognised Alfie's coat, assumed that the man in it was actually Alfie, and took no further notice of him. He was accustomed to Alfie camping out in the corner of the grass field.'

'This man, whoever he was, could have been behind the wall at seven minutes past one,' Dr Priestley suggested.

'Yes, if he ever existed, which I don't believe he did. I believe the doctor invented the story to put us off the track. He knew that Alfie used to hang about the field, and thought it quite safe to say that he'd seen him coming out of it. What he didn't know was that Alfie had been located three miles and more away twenty minutes earlier. It's my belief that if anybody came out of the field at that time, it was the doctor himself.

'Then there's no doubt that Alfie must have got those cigarettes from the doctor himself or from one of his household. The Adderminster Police made a house-to-house inquiry through the town, and couldn't find anybody who had so much as heard of Black's Russian Blend. I asked Mrs Thornborough about them, and she said she had never seen the brand until a box of a hundred arrived about a week before the crime. There was nothing in the box to show who had sent them, but she assumes that it must have been her uncle. He often used to send her cigarettes and chocolates and things like that. The address was type-written on an adhesive label, she remembered, and she supposed the parcel had been sent straight from the shop where the cigarettes were bought. She said that her uncle sometimes sent her things that way. She hadn't kept the paper in which the parcel was wrapped, and she hadn't smoked many of the cigarettes because she hadn't liked them.

'I talked to Alfie, who struck me as being a very decent hard-working chap, at least when he's normal. He says he remembers nothing whatever of that particular Saturday, and I believe him. But the Adderminster Police have tried to trace his movements. There's no doubt about his call upon Colonel Exbury at a quarter to one. He was seen by at least three people walking through the town in the direction of Gunthorpe Road shortly before two o'clock. It would have taken him just about that time to walk from Colonel Exbury's, and it corresponds with his call upon Mr Willingdon some time after two.

'Then we come to the coat. Colonel Exbury says definitely that Alfie was not wearing it when he saw him. Two of the people who saw him in Adderminster an hour later noticed that he wasn't wearing the coat, a fact which surprised them, since they'd never seen him without it before. On the other hand, Willingdon's description to Jimmy leaves no room for doubt that Alfie was wearing the coat when he called at the cottage. I don't think myself that there's any mystery involved there. Alfie's story of the man with the torch who bought his coat for half a crown and a handful of cigarettes is all moonshine. In his disordered state of mind, he may very well have dreamt the whole thing. On the Friday night he slept, probably with the coat wrapped round him, in the corner of the field. On Saturday morning he discarded it and walked to Colonel Exbury's place and back. He returned to the field, put his coat on and then, discovering an urgent need for more cigarettes, walked across to the cottage and demanded some. Later in the evening he again discarded his coat and wandered down the town, dreaming again that he had sold it. We know what happened to him after that, and Jimmy found the coat next morning where he had left it.'

'Then in your opinion neither Alfie Prince nor his coat have any connection with the crime?' Dr Priestley asked.

'None whatever. The next person to be considered was Coates the chauffeur. As you know, professor, both Jimmy and I were a little bit doubtful about him. The doctor, as Mr Fransham's executor, gave Coates a month's wages and told him that he was free to look for another job. He told him at the same time of the amount of the legacy that was coming to him. Coates went straight down to his brother's place somewhere near Winchester, and set to work upon the filling station which Jimmy had heard about. As Mr Redbourne, Mr Fransham's solicitor had backed out of the affair, the doctor employed another lawyer, who got probate of the will without difficulty. His legacy was paid to Coates about three weeks ago. I'm pretty well convinced by now that he had no share in the crime.

'Finally, there was that list of Mr Fransham's friends which Stowell gave to Jimmy. They have all been interviewed, and they've all got absolutely watertight alibis. None of them can have been anywhere near Adderminster at the time of the crime. There was nobody among them who had anything to gain by Mr Fransham's death or could suggest anyone but the doctor who had any motive for murdering him. In fact, professor, it comes to what you would call a process of elimination. It's ridiculous to suppose that a total stranger killed Mr Fransham just for the fun of the thing. Besides, how could he have done it?'

'How do you suggest that Dr Thornborough did it?' Dr Priestley asked quietly.

Hanslet sighed heavily. 'If I could make a reasonable suggestion the doctor would be in quod now awaiting his trial,' he replied. 'I'll be quite frank with you, professor. When I first took the case over, I thought there must have been a pretty bad blunder somewhere. It seemed to me that Mr Fransham must have been plugged from the further side of the wall and that Linton, in spite of what he had said, had somehow allowed the doctor a chance of picking up the missile and disposing of it. But I turned Linton inside out. I even went so far as to make a most improper suggestion to him. I told him that if he admitted that the doctor had had a chance of picking up the thing, whatever it was, it wouldn't hurt him and would justify the doctor's arrest. I didn't of course, make any definite promises, but I hinted that policemen concerned in a case like that stood a very good chance of promotion. I wasn't encouraging the man to tell a deliberate lie, but I wanted to give him a chance of confessing that he hadn't been so alert as he made out. But Linton stuck to his guns in spite of everything. He maintained, and still maintains for that matter, that not so much as a pin could have left that cloakroom without his knowledge.'

Dr Priestley smiled faintly. 'And you are driven to believe him?' he said.

'I've no option, since I absolutely refuse to entertain the only possible alternative. It might be suggested that Dr Thornborough had offered to buy Linton's silence. I'll admit that policemen have been known to take bribes for winking at offences against footling things like the licensing laws. But I absolutely refuse to believe that any policeman, from the humblest village constable upwards, would consider for a moment the acceptance of a bribe where a capital charge was concerned.'

'I heartly agree with you,' Dr Priestley replied, still with the same enigmatic smile. 'I am quite sure that you need have no hesitation in accepting Linton's statement.'

'Then in that case Fransham can't have been killed by anything thrown at him,' said Hanslet. 'Someone must have hit him through the window, though that sounds incredible in view of the evidence. Can't you suggest some answer to the puzzle, professor?'

Dr Priestley shook his head. 'Not at present,' he replied. 'What is the position as regards Dr Thornborough's house at Adderminster?'

'It's empty and is to be let unfurnished. The doctor cleared out all his stuff when he left the town. But after what happened there, it will be some time before the place finds a tenant.'

'Is the cottage on the opposite side of Gunthorpe Road occupied?'

'Yes. The owner and his wife, Mr and Mrs Whiteway, are back there.'

'I gather that under the terms of Mr Fransham's will, the remainder of the lease of the house occupied by him, No. 4 Cheveley Street, would fall to his niece Mrs Thornborough. She would presumably also acquire the contents of the house?'

'All I know is that the house is empty. The Stowells went away a month ago and the furniture was removed a few days later. As the Thornboroughs have taken a flat in Mayfair, I don't suppose they mean to renew the lease.'

'Mayland could tell you how matters stand in that respect,' Oldland suggested.

'Is the point of any particular importance, professor?' Hanslet asked.

'That is for you to judge,' Dr Priestley replied. 'I should have thought that any transaction in which Dr or Mrs Thornborough were engaged would be of interest to the police.'

'Well, I'll make it my business to find out,' said Hanslet. 'It's getting pretty late now, so I'll be off. But I'll let you know if I hear anything fresh that's likely to interest you.'

CHAPTER III

It was not until the following Monday, August 9, that Hanslet found leisure to interview Anthony Mayland. That morning, shortly before ten o'clock, he called at No. 3 Cheveley Street, and was informed by Grace that Mr Mayland was at home. He was shown into the study, where, within a couple of minutes, a tall young man dressed in black joined him. He was pale and harassed-looking and his eyes looked tired behind their horn-rimmed glasses.

'My name is Mayland,' he said in a low, but rather harsh voice. 'Is your visit in connection with the death of my stepfather, superintendent?'

'No, it isn't, Mr Mayland,' Hanslet replied. 'In fact, I must apologise for troubling you at such a distressing time. But I am anxious for certain information about the house next door, formerly in the occupation of Mr Fransham.'

Mayland looked very much astonished at this.

'The house is empty, and has been for some little time,' he replied.

'So I understand. The lease expires at Christmas, does it not?'

'It would have done in the ordinary way. But an arrangement was made whereby the lease was surrendered on July 24.'

'Can you tell me how that arrangement came to be made, Mr Mayland?'

'I can, for I happen to know the circumstances. I don't know whether you are aware of it, but I am an architect, and my stepfather always consulted me about his property. At the time of his death, Mr Fransham had not come to any decision regarding the renewal of his lease. My stepfather was perfectly willing to grant him a renewal if he desired it. He had always proved to be in every way a perfectly satisfactory tenant.

'On the other hand, my stepfather had decided what he would do in the event of Mr Fransham not wishing to renew. He had talked the matter over with me, and we had come to the conclusion that it would be more profitable for him to modernise the house before offering it to a fresh tenant. The increased rent which he would be justified in asking would compensate for the cost of the alterations.

'Shortly after Mr Fransham's death I made a suggestion. It seemed unlikely that his heirs would wish to occupy the house for the remainder of the lease, or to renew it when it expired. The suggestion was that my stepfather should write to Mrs Thornborough, whom, of course, he knew, offering to accept an immediate surrender of the lease. This would enable us to gain possession and to carry out the proposed modernisation before Christmas. My stepfather approved of the suggestion, but refused to have any direct communication with either Mrs Thornborough or her husband. However, he instructed his solicitor, Mr Emscott to make the offer, which was accepted.'

'Why did Sir Godfrey refuse to communicate with Dr or Mrs Thornborough?' Hanslet asked.

Mayland hesitated. 'I have no idea what view the police take of Mr Fransham's death,' he replied. 'Nor have I any first hand knowledge of the circumstances. But my stepfather was firmly convinced that either Dr Thornborough or his wife were responsible.'

'Had he any definite reason for this conviction?'

'I don't know that he had any special knowledge of the circumstances. But Mr Fransham was killed in the Thornborough's house, and they are the only people who have benefited to any appreciable extent from his death.'

'Did you ever meet Dr Thornborough, Mr Mayland?'

'I don't remember doing so. But I knew Betty Thornborough pretty well at one time. We always used to get on very well together. Unless she's changed a lot since then, I can't imagine that she can have had any hand in the crime.'

Hanslet was not particularly anxious to discuss the implications of the Adderminster murder with a stranger. He hastened to change the subject.

'You knew Mr and Mrs Stowell, the married couple who had been with Mr Fransham for so many years, I expect, Mr Mayland?' he said.

'Oh, I knew them well enough, but I hadn't seen much of them recently,' Mayland replied. 'You see, for the last three or four years, I haven't spent much of my time here. For one thing I had my own work to attend to, and for another I didn't live in this house, though a room was always at my disposal if I wanted it.'

'You have rooms of your own, I understand?' Hanslet suggested.

'I have. But I don't want you to draw the conclusion that there was the slightest estrangement between my stepfather and myself. We were always on the very best of terms, and I used to come and see him here at least once or twice a week. But so long as I lived here with him, things were awkward for both of us. He was of an exceptionally sociable nature, and I'm afraid I'm not. At least, I didn't care about associating with some of his friends. The result was that I was apt to be a bit of a wet blanket at his parties. On the other hand, I found his routine a bit trying. He never went to bed before midnight, and refused to have breakfast before half-past nine in the morning.'

'Hardly suitable hours for a professional man like yourself, Mr Mayland.'

'That's just it. I found I couldn't keep pace with my work under those conditions. So I suggested to my stepfather that I should find a room for myself, and he rather jumped at the idea, though he tried not to show it. And I really believe that since then we got on better than we ever had before. His death is a terrible blow to me. I feel that I have lost the best friend that I am ever likely to have. You've heard how it happened, I expect, superintendent?'

'It is part of my job to study reports of inquests,' replied Hanslet diplomatically. 'Sir Godfrey was to have been married very shortly, was he not?

Mayland frowned. 'He was,' he replied shortly; and then after a pause he added, 'That's the one spark of comfort that I can derive from his death. He's been spared a lot of unhappiness.'

'In your opinion then his intended re-marriage was a mistake?'

'It would have been more than a mistake—it would have been a disaster. Of course you think I'm prejudiced, since my mother was Branstock's first wife. But it isn't that at all. I should have been delighted if he had married a suitable woman, who would have made him happy. But this particular woman would have ruined his life. After he'd lived with her for a bit and the glamour had worn off, he would have found out what she really was like. As I say, it's a blessing he's been spared that disillusion.'

'Do you know anything definite against the lady?' Hanslet asked.

'I do,' Mayland replied with considerable emphasis. 'Things which I don't propose to repeat, however.'

'Did you make any attempt to dissuade your stepfather from the marriage?'

Mayland's thin lips curled in a faint smile. 'You didn't know him,' he replied. 'He was one of those people who are roused to fury by the slightest show of opposition. If I had breathed a single word against Nancy Lanchester he would have carried her off to the nearest registry office and married her out of hand. Just as a lesson to me to mind my own business in future. Besides, although perhaps you don't realise it, my position was, and still is, for that matter, very delicate.'

'How delicate, Mr Mayland?'

'In the sense that I don't know whether I have any right to be in this house at all. You see, although for years everybody has regarded me as Branstock's son, in reality I am nothing of the kind. There's no question of my being his next of kin, for he and I were not related in any way.'

'But you are no doubt aware of the terms of Sir Godfrey's will?'

'That's just exactly what I'm not. Between ourselves, superintendent, it's the very devil. The only person who knows is my stepfather's solicitor, Emscott, and he's in America. I got on to his office on Thursday morning and they cabled him, but he can't be back before next week. To add to the complication they tell me that Emscott's managing clerk is down with pneumonia and that there's nobody in the place who knows or can do anything. Meanwhile, I'm holding the fort as best I can in spite of the fact that I may be slung out eventually as a usurper.'

'Who are you holding it against, Mr Mayland?'

'Nancy Lanchester, or rather her family. She, I am told, is too prostrate with grief to stir from her bed. That may be true, but it's disappointment, not grief, that she's suffering from. She sent her cousin, by name Christopher Portslade, to represent her at the funeral on Saturday. And the insufferable young cub had the sauce to gate-crash here afterwards.'

'What did he want?'

'Oh, quite a lot of things. Although it didn't transpire at the inquest, he, together with his sister and Nancy Lanchester, were in the house when my stepfather's death was discovered. Dr Oldland, to whom I can never be sufficiently grateful, put the three of them out of the house on the pretext that Branstock had been taken ill. It wasn't until next morning when she rang up that Nancy Lanchester was told that my stepfather was dead.

'Young Portslade wanted an explanation of this. He said that his cousin had more right in the house than anybody else at such a time and that to treat her in such a way had been an insult. Then he went on to say that in the hearing of himself and his sister, Branstock had promised to present Nancy Lanchester after dinner on Wednesday with a cheque for a thousand pounds to celebrate his birthday. I asked him when this promise had been made, and he told me that it was a couple of days before, when they were all together. I said that I could do nothing about it, and that he'd better approach Branstock's executors on the matter.

'That brought him to his next point. Where was the will, and why had he not been invited to hear it read? He seemed to think that the proper sequel to any funeral was the reading of the will. I told him about Emscott's absence, and explained that we should all have to wait until his return. And then if you please, he had the sauce to say that that wasn't at all necessary. He knew for a fact that Branstock had made a will leaving everything he possessed to Nancy Lanchester. I asked him how he knew that and he told me that Branstock himself told him at least a couple of months ago.'

'Do you suppose that he was telling the truth?' Hanslet asked.

Mayland shrugged his shoulders. 'I should be very loth to believe anything that Christopher Portslade told me,' he replied. 'For all I know it may be true, but I wasn't going to be bluffed into leaving Portslade in possession, which was obviously what he wanted. I feel responsible for the safe custody of everything in this house until the executors can take over. Don't you think I'm right, super-intendent?'

'Under the circumstances, I certainly do,' Hanslet replied.

'I'm very glad to hear you say that. You've strengthened my hand a lot. I don't even know who Branstock appointed as his executors. But Emscott himself is pretty sure to be one of them. I shall be very much relieved when he gets back to England, I can tell you. But to get back to Portslade; his final demand was that he should be allowed to take over the management of the house as the representative of his cousin. I told him quite politely that if he made any attempt in that direction I should take him by the scruff of the neck and throw him out of the front door. He didn't seem to relish that prospect and departed vowing that he would seek legal advice. I haven't seen or heard anything of him since.'

At this moment Grace entered the room bearing a card on a tray. She handed it to Mayland who picked it up and glanced at it. 'All right, Grace, show him into the dining-room and ask him to wait for a couple of minutes, will you? I'm awfully sorry, superintendent, but that's the district surveyor. He's come to try and find out how the foul gas got into the cellar and he wants me to show him round. Is there anything else you would like to ask me?'

'I don't think so, thanks very much, Mr Mayland,' Hanslet replied. 'I won't keep you from your appointment.'

Mayland saw the superindendent to the front door, and then walked into the dining-room where the district surveyor was awaiting him. 'Good-morning, Mr Sandling,' he said. 'My name is Mayland. Sir Godfrey Branstock was my stepfather and I am temporarily in charge here. As it happens I am very well acquainted with the premises. I am an architect by profession, and was responsible for the modernisation of the house. You would like to inspect the cellar first, I dare say?'

'I should,' the surveyor replied. 'And I should be grateful

if you could come with me, Mr Mayland, since you are familiar with the details.'

'I'll certainly come with you, if you like. But I can't claim to be familiar with the cellar. I don't remember ever having been into it. My stepfather didn't like anybody else going down there and always kept the key himself.'

'I see. It might be advisable for us to have a lighted candle in readiness.'

'There's a candle in the basement. I'll show you the way, Mr Sandling.'

They descended to the basement, where Mayland found the candle which had been used on a previous occasion. He was about to open the cellar door when the surveyor stopped him. 'Better be careful,' he said. 'When was that door last opened?'

'It hasn't been opened since Friday, when Dr Oldland and the analyst tested the air,' Mayland replied.

'The cellar has been closed for three days, then. We'd better light that candle and lower it to the floor before we go on.'

The candle burnt brightly enough until it was within two or three inches of the floor, then the flame grew dim and finally expired.

'Still pretty foul down there,' said Mr Sandling. 'We'd better leave the door open for a few minutes before we take any risks. Was this cellar in constant use before Sir Godfrey's death?'

'It's been used for the storage of wine ever since I can remember. When the house was modernised, Branstock insisted that the cellar should be left untouched. He said that we should never be able to build a room above ground which would keep wine so well.'

'Sir Godfrey was the only person who entered it, you tell me. Did he ever complain of feeling ill effects after he had done so?'

'Only once, to my knowledge. That was about a fortnight ago, when I was dining here; he told me almost jokingly that he thought he must be getting old, for when he had stooped down in the cellar to get a bottle of wine out of one of the bins, he had felt a sensation of giddiness and tightness in the chest. He said that the sensation had passed off very quickly, and as I knew that Dr Oldland had been treating him for high blood pressure, I thought that might have been one of the symptoms. The idea that the air in the cellar could be foul never occurred to me.'

'There is nothing in the cellar but wine, I suppose? Nothing that could have fermented and caused an accumulation of carbon dioxide?'

'That we shall discover for ourselves. So far as I know, Branstock only stored the best of his wine there. Lighter wines, beers, spirits and so forth, were kept in a smaller cellar upstairs.'

All this time the surveyor had been swinging the cellar door backwards and forwards. 'That ought to have fanned some of the stuff out,' he said. 'Let's try the candle again.'

At the second attempt the candle remained alight even when standing on the floor.

'I think we can go down now, Mr Mayland,' said Sandling. 'But let me know immediately if you feel any oppressive symptoms.'

The cellar was about twenty feet square and just over six feet high. On three of its sides the walls were occupied from floor to ceiling with wine bins. The fourth side, against which were the stone steps, was vacant.

Mr Sandling tested the flags of the floor with his feet. 'Everything seems to be sound enough,' he remarked. 'Of course, we can't tell what may be behind those bins. We shall have to get them all shifted, I'm afraid. Hullo, what's this?' He pointed to a spot at the bottom of the unoccupied wall. 'There's a brick out there by the look of it,' he said. 'Do you happen to know what is beyond this wall, Mr Mayland.'

'The cellar of No. 4, I fancy. The two houses were originally built upon the same plan. But this one has been modernised and the basement is no longer used except for storage purposes. But in the case of No. 4, the basement, and for all I know, the cellar too, was in use until a short time ago.'

Upon examining the hole in the wall together, they soon came to the conclusion that it was not a question of a brick having been removed at any time. A nine inch wall separated the two houses and when this had been built, an orifice had purposely been left at the cellar floor.

'There's nothing very surprising about that,' the surveyor commented. 'At the time when these houses were built it was quite a common practice to have common drainage to two or even more cellars. It was then only necessary to fit a gully in one of them, for an orifice like this would enable water collecting in any of the others to flow to the gully. The gully is usually in the centre of the floor, which is made to slope down from the walls towards it. There's nothing of the sort in this cellar. Perhaps there is in the one next door, Mr Mayland?'

'I can't tell you, off hand. I've been making a preliminary survey of No. 4 recently, with a view to having it modernised on the same lines as this house. But I didn't penetrate into the cellar. No. 4 is empty, as of course you know, and the keys have been handed over to my stepfather. I think I could find them if you would like to explore the other cellar.'

'Well, I don't see any possible source of foul gas here,' the surveyor replied. 'On the other hand, it's possible that the gas found its way in through that orifice at the foot of the wall. I think that if it's convenient we ought to investigate the conditions in the cellar of No. 4.'

It took Mayland a few minutes to find the keys of No. 4, but he eventually located them in a desk in Branstock's study.

'How long has this house been empty?' asked the surveyor as they entered it.

'Nearly a month now,' Mayland replied. 'I think it was on the 12th June that Mr Fransham was killed. He had a married couple living in the house. They stayed on for some weeks after his death and finally superintended the removal of the furniture.'

'That was an amazing affair!' exclaimed Mr Sandling. 'I knew Mr Fransham slightly and, of course, I followed the case in the papers very carefully at the time. I can't think why the police haven't taken action long before this. There doesn't seem to be the slightest doubt who did it.'

Mayland smiled. 'I don't suppose there is very much doubt,' he replied. 'But the police are much too cautious to make an arrest until they're absolutely certain. The guilty man might be acquitted and then even if conclusive evidence against him turned up later, he couldn't be tried again. Superintendent Hanslet of the Yard was with me when you arrived just now. He wanted a few particulars about this very house we're in. That shows they're still on the scent, I take it.'

No. 4 presented the usual forlorn appearance of a house which has been empty even for a short time. They descended to the basement, which was littered with unconsidered trifles, wisps of straw, torn fragments of newspaper and so forth. 'It wasn't worth while having the place cleared up,' Mayland explained. 'You know for yourself what a mess builders make about a place. My stepfather was anxious to get the alteration work done as soon as possible. He meant to throw out a new set of kitchen premises on the ground floor, as he did in the case of No. 3 a little time ago. The same plans and specifications would have done with slight alterations. In fact, I hoped to get them prepared this week and submit them to your office for approval.'

'What will become of the premises now?' Sandling asked.

'That's more than I can tell you,' Mayland replied grimly. 'Nobody knows yet who they belong to. Technically, I suppose I'm trespassing. The arrangement of this basement is exactly the same as at No. 3, only of course the other way about. Here's the cellar door and the key's in the lock.'

He turned the key, which grated rustily, and the door opened with a reluctant creaking.

'It doesn't seem to have been opened for some time,' he remarked. 'Hullo, seems a bit queer down there, doesn't it?'

The surveyor approached the doorway and sniffed. 'Sulphuretted hydrogen!' he exclaimed. 'I thought I detected a faint trace of it in the cellar next door, but I wasn't sure. I shouldn't wonder if that was the clue. We'd better try to get this cellar ventilated like we did the other one.'

'There's no electric light in this one, I see,' said Mayland. 'We'll have to use the candle in any case. But we'd better give the atmosphere a chance to clear before we go down. The coroner's guess was a pretty shrewd one, it seems to me.'

'Yes, that smell of sulphuretted hydrogen certainly suggests the presence of sewer gas,' the surveyor replied. 'It would naturally be more noticeable here than at No. 3 since this door has been closed for a longer time. You have no idea when it was last opened, I suppose?'

Mayland shook his head. 'I don't know whether the cellar was used in Mr Fransham's time. But in any case, it's very improbable that this door has been opened since the Stowells left. The keys of the house were handed over to my stepfather by Stowell himself when he left. And they are not likely to have been out of his possession since then, except on the day when he handed them over to me to examine the premises. I certainly didn't open this door then. So I think we may safely assume that it hasn't been opened for at least a month.'

They waited for a few minutes longer and then, having lighted the candle, descended into the cellar. It was similar in size to the one which they had already inspected. But it contained no wine bins, and was empty but for a few mouldering crates, all of which proved to be empty. And in the middle of the floor was a gully towards which the floor sloped on all sides.

The surveyor pointed to this triumphantly. 'There you are!' he exclaimed. 'That's just exactly what I expected. That gully was originally intended to drain both cellars, hence the aperture in the foot of the wall dividing them. No doubt the gully has become defective through want of attention, and now allows gas to escape from the sewer.'

'I thought all sewers were so well ventilated nowadays that no accumulation of gas could occur?'

'Main sewers are, certainly. But in old premises like these, you will often find household drains which don't conform to modern requirements. And with a defective gully like this, there's always the danger of an infiltration of sewer gas from them. Sewer gas usually contains more or less sulphuretted hydrogen, by which its presence may be detected. But it doesn't necessarily follow that that particular gas should be present. Carbon dioxide alone or mixed with nitrogen would be equally fatal if sufficiently concentrated. Any sulphuretted hydrogen present would tend to rise, which accounts for our detecting it when we opened this door. But the carbon dioxide, if undisturbed by ventilation, would collect at the bottom of the cellar.'

'I see,' said Mayland thoughtfully. 'Now I come to think of it my stepfather had a very feeble sense of smell. He could not, for instance, detect the scent of flowers unless they were very powerful. I don't believe he noticed the particularly revolting perfumes which some of his friends used. Even if there had been any sulphuretted hydrogen about when he went down to the cellar the other night, I don't think he'd have been aware of it. And the door had been left open for some little while before anybody else arrived upon the scene.'

'If he had smelt the sulphuretted hydrogen he might have been alive now,' said Mr Sandling gloomily. 'Well, Mr Mayland, I'm very glad that you were able to give me your assistance. As an architect yourself, you will appreciate the position, of course. I shall have to make a report to the local authorities. They, I expect, will serve a notice upon the owner of the premises to the effect that this gully must be repaired or abolished altogether. Personally, I should favour the latter course. Both these cellars seem to be perfectly dry and no real need for drainage exists.'

'Yes, I fully appreciate that,' said Mayland. 'Do you know, I can't help feeling responsible in a way for what happened. If I had opened this cellar door that day when I was looking over the house, I should have noticed that something was wrong and had immediate steps taken to put it right.'

'I don't think you can blame yourself for that, Mr Mayland. I expect that the gas has been accumulating here for a considerable time. Judging by the appearance of this cellar it was not regularly used in Mr Fransham's time. The door may not have been opened for months, in which case the cellar would have remained unventilated all that time. The symptoms mentioned by Sir Godfrey on the previous occasion suggest that there was no sudden influx of gas.'

'No, he didn't realise what the trouble was, and nobody with a keener sense of smell had the chance of enlightening him. His cellar was one of his pet fads. He never would let anybody else go down there. It wasn't that he was afraid they might steal a bottle of wine, but thought that they might disturb one of his favourite vintages. Even when his wine merchants delivered a fresh consignment, he always insisted upon being present himself, to see that they put each bottle in exactly the right place. And I don't suppose that happened more than once in a couple of years, for he always bought in large quantities. Is there anything else you would like to see while you're here, Mr Sandling?'

The surveyor expressed himself satisfied and they returned to No. 3.

CHAPTER IV

Ten days later, on the morning of Thursday, August 19, Harold Merefield was shown into Hanslet's room at Scotland Yard.

The superintendent, with whom the appointment had been made by telephone on the previous evening, looked up as his visitor entered. 'Come in, Mr Merefield,' he said. 'Sit down and make yourself comfortable. It would be pretty safe to guess that you've come to see me on behalf of the professor, I suppose?'

Harold laughed. 'I'd hardly venture to intrude upon my own account,' he replied. 'My old man has been pretty busy with his own affairs lately, but yesterday he knocked off and began talking about that Adderminster business. It's been at the back of his mind all the time, I know that perfectly well.'

'I'm jolly glad to hear it,' said Hanslet warmly. 'He hasn't by any chance found out how Mr Fransham was killed, has he?'

'If he has, he hasn't told me. Yesterday he was concerned

187

with that elusive fellow Alfie Prince. He made me look up my notes about him and settled upon those cigarette ends that Jimmy found in the corner of the field.'

Hanslet sighed. 'I thought I'd made that point pretty clear to the professor when I last saw him. They must have come from the box which we know to have been in Dr Thornborough's house at the time. I'm quite satisfied with the evidence that nobody else in Adderminster possessed any of Black's Russian Blend.'

'Well, my old man's got it into his head that those cigarettes might provide a valuable clue. He wants you to find out for certain whether or not Mr Fransham sent them to Mrs Thornborough.'

'Oh he does, does he? He's forgotten, I suppose, that Mr Fransham was buried a couple of months ago, and that dead men tell no tales.'

'No, he hasn't forgotten that. You ought to know by this time that there isn't much that he does forget. According to Mrs Thornborough, as you told him, the cigarettes appear to have sent to her straight from the shop. Jimmy said that these particular cigarettes could only be obtained from one of Black's branches. He set me to work to look up the addresses of these branches. The nearest one to Cheveley Street is in Knightsbridge. Got it?'

'Yes, I've got it. Make inquiries at the shop. But I can't see that it matters a damn whether the cigarettes were sent by Mr Fransham or by someone else.'

'No more can I, between ourselves,' Harold replied. 'But there you are, that's what I was to suggest to you. And I was to add that if you care to come to dinner tonight at Westbourne Terrace, the old man will be delighted to see you.'

Hanslet grunted. 'Give him my best thanks and tell him that I'll come, by all means. And between now and then I'll make an opportunity of inquiring about his confounded cigarettes.'

The superintendent was as good as his word. That afternoon he went to Black's Branch in Knightsbridge and asked to see the manager. From him he learnt that Mr Fransham had been a very good customer.

'He bought practically all his cigars and cigarettes from us,' the manager said. 'The cigarettes were for his friends, I suppose, for he never touched them himself. He always smoked cigars, and a very particular brand of them at that.'

'Did he ever ask you to send cigarettes direct to his friends by post?'

'Yes, occasionally. Always to the same address, if I remember right; a lady in the country whom he told me once was his niece, I believe. I can't remember the name for the moment.'

'Was it Thornborough?'

'Why, yes, of course it was. It was while he was visiting her that Mr Fransham was killed.'

'Can you tell me if you sent Mrs Thornborough a box of cigarettes sometime at the end of May or the beginning of June last?'

'I dare say I can if I look in the order book,' the manager replied. He produced the volume and turned over the pages. 'Yes, here you are,' he continued. 'On May 31, we posted a box of a hundred of our Russian Blend to Mrs Thornborough, *Epidaurus*, Adderminster. I remember the incident now, and being slightly surprised at the time.'

'Why surprised?' Hanslet asked.

'At the particular brand which Mr Fransham had ordered. He had told me once that smoking Virginia cigarettes was a very bad habit, but that smoking anything stronger was tantamount to suicide.'

'Did he order the cigarettes in person?'

'No, the order came on a postcard, if I remember right.'

'Is that postcard still in existence?'

'I'm not sure that it is,' the manager replied doubtfully. 'It would have been kept as our authority for supplying the goods until the account had been settled. Mr Fransham had a quarterly account with us, and he always settled regularly. The last account was settled by his executors about a month ago, and it is quite likely that the postcard was destroyed then. It may still be in the files, though. I'll have a look.'

In spite of the manager's fears the search proved successful. 'Here it is,' he said. 'You're welcome to it, if it's any use to you.'

Hanslet took the card and examined it closely. It was an ordinary stamped postcard, upon which a communication had been typed. This communication bore no address and was in the third person.

'Mr Robert Fransham would be obliged if Messrs. Black would post immediately one hundred of their Russian Blend cigarettes to the following address, and charge the same to his account: Mrs Thornborough, *Epidaurus,* Adderminster.'

On the reverse side of the card was typed the name and address of the firm. The postmark, creditably distinct, was, Adderminster, May 29.

That evening, in Dr Priestley's study after dinner, Hanslet repeated the story of his visit to the shop.

'Immediately I saw that postcard I had my suspicions,' he said. 'I took it back to the Yard and got the experts to have a look at it. They compared it with the letter found in Mr Fransham's pocket after his death. As usual, they won't swear to anything definite. But from what they tell me I think there's very little doubt that the two were typed upon the same machine. And there's that postmark, Adderminster, plain enough for all the world to see. There's not a shadow of doubt that it was the doctor who sent the postcard. But what he did it for, I'm blest if I can make out.'

'What makes you so certain that it was Dr Thornborough who sent the postcard?' Dr Priestley asked.

'Common sense, professor,' Hanslet replied crisply. 'To begin with, there's the evidence of the typewriter. It's not conclusive, I know, but it's highly suggestive, if nothing more. And then there's the postmark. Who else in Adderminster but the doctor can have known where Mr Fransham bought his tobacco? Finally, there's the fact that the executors paid the account without question. And the principal executor, as no doubt you remember, was the doctor.'

Dr Priestley smiled faintly. 'In any case you are satisfied that the order for these cigarettes did not originate with Mr Fransham?' he asked.

'Of course, and that brings me to another point. In the ordinary way, one would suppose Mrs Thornborough would have written to her uncle to thank him for his present. He would have replied asking her what she was talking about and the fat would have been in the fire. But if it was the doctor who ordered the cigarettes, everything would have been easy. He only had to offer to post his wife's letter of thanks and then to destroy it.'

'Have you gathered anything of the relationship existing between Dr Thornborough and his wife?' Dr Priestley asked.

'From everything I've heard they seem to have got along pretty well together. When a married couple don't hit it off, they usually take a delight in repeating their grievances to their neighbours. But in this case nobody has suggested anything of the kind. And Mrs Thornborough has stuck to her husband, which is more than most women would have done under the circumstances.'

'Would you describe Mrs Thornborough as an attractive woman?'

'She's a very good-looking woman and I dare say a lot of people would be attracted by her. Of course, I haven't met her under the most favourable circumstances. No doubt she looks upon me, quite rightly, as a policeman who's trying to lay her husband by the heels. But when all that's said and done there's something about her that rather puts me off. I don't know how to explain it, except by saying that she seems distant somehow.'

'Distant in her manner, do you mean?' Dr Priestley asked.

'And in her mind as well. She gives you the impression when you talk to her, that she's thinking all the time about something quite different. I don't mean that she's dreamy— far from it. She gives you the impression that she's got something far more important to think about even than the murder of her uncle.'

'Has it occurred to you to associate Mrs Thornborough with the motive for Mr Fransham's murder?'

Hanslet looked slightly puzzled. 'I don't quite know what you mean, professor,' he replied. 'She can't have done the job herself. Linton's quite sure that she was upstairs at the time.'

'That was not my meaning,' said Dr Priestley. 'I will express myself differently. Have you considered the possibility that the murderer's aim may have included Dr Thornborough?'

Hanslet looked more puzzled than ever. 'Well, no, I haven't,' he replied. 'I may be a bit slow in the uptake, but I don't see what you're getting at, professor.'

Dr Priestley smiled. 'What is your principal reason for believing in Dr Thornborough's guilt?' he asked.

'Motive,' replied Hanslet promptly. 'Nobody but the doctor and, of course, his wife, have benefited in the slightest degree by Mr Fransham's death.'

'But suppose that Mr Fransham's murder was only the first stage in a carefully-prepared scheme? Mr Fransham may have been a total stranger to the murderer, and yet the former's death may have facilitated the latter's aims. Do you follow me?'

'Not altogether, I'm afraid, professor,' Hanslet replied warily.

Dr Priestley made a gesture of impatience. 'You force me into putting a purely hypothetical case in support of which there is not the slightest evidence. Let us suppose for a moment that Mrs Thornborough was the ultimate object of some unknown person's designs. He may have been inspired by a passion for her appearance or her expectations or for both. A necessary preliminary to the realisation of her expectations was her uncle's death. And before the unknown person could marry her, he must contrive to separate her from her husband. Since apparently she had not the desire to divorce Dr Thornborough, this separation could only be achieved by the latter's death.

'Our unknown, and as I must emphasise again, entirely

hypothetical, murderer was thus faced with the problem of the removal of two individuals. His attempt to solve this problem was not devoid of ingenuity. Having contrived to murder Mr Fransham under circumstances which threw suspicion upon Dr Thornborough, he believed that the subsequent removal of the doctor could safely be left in the hands of Justice. You admit yourself, superintendent, that but for a single gap in the evidence, Dr Thornborough would have been arrested shortly after the crime. And had your evidence been complete, there is very little doubt that he would have been convicted.'

The superintendent stroked his chin reflectively.

'That's all very well, professor,' he replied after a pause. 'I admit that your theory gets round the difficulty of motive. But my suspicions of the doctor don't rest only on that. Who else could have had such an intimate knowledge of all the people and circumstances concerned?'

'Anyone who possessed the necessary facilities for observation,' Dr Priestley replied. 'Sir Godfrey Branstock, for instance.'

Hanslet almost leapt out of his chair. 'Sir Godfrey!' he exclaimed. 'You're not suggesting that he was after Mrs Thornborough, are you, professor? Why, he was engaged to be married to another girl next week. Besides, there's never been any suggestion that he was at Adderminster when Mr Fransham was killed.'

'Has there been any suggestion that he was not?' Dr Priestley asked dryly.

'Well, no, there hasn't. Except that you remember he told Jimmy that he saw Mr Fransham start off that morning. According to Coates he didn't hurry on the road and I suppose that Sir Godfrey could have got to the doctor's house before Mr Fransham's car arrived. But somehow, the idea doesn't seem likely to me. Can't you suggest someone else, professor.'

'Certainly,' Dr Priestley replied. 'Young Mayland, who we are told, was brought up in Branstock's house.'

'Ah now, that's just a shade less impossible,' Hanslet exclaimed. 'I didn't tell you that I had a conversation with Mayland last week, did I? He told me himself that he had known Mrs Thornborough before her marriage and got on very well with her then. But he doesn't seem to have seen much of her since. And apart from that there's nothing whatever to connect him with the crime.'

'I am afraid you are inclined to attach too much weight to my entirely imaginary hypothesis. It is not at all necessary that Mrs Thornborough should have been the murderer's ultimate objective. All I wished to point out was that Mr Fransham's removal may have been the first step in a considered plan, and not its ultimate aim. You have heard no more of the tenant of the cottage in Gunthorpe Road, I suppose?'

'Young Willingdon?' Hanslet replied. 'Oh yes. Like everyone else concerned he has been kept under observation. Not directly, of course. We have merely asked the Leeds police to make a few inquiries and keep an eye on his movements. They report that his troubles have blown over, thanks to his father, who had to dip his hand pretty deeply into his pocket. Frank Willingdon has settled down in Leeds to whatever job he holds in the old man's business. We can count him out as far as Mr Fransham's death is concerned.'

'And yet I think it not improbable that he is in possession of certain facts which you would find extremely valuable,' Dr Priestley remarked quietly.

Hanslet looked doubtful. 'Jimmy had a talk with him at the time, you remember, professor. If he knew anything likely to be useful, why didn't he divulge the facts then?'

'Possibly because the inspector's questions did not cover a wide enough ground,' replied Dr Priestley dryly. 'Was Willingdon asked, for instance, whether he was acquainted with Miss Nancy Lanchester?'

'He certainly wasn't,' Hanslet exclaimed in considerable astonishment. 'To the best of my recollection we hadn't so much as heard of the lady's name at that time. And even if Willingdon did know her, I don't see what possible bearing the facts could have had on Mr Fransham's death. I wonder what on earth you're driving at, professor?'

Dr Priestley brushed the question aside with a characteristic gesture. 'By all accounts Willingdon was not averse to youthful and somewhat dubious society,' he continued. 'During his enforced visit to London, he is said to have mixed with a set which my generation would stigmatise as fast. Sir Godfrey Branstock, it appears, dispensed hospitality to people of very similar tastes and habits. It would not surprise me to learn that Willingdon had become acquainted with one or more of the people who frequented Sir Godfrey's house.'

'It's more than likely,' Hanslet agreed. 'But what of it? You're not suggesting that Sir Godfrey's bright young friends had anything to do with Mr Fransham's death, are you, professor?'

Dr Priestley shook his head gravely. 'I make no direct suggestion of the kind. You were present in this room rather more than a week ago when Oldland described the circumstances of Sir Godfrey's death. He maintained then that it would be ridiculous to speak of coincidence in connection with the deaths of Mr Fransham and Sir Godfrey. And he was perfectly correct. No question of coincidence arises when a second event follows naturally upon a first.'

Hanslet scratched his head, then sought inspiration in the glass of beer which stood on the table beside his chair.

'You're getting a bit beyond my depth, professor,' he said. 'I suppose when you speak of two events, you mean that Sir Godfrey's death followed naturally upon Mr Fransham's, but I'm blest if I can see what makes you say that. The only connection between the two men was that they happened to live next door to one another and so became acquainted. Their interests were so different that this acquaintanceship never ripened into anything closer. I'm pretty certain that if there had been any intimacy between them we should have heard of it by now. From what I can make out, neither of them went out of his way to cultivate the other, although they were perfectly friendly when they met.'

'I do not question the accuracy of your knowledge of the relationship which existed between them. It is most unlikely that any real intimacy existed. But, all the same, I have more than a suspicion that had Mr Fransham not been murdered, Sir Godfrey Branstock would be alive today.'

'I can't follow you there, professor,' Hanslet objected. 'How on earth could Mr Fransham, alive or dead, have prevented the accident which proved fatal to Sir Godfrey?'

'That is a matter which I do not yet feel competent to discuss. But I cannot dismiss the possibility that the study of Sir Godfrey's death may eventually be the means of throwing light upon the murder of Mr Fransham. I would therefore recommend you not to lose sight of the members of what I may call Sir Godfrey's entourage. And while we are upon that subject a point of some interest occurs to me. Have you learnt whether Miss Lanchester or her family have benefited in any way under the terms of his will?'

'No, I haven't, but the solicitor ought to have got back from America by this time, and I can very easily find out. I'll call at No. 3 tomorrow, and if Mr Mayland's there he'll tell me all about it.'

'That piece of information is worth acquiring, I think,' said Dr Priestley, in a tone suggesting that the matter had very little further interest for him. 'Ah, I see that you have finished your beer. Harold, perhaps you will be good enough to fetch another bottle for the superintendent. Since you know where to find it, there is no need to trouble Mary.'

Harold left the room, to return a minute later with a bottle which he set down beside Hanslet. The latter opened it, poured some of the beer into his glass and tasted it.

'By jove, that's good!' he exclaimed. 'Although you don't drink beer yourself, professor, you certainly know how it should be kept.'

'I always endeavour to study the tastes of my guests,' Dr Priestley replied stiffly. 'Mary has orders to place the beer in the refrigerator shortly before it is likely to be required. I have always maintained that a domestic refrigerator is one of the greatest boons conferred upon us by science. Its influence upon health and comfort is so great that I should no more think of being without one than I should of being without a bath. You have no doubt studied the subject of refrigerators, superintendent?'

'Well, I can't say that I have,' Hanslet replied, amused

at Dr Priestley's enthusiasm. 'Not deeply, at all events. But I'm thoroughly grateful to this particular one, I assure you. Talking of Mayland, is there anything else you would like me to ask when I see him?'

But Dr Priestley was not thus to be ridden off his topic. 'You have not studied the subject?' he said in a tone of mild surprise. 'And yet the prominent place occupied by the refrigerator in a modern household cannot have evaded your attention. You cannot escape the ubiquity of this most convenient instrument. For instance, a refrigerator was mentioned in the course of the inquest on Sir Godfrey Branstock. The cook, as you may remember, in describing her discovery of the body, mentioned a buzzing in her head, which she attributed at the time to the sound of the refrigerator motor, but which was subsequently explained as being due to the effects of the foul air. We know then that a refrigerator is installed at No. 3 Cheveley Street. Do you happen to be aware if Mr Fransham also possessed one?'

'I really couldn't say,' the superintendent replied with a touch of impatience.

But Dr Priestley appeared not to notice his guest's symptoms of irritation. 'The point would be of interest from a statistical point of view,' he said dreamily. 'Here we have an example chosen at random. In connection with the murder of Mr Fransham, four houses have been mentioned, two situated in London and two in the country. An examination of these four houses would provide an enlightening test of the popularity of the refrigerator. In how many of them had one been installed, I wonder?'

Hanslet shrugged his shoulders. But it was always wise to humour the professor, however extravagant his whims might appear. 'I don't know,' he replied. 'But if you're really interested, I can easily find out.'

Dr Priestley's voice and expression suddenly became more alert. 'Ah!' he exclaimed. 'So you are still in a position to ascertain fresh facts, however trifling? And how would you proceed to obtain the necessary information in this particular case, may I ask?'

Hanslet smiled. 'You won't catch us out as easily as that, professor,' he replied. 'Although no active steps have been taken recently, it doesn't follow that matters are being allowed to slide. We are still in close touch with all the people who came under our notice at the time of Mr Fransham's murder. You ask how I could find out which of those four houses, two of which are now empty, had refrigerators installed? Well, I'll tell you.

'In the case of Mr Fransham's house, No. 4 Cheveley Street, I should send a man round to ask the Stowells. On the strength of the annuity which they enjoy under his will, they have retired from service and are living in a house at Hammersmith.

'In the case of Dr Thornborough's house, *Epidaurus*, I should get Superintendent Yateley on to the job. When Dr and Mrs Thornborough left Adderminster, they asked their cook and parlourmaid to come with them, but they refused; one can easily guess why. They are now both in service in Adderminster. The cook, for instance, is now with Colonel Exbury, whose name was mentioned in connection with Alfie Prince. The parlourmaid has taken a situation at the local inn, the Red Lion.

'With regard to the cottage in Gunthorpe Road, Yateley would only have to ask the owners, Mr and Mrs Whiteway, who are now living there. But as it happens that would not be necessary, for Jimmy, who went over the place with Didcot the house agent, mentioned in his report that it was fitted up with every modern gadget, refrigerator included.'

'Excellent!' Dr Priestley exclaimed. 'It is very satisfactory to learn that the police are in a position to ascertain fresh facts or to verify old ones. They could, for instance, find out where Mr Fransham's car was kept when it was not in use?'

'They know that already, professor,' Hanslet replied. 'When I took over the case from Jimmy, I went to No. 4 Cheveley Street as a matter of routine, and had a good look over the premises. Behind the six houses, there is a range of mews which consisted originally of coach houses and stabling with rooms above. The range was divided into six portions, one being allotted to each house, on to which they backed. The entrance to the mews is between numbers 4 and 5 and runs down at rather a steep pitch. The result of this is that the surface of the ground in the mews is on a level with the basements of the houses. In the case of No. 4 and possibly of the others, there was a communicating door between the basement and the stabling, but Stowell, who was there when I looked over the place, told me that it was never used.'

'Is there a similar door in the case of No. 3?'

'There may have been at one time, but there isn't now. The stabling belonging to No. 3 was pulled down when the house was modernised, and new kitchen premises were built on the site. In the case of the other five houses, the stabling remains much as it was, but only the coach houses are now in use as garages. Mr Fransham kept his car in the coach house belonging to No. 4.'

'Do you happen to know if any of the rooms above these coach houses are now occupied?'

'I noticed that in one or two cases chauffeurs seemed to be living in them. But Coates didn't. Stowell told me that Mr Fransham preferred him to live in the house itself.'

'Since the kitchen premises of No. 4 are still situated in the basement, access can presumably be obtained to the house by means of the area?'

'That's right, professor. There were originally three ways of getting into the house—by the front door, the area door and the door leading into the mews. But, as I told you, Stowell said that the third one was never used in Mr Fransham's time.'

Dr Priestley nodded thoughtfully. 'You asked me a few minutes ago what questions you should put to Mr Mayland when you called upon him,' he said. 'It would be interesting to know precisely how many keys of No. 4 were handed over to Sir Godfrey Branstock on the conclusion of Mr Fransham's tenancy. Also whether these keys were delivered to him in person and, if so, by whom? And one thing more: Perhaps you could ascertain whether Sir Godfrey Branstock's executors would consider letting or selling No. 4, and if so under what conditions?'

CHAPTER V

Early next morning, Friday, August 20th, Hanslet went to No. 3 Cheveley Street and asked for Mr Mayland. He was shown into the study, where Mayland was sitting surrounded by a mass of papers.

'Come in, superintendent,' he said cheerfully. 'You must excuse this litter. I'm trying to sort out my stepfather's papers, and it's not a very easy job.'

'I'm sorry to disturb you,' Hanslet replied. 'I dropped in to ask you a few questions; but if you're busy I can easily come back another time.'

'I'm not so busy that I can't make time to talk to you. Try one of these cigarettes. I've just come across the box in one of the drawers of this desk, and they don't seem at all bad.'

As Hanslet took one of the proffered cigarettes, he glanced at the box. It bore the inscription: 'Black's Finest Virginia, No. 10.'

'Did Sir Godfrey smoke this brand of cigarettes habitually?' he asked.

'He never smoked much at any time, though he had cigars and cigarettes on hand for his guests. For the last few years he always went to Black's in Knightsbridge for them.'

'Do you know why he favoured that particular firm?' Hanslet asked.

'I suppose because he found that they suited him,' Mayland replied. 'As a matter of fact, I believe it was Fransham who originally recommended him to go there. But I don't suppose you came here to discuss tobacconists with me, did you, superintendent?'

'Not entirely,' said Hanslet. 'My principal object in calling was to ask if you had had any further trouble with Miss Lanchester or her family?'

Mayland's face wrinkled into an expression of distaste. 'I had nothing but trouble until Emscott got back on Wednesday evening,' he replied. 'That confounded Lanchester woman has done everything she could to establish herself here. She and her relations became such a nuisance that I felt inclined to ring you up and ask for police protection. But my difficulty was that I didn't know whether I had any right here myself. It would have been devilish awkward if it had turned out in the end that I was the intruder and not she.'

'Did Miss Lanchester come to see you herself?'

'Did she not! I expected her to rage like a fury, but she didn't do anything of the kind. She adopted a superior and even forgiving attitude. She even apologised for her cousin Chris. I mustn't take anything he had said too seriously. He was an impulsive boy who had been very fond of my stepfather, whose death he had taken deeply to heart. Then she went on to say that there was no reason why she and I could not come to some amicable arrangement.'

'What exactly did she mean by that?' Hanslet asked.

'She meant, I fancy, that I could be bribed to clear out, and give her the free run of the place. She told me that to her certain knowledge my stepfather had made a fresh will since he and she had become engaged. Under the terms of this will, all his property was to revert to her upon my stepfather's death. Of course, I wasn't going to accept her statement without proof. I asked her where this will was, and she told me that to the best of her belief it was deposited with my stepfather's solicitors. I told her that I had had a cable sent to Emscott, who was then on his way back from America. Until his return, I felt it my duty to hold myself responsible to the executors for this house and its contents.'

'How did Miss Lanchester take that?'

'She didn't like it a bit. But she tried persuasion. She said it would be ridiculous for she and I to quarrel. She knew that Godfrey—she always referred to my stepfather as Godfrey, which for some reason irritated me profoundly—had always been very fond of me. When he had drawn up this fresh will she had tried to induce him to make some provision for me. But, according to her, my stepfather had said that I was already provided for, and that if at any future time I wanted help, he could trust her to give it to me. And she had the sauce to say that of course she would always be perfectly willing to do this. Meanwhile, as the house and everything in it really belonged to her, it would be far simpler if I walked out and left the direction of affairs to her. She and her cousins the Portslades would take possession at once, and so save me any further trouble. I must find this interruption to my work a terrible nuisance. And when I frankly refused to budge she lost her temper at last and said she was going to fetch the police and have me turned out. I don't know whether she did actually approach the police, but anyhow she went away, which was all I cared about.'

'Since you are still here, the story of the fresh will was untrue, of course?'

Mayland smiled. 'That's just the odd part of it,' he replied. 'Nancy Lanchester's statement that my stepfather had made a fresh will was perfectly correct. But, unfortunately for her, he hadn't signed it. Emscott told me the whole story on Wednesday evening. But I don't suppose you're sufficiently interested for me to repeat it?'

'I'd like to hear about Miss Lanchester's discomfiture,' said Hanslet.

'Then I'll tell you the story as Emscott told it to me. According to him, when Branstock married my mother in 1919, he hadn't made a will at all. He went to Emscott and told him to draw one up for him. When Emscott asked him about its provisions, he told him that he wished to leave his estate to my mother, or if she died before him to her children in equal shares.

'Emscott was perfectly frank when he explained all this to me the other evening. He told me that he had pointed out to Branstock at the time that this would include me equally with any children that he might have of his own. Branstock had told him that he fully understood this, and that it was only fair that his wife's son should share with his own family.

'Now, as it happened, my mother died two years after her second marriage, before she had had any more children. Emscott tells me that after a decent interval he pointed out to Branstock that I, no relation of his, was actually his sole heir. Branstock replied that I might just as well be his heir as anybody else. He had no relations of his own for whom he cared a brass farthing, and that although I was no relation, I was after all the son of his dead wife.

'So matters rested until one day last spring when Branstock went to see Emscott in his office. After much humming and hawing, my stepfather announced that the time had now come when he must reconsider the terms of his will. He had proposed to a very charming lady and had been accepted. They were to be married in August, and it was only fair that his future wife and their prospective children should inherit his estate. Emscott congratulated him, and naturally asked who the bride was to be.

'When he heard that my stepfather was to marry Nancy Lanchester, he was appalled. It appears that he had met her one evening when he was dining here and had formed a most unfavourable opinion. For one thing, she had tried, unsuccessfully, of course, to pump him as to the extent of my stepfather's means. Emscott regarded her as a gold-digger pure and simple, out to get as much as she could from my stepfather. But, as he told me, he never had thought that he would be such a fool as to make her the second Lady Branstock.

'Emscott, by his own account, was as tactful as he dared be. But he very soon discovered that my stepfather had made up his mind, and that no suggestions would move him. If he had refused to draw up a fresh will, Branstock would have got someone else to do it. Nancy Lanchester wasn't lying when she told me that a fresh will had been made in her favour. But Emscott was successful in persuading my stepfather not to sign it until the wedding had taken place.'

'It's very fortunate that he did so,' Hanslet remarked.

'It's very fortunate for me, certainly. For now, of course, the original will stands and I become the sole heir. It turns out that my stepfather had appointed as executor a cousin of his who lives in the country, and Emscott himself. I have been asked to wind up the household on their behalf, and that's what you see me doing now.'

'You don't propose to live here yourself, then, Mr Mayland?' Hanslet asked.

Mayland shook his head. 'These old-fashioned houses don't appeal to me,' he replied. 'I shall sell this property and build myself a house somewhere according to my own ideas. I'm an architect by profession, you must remember. I shall, of course, continue to practise, and with a little capital behind me I shall be able to carry out one or two schemes which I've often thought of.'

'Is Miss Lanchester aware of the position?'

'Emscott told me that he would write to her at once and break the news. Later on I shall make it my business to see that she's provided for. After all, whether she imposed upon my stepfather or not, he had asked her to marry him. If only out of regard for his memory she ought to get something.'

'It isn't everybody who would look at it that way, Mr Mayland. Now, I wonder if I may take up your time with a few further questions?'

'Fire away and I'll do my best to answer them,' Mayland replied.

'That's very kind of you. To begin with, the keys of No. 4 are in your possession, I understand?'

'I've got them here if you want them,' Mayland replied, opening a drawer in the desk at which he was sitting.

'Three keys, all of which fit the Yale lock on the front door.'

'Where are the keys of the area door and the door leading into the mews?'

'In the locks on the inside of the doors, I fancy. I am pretty sure that I saw them there when I looked over the house with a view to the proposed alterations.'

'Do you happen to know if these three keys were handed to Sir Godfrey in person?'

'Yes, they were. My stepfather told me that Stowell brought them to him when he left the house. It was a couple of days later that he had asked me to go over the place and see about the alterations. And I've blamed myself ever since that I didn't go down into the cellar then. I should have found out that there was something wrong and had it seen to. We know now that the accumulation of gas was due to a defective gully in No. 4 which made its way through an opening into the cellar of this house. I've had the gully filled up with cement for good and all. But it's like locking the stable door after the horse has been stolen.'

'Would you consider the sale of No. 4 to a suitable purchaser, Mr Mayland?'

'I mean to get rid of both houses, either separately or together. If you know of anyone likely to buy No. 4, by all means send him along.'

As Hanslet sat in the district train between Sloane Square and Hammersmith, he pondered what Mayland had told him, in regard to his own conversation with Dr Priestley on the previous evening. It was the professor's remark that Sir Godfrey's death had followed naturally upon Mr Fransham's which worried him chiefly. Until at last some inkling of the professor's meaning dawned upon him.

The argument, as the superintendent saw it, was this: If Mr Fransham had not been murdered, No. 4 would have been occupied on the date of Sir Godfrey's death. In that case the accumulation of foul air in the cellar would probably have been detected, and steps would have been taken in the matter. In that respect, then, it might be said that Sir Godfrey's death was an indirect result of the murder of Mr Fransham.

But the professor's corollary that the circumstances of the second event might throw light upon the first, seemed utterly fantastic. There could be no doubt that Sir Godfrey's death had been due to sheer accident. Nor would it help matters to suppose that this accident had been criminally contrived, that the gully had been deliberately damaged so as to admit foul air to the cellar. What possible connection could exist between this act and the murder of Mr Fransham?

Hanslet was still meditating upon this question when he reached the Stowells' house. He found Stowell at home, busily engaged on some business of domestic carpentry.

'Good-morning, sir,' he said respectfully. 'Is there any fresh news about Mr Fransham?'

'Not yet,' Hanslet replied. 'I've just dropped in to ask you a few questions. To begin with, do you remember handing over the keys of No. 4?'

'Perfectly, sir. I took them in myself to Sir Godfrey, and got a receipt for them, which I sent to Dr Thornborough.'

'How many keys did you hand over?'

'Three, sir—the three keys of the front door. The one which used to belong to Mr Fransham, the one I took from Coates before he left, and my own.'

'Were there any other keys of the front door in existence?'

'No, sir. Those were the only three all the time I lived there.'

'What became of the keys of the other two doors?'

'I left them in the locks on the inside, sir, and bolted the doors before I shut the house up. I told Sir Godfrey at the time that I had done so, and he seemed quite satisfied.'

'When did you last open the cellar door?'

'The cellar door, sir? I don't suppose that's been opened for ten years or more. When I first went to Mr Fransham, I used to keep the wine down there, but I soon gave it up. The steps were very awkward, and Mr Fransham didn't care to go to the expense of having a light put in the cellar. I was afraid of breaking my neck every time I went down there. So, for the little quantity of wine that Mr Fransham used to keep in the house, I used the cupboard under the basement stairs.'

'I see. Did you ever notice an unpleasant smell in the cellar? Or feel giddy after you had been down there?'

Stowell shook his head. 'I can't say that I did, sir,' he replied. 'I was talking about that very thing to my wife after we'd been reading in the paper about what happened to Sir Godfrey. And I was saying to her that it was lucky we gave up using the cellar when we did, even though I had never noticed anything wrong with it.'

'It may have been lucky or it may not,' said Hanslet thoughtfully. 'One thing more,' he continued. 'Was there a refrigerator installed at No. 4?'

'No, sir, there wasn't. It's one thing my wife wanted badly, and I spoke to Mr Fransham two or three times about it. But all I could get him to say was that he'd think about it. He never liked spending money upon anything he didn't think absolutely necessary.'

Hanslet's next visit was to Mr Sandling, the borough surveyor, from whom he elicited an account of his inspection of the gully in the cellar of No. 4.

'There's no doubt that some defect in the connection was responsible for the accumulation of foul air in the cellar,' said Mr Sandling. 'There was distinct evidence of the presence of sewer gas there when Mr Mayland and I examined the place. Faulty ventilation must have allowed an accumulation of gas in the drainage system, and this must have found its way back through the gully. Although such an occurrence is fortunately very rare, there is always a possibility of its happening, especially in the case of cellars which are kept closed and have no means of ventilation apart from the door.'

'I suppose that there is no possibility of the gully having been tampered with deliberately?' Hanslet asked.

Mr Sandling laughed. 'My dear sir!' he exclaimed. 'I know that it is the business of the police to be suspicious, but in this case you may set your mind at rest. I suppose your idea is that someone with designs on Sir Godfrey Branstock's life might have interfered with the gully. Well, I don't suppose that a more unpromising method of murder could be imagined. It might have been years before conditions in the drainage system became such that an accumulation of gas occurred.

'Besides, as soon as Mr Mayland and I opened the cellar door of No. 4 I could see at once that nobody had been down there for a very long time. The floor was at least half an inch thick in dust which would have shown the lightest footprints. In fact, the gully itself was so choked with debris that it is a wonder the gas managed to percolate through it at all.'

'You've no doubt, however, that the foul air did actually find its way into the cellars through the gully?'

Mr Sandling shrugged his shoulders. 'The circumstances don't leave any room for doubt,' he replied. 'Look here, superintendent, you're sufficiently intelligent to appreciate the facts. Here they are in logical sequence. The medical examination revealed that the cause of Sir Godfrey Branstock's death was suffocation by carbon dioxide. Next day the Home Office analyst found a large proportion of carbon dioxide in the atmosphere of the cellar of No. 3. When I inspected the cellar of No. 4, I found evidence not only of carbon dioxide, but of sulphuretted hydrogen as well. The association of these two gases is a certain indication of sewer gas. Sewer gas, as its name implies, originates in drains. In the cellar of No. 4 was a gully connected to the drainage system. On at least one previous occasion when Sir Godfrey had entered the cellar of No. 3 he had experienced peculiar symptoms, though the cause of these was not suspected at the time. The presence of sewer gas can nearly always be detected by the characteristic odour of sulphuretted hydrogen, one of its constituents. Sir Godfrey, the only person who had access to the cellar of No. 3, was deficient in his sense of smell. It seems to me that these facts tell their own story with unusual clarity.'

Hanslet, back once more in his room at Scotland Yard, made yet another attempt to unravel the meaning of Dr Priestley's cryptic remark. Each fresh inquiry seemed to make it less likely that Sir Godfrey Branstock's death had followed naturally upon the murder of Mr Fransham. Even if Mr Fransham had still been in residence, the accumulation of gas would not have been discovered, since the cellar of No. 4 was disused. And any possibility that the accumulation had been caused deliberately was ruled out. Upon that point at least the borough surveyor had been emphatic.

On the other hand, there was that curious story of the two wills which Mayland had unfolded. The significance of the situation had not escaped the superintendent. He had very little doubt that Sir Godfrey had told Nancy Lanchester that he had drawn up a will in her favour. But it was most unlikely that he had revealed to her that he had been persuaded by his solicitor not to sign it until after the wedding. She, believing the will to be already valid, would thus have a motive for getting Sir Godfrey out of the way, and so avoiding the necessity of marrying a man very many years older than herself. For it was quite obvious to Hanslet that her object had been not Sir Godfrey himself, but his money.

But, once embarked on this line of thought, he recalled to his memory the details which Dr Oldland had given him of the affair. Nancy Lanchester and her two cousins had been in the house at the time of Sir Godfrey's death. That in itself was a suspicious circumstance. And, although the medical evidence as to the cause of Sir Godfrey's death had been unquestioned at the time, the bare possibility remained that a mistake had been made. Was it too fantastic to imagine that he might have been over-powered and suffocated, and his body subsequently deposited in the cellar?

But even if this wholly unsupported theory could be maintained, Dr Priestley's suggestion remained as obscure as ever. What connection could be established between the two murders? On the one hand Dr Thornborough could not possibly have contrived Sir Godfrey's death, nor had he any conceivable motive for wishing to do so. On the other hand, though by a stretch of the imagination it might be possible to suppose that Nancy Lanchester and her friends could have contrived the death of Mr Fransham, what possible object could they have had in doing so?

Nor was there any similarity in the causes of death in either case. Even allowing for errors of detail in diagnosis, there could be no doubt that Sir Godfrey had died of suffocation. It had been established with absolute certainty that Mr Fransham had died as the result of a fractured skull. How the injury had been inflicted was still a mystery, but that did not alter the fact.

That afternoon a reply came to the message which Hanslet had dispatched to Adderminster earlier in the day. Superintendent Yateley reported that he had made inquiries as requested. The result of these showed that at the time that *Epidaurus* was completed Dr Thornborough had had a refrigerator installed there. It was the pattern known as the 'Icicle', Type 15. The refrigerator had now been removed from the house together with the rest of the doctor's belongings. A refrigerator was also installed in the cottage owned by Mr Whiteway. This was a 'Snowflake', Type Z7.

Hanslet called upon Dr Priestley that evening and gave him an account of his activities during the day.

'You see how it is, professor,' he said. 'There's only about one chance in ten thousand that Sir Godfrey's death was due to foul play. His bedroom and dressing-room are on the same floor as the lounge where his guests were assembled that evening. I suppose it's just within the bounds of possibility that he was attacked and suffocated in one of these rooms. Nancy Lanchester and her two cousins might have been capable between them of carrying his body down to the cellar. But how on earth they could have done so in a house full of servants is more than I can imagine. And the only other alternative is that his death was due to sheer accident.'

'I do not think that is the only other alternative,' Dr Priestley replied gently. 'However, that point need not detain us at present. I understand that Mr Mayland and Stowell are in exact agreement as to the keys of No. 4 handed over to Sir Godfrey?'

'Their statements coincide exactly,' Hanslet replied.

'Then we may, for the present, accept them as correct. Again, the evidence that the cellar of No. 4 had not been entered for some considerable period before Sir Godfrey's death appears to be incontrovertible. We have Stowell's statement to that effect, which appears to be confirmed by the dust observed by the district surveyor. Really, superintendent, I envy you an investigation which offers so much scope for pure detection.'

Hanslet laughed. 'There's no question of any official investigation into the cause of Sir Godfrey's death,' he replied. 'The coroner's jury brought in a verdict of accidental death, and up to the present I've found no cause to disagree with that verdict. So that if you envy me the job, there's no earthly reason why you shouldn't take it over.'

'Do you mean that seriously?' Dr Priestley asked.

'Perfectly seriously, professor.'

'In that case I may possibly do so,' said Dr Priestley quietly. 'Did you ascertain Mr Mayland's intentions regarding No. 4?'

'He means to sell both houses,' Hanslet replied. 'And he

told me that if I knew of a likely purchaser, he'd be glad if I'd send him along. And there's just one more thing, professor; you remember that test question of yours last night about the refrigerators. Well, just to demonstrate that the police are always in a position to find out details, no matter how unimportant, I've got the answer for you. Not only can I tell you which of the houses were fitted with refrigerators, but I can supply the make and type.'

'I congratulate you, superintendent. Can you repeat the particulars?'

Hanslet took a piece of paper from his pocket. 'Here they are,' he replied. 'There was no refrigerator in No. 4, apparently because Mr Fransham was too mean to buy one. Sir Godfrey in No. 3 had a "Storfresh", Type A.D. Dr Thornborough at *Epidaurus* had an "Icicle", Type 15. Mr Whiteway in the cottage at Gunthorpe Road has a "Snowflake", Type Z7. You were apparently quite right about the popularity of the domestic refrigerator. Three out of these four houses had one installed.'

'That is most interesting,' said Dr Priestley. 'Perhaps you will allow Harold to copy those particulars?'

'He needn't trouble about that,' Hanslet replied. 'He can have this paper that I've written them down on. And now if you don't mind, professor, I'll be getting back to the Yard. Having been out all the morning, I've got some arrears to make up before I go home.'

CHAPTER VI

Anthony Mayland had barely finished his breakfast next morning, Saturday, August 21st, when Grace, the parlour-maid at No. 3, brought him a card on a silver salver.

'There's a gentleman just called, sir,' she said. 'And he'd like to see you if it's convenient.'

Mayland picked up the card and looked at it. 'Never heard of him,' he replied, 'but I'd better see him, I suppose. All right, Grace, show him into the study and tell him that I'll be along in a moment.'

A couple of minutes later he entered the study to find his visitor standing in the middle of the room. 'Good-morning, Mr Merefield,' he said. 'Won't you sit down? That's right. Now, what can I have the pleasure of doing for you?'

'I've called on behalf of my employer, Dr Priestley,' Harold replied. 'Superintendent Hanslet, whom I believe you know, has told him that you are anxious to sell the house next door.'

'Yes, I know the superintendent,' said Mayland. 'He was

218

here yesterday, and I told him that I wanted to sell both houses. Am I to understand that Dr Priestley is interested in No. 4?'

'He thinks from what the superintendent has said that it might suit him. Between ourselves, I think he's rather keen. Anyhow, he's waiting outside in a taxi now. He sent me in to ask you if you would allow him to look over the house.'

'I'd be delighted,' Mayland replied with a glance at the clock. 'The only thing is that I've got an appointment at my solicitor's in half an hour, and I can't possibly spare the time to show you over the place. But if you like to take the keys and look over the house by yourselves, you're quite welcome. You can hand them back again to my maid when you've finished. But I warn you that the place is in a bit of a mess. I was contemplating certain alterations, and so did not trouble to have the place cleaned out after the last tenant left.'

'Dr Priestley won't mind that,' said Harold. 'I'd be very glad of the loan of the keys, and they shall be returned as soon as we've seen over the place.'

Mayland took the three keys from the desk and gave them to Harold. 'It doesn't matter which you use,' he said. 'They all fit the front door. When you've done with them, just ring the bell and hand them into the parlourmaid, will you?' He escorted Harold to the door and glanced at the taxi standing outside No. 4. He could see the somewhat severe face of the elderly gentleman sitting in it.

Dr Priestley got out of the taxi, which drove away after Harold had paid the driver. 'You saw Mr Mayland?' he asked.

'Yes, sir. Unfortunately he has an appointment which

prevents him from showing us over the place himself. However, he gave me the keys. Here they are.'

Dr Priestley took the keys and approached the front door. It was characteristic of him that he should try each key in the lock in turn to find that they opened it with equal facility. He and Harold entered the house and shut the front door behind them. They then proceeded to inspect the house in complete silence, beginning at the top floor. Dr Priestley did not seem inclined for conversation, and Harold naturally respected his wishes.

It was not until they had completed their tour of the ground floor that Dr Priestley made any remarks. 'A very comfortable house of the old-fashioned type,' he said. 'Its main disadvantage, of course, is that the kitchen premises are situated in the basement. Sir Godfrey Branstock was well advised when he had his own house modernised. However, while we are here we had better inspect the basement and ascertain its possibilities.'

Access to the basement in No. 4 was, as in the case of No. 3, obtained by means of a door in the hall, beyond which was a flight of stairs. Indeed, the internal arrangement of the two houses was exactly similar. Dr Priestley and Harold descended these stairs, to find themselves in a wide passage off which several doors opened. They inspected in turn, the kitchen, the servants' hall, the scullery, the pantry and the larder, to find these all empty. Only three doors then remained unopened. One by the foot of the stairs and one at each extremity of the passage. All these three doors were locked, with the keys in position. The two latter were bolted as well.

Dr Priestley turned his attention to the first of these doors, which had been heavily made of thick boards and fitted with a massive lock. But age and the dampness of the basement had done its work, and at the bottom of the door the wood had rotted away in places from the nails which secured it. Dr Priestley, investigating this, found that at one place the boards could be pushed away from the framework of the door, leaving an orifice several inches wide. Through this orifice could be seen, by the help of an electric torch produced by Harold, a flight of stone steps. This, then, was evidently the door giving access to the cellar.

Harold was about to turn the key, but Dr Priestley restrained him. 'We need not open that door,' he said. 'We have ascertained that it leads to the cellar, which is sufficient for us. It is possible, though extremely unlikely, that there may still be some foul air present. We will make a note that this door needs repairing. We will now turn our attention to the other two.'

As could be seen through a small window beside it, the door at the farther end of the passage led into the area. Dr Priestley, after glancing at the bolts which secured it, shook his head.

'We need not open that,' he said. 'But the door at this end of the passage should lead into the mews, and I particularly wish to inspect the accommodation available there. Unfortunately, according to Stowell, this door was never used in Mr Fransham's time, and we may therefore find difficulty in opening it.'

'I'll have a shot at it, anyhow,' Harold replied. He applied himself to the upper bolt, which drew back with surprising ease. Nor did the lower bolt offer any greater resistance. He turned the key, which moved smoothly in the lock. Finally, at a pull upon the handle, the door swung open noiselessly upon its hinges. 'It looks to me, sir, as though the fastenings of this door have been oiled not very long ago,' Harold exclaimed.

'And what does that suggest to you, my boy?' Dr Priestley asked good-humouredly.

'That someone was in the habit of using it to get in or out of the house secretly, sir. Probably, I should think, Coates the chauffeur. We know that he had a key of the front door, but every time that he came in or out of that way he would be pretty sure to be seen. Whereas he could slip through this door into the mews without anyone being the wiser.'

Dr Priestley made no comment upon this. 'Let us see what is beyond the door,' he said.

They passed through the doorway and found themselves in what had originally been the harness-room of the stabling. It contained a tortoise stove, which had long ago been dismantled and pushed away in a corner. Beside it lay a six-foot length of four-inch stove pipe, very rusty, and a couple of bends. During Mr Fransham's occupation of No. 4, this room had evidently been used by Coates as a place in which to deposit unwanted rubbish. Lying about the floor, or hanging up on various projections from the wall, were a number of empty oil drums and half a dozen disused motor-car tyres.

The harness-room possessed three doors in all. These were: the one communicating with the house, by which they had entered the harness-room, a second outside door leading into the yard of the mews, and a third opening into the coach-house lately used as a garage. The second of these was locked, with the key in position on the inside, and the third was open. A flight of wooden steps led from the harness-room to the floor above. There was no interior connection between the stalls which stood beside the coach-house and the rest of the stabling.

They proceeded first to investigate the coach-house, which was large enough to contain two cars of medium size. Dr Priestley directed his attention to the double doors leading into the yard. One of these doors was secured by internal fastenings, and the other was locked to it, but the key was not in the lock. Having satisfied himself of this, Dr Priestley examined the floor as though searching for some object. He found nothing, for the floor presented a surprising contrast to the unkempt appearance of the rest of the establishment. It was, in fact, remarkably clean, as though it had been washed not very long before.

Dr Priestley called Harold's attention to this. 'It is curious that the garage should have been cleaned out, and the harness-room left in such a terribly untidy state,' he said. 'But what is even more curious is the absence of the key of the coach-house door. The dimensions of the lock indicate that it must be of considerable size. It is unlikely, therefore, that it has been overlooked. Yet neither Mr Mayland nor Stowell have made any mention of it having been handed over to Sir Godfrey Branstock. Would you be good enough, Harold, to mount that flight of wooden steps in the harness-room and explore the floor above?'

Harold returned from his explorations to find Dr Priestley still standing in the coach-house, apparently absorbed in thought. 'There is nothing to be seen upstairs, sir,' he reported. 'There are two good-sized rooms, both completely empty. And, judging from the thick layer of dust covering the floor, I should say that nobody had been into them for ages. You remember that we were told that Coates lived in the house itself.'

Dr Priestley nodded. 'I should like to inspect the yard,' he said. 'We could reach it by unlocking the door in the harness-room, but perhaps it is better not to do so. We will re-enter the house by the way we came.'

They did so, Dr Priestley insisting that the intercommunicating door should be left exactly as they had found it. Harold therefore bolted it and turned the key. They then left the house by the front door and walked down the approach between Nos. 4 and 5 into the mews.

A couple of chauffeurs were standing in the yard, smoking cigarettes and exchanging reminiscences. Dr Priestley walked up to them. 'Do either of you know a man called Coates?' he asked abruptly.

The chauffeurs stared at this elderly gentleman, who had so unceremoniously interrupted their conversation. 'Coates, sir?' one of them replied. 'Yes, if you mean him that used to drive the car for the gentleman in No. 4. I knew him well enough, and a surly sort of chap he was. It was as much as he could do to pass the time of day with anyone. But he's not here now. He left soon after his guv'nor was killed. And to the best of my belief he went down into the country somewhere.'

'You have not seen him about here since then?'

'The chauffeur shook his head. 'There wouldn't be any occasion for him to come back,' he replied. 'His guv'nor's car was never brought back here, and I don't suppose the garage belonging to No. 4 has been so much as opened for a couple of months or more.'

The second chauffeur, who had not yet spoken, took his cigarette out of his mouth.

'That's just where you're wrong, Jack,' he said complacently. 'There was a car, or a van rather, in that garage not
a week ago.'

'Well, I didn't know that,' said the one who had been
addressed as Jack. 'A van, you say? Bringing over some
builder's stuff, likely enough. I've heard it said that now
No. 4's empty they're going to alter it the same as they
did No. 3.'

'That's just what I thought when I saw the van draw
out. Last Sunday morning it was, round about four o'clock,
just as it was getting light. You remember that terrible
toothache I had, Jack? When I went to see the dentist
about it on the Monday morning he said I'd got an abscess.'

'Of pain, no doubt,' said Dr Priestley politely. 'You have
my hearfelt sympathy. But you were saying something
about a van?'

'That's right, sir. It was owing to the toothache that I
came to see the van, as I was going to tell you. What with
the pain, I couldn't sleep a wink all night and when I heard
an engine start in the yard I got up and looked out of the
window. I sleep over the garage that belongs to No. 2, if
you understand me, sir. And Jack here, who's employed at
No. 5, sleeps over his garage the same as I do. We're the
only two who sleep on the mews, for No. 1 and No. 6
don't keep cars. No. 4's empty, and the garage belonging
to No. 3 has been done away with, as you can see for
yourself, sir.'

'Yes, I have noticed that,' said Dr Priestley. 'What exactly
did you see when you looked out of your window on
Sunday morning?'

'The first thing I saw was that the doors of No. 4 garage
were open. And I thought that was funny, for knowing the

house had been empty for some weeks, I couldn't think who it could be. And while I was still looking a van came out. One of those Comet thirty-hundredweight vans that you see about, it was. Naturally, it being a closed van, I couldn't see what was in it. And when the van was out in the yard, the driver got down, shut the garage doors, locked them and put the key in his pocket. Then he drove off, and that's the last I saw of him.'

'You did not recognise him?' Dr Priestley asked. 'He could not have been Coates, by any chance?'

The chauffeur shook his head. 'It wasn't Coates, sir, whoever it was,' he replied. 'It was a much younger chap than him. I couldn't see his face properly, being right above him as you might say, and the light none too good. But I could tell he was a youngish man by the way he walked.'

'Did either of you know that there was a van in the garage?'

Both shook their heads, and Jack took upon himself to answer the question. 'I didn't know and Fred says that he didn't either. But there's nothing remarkable about that. We both happened to be out on the Saturday afternoon and if the van drove in then there wouldn't be anybody about to take notice. If often happens that there's nobody in these mews for hours on end.'

'Did you notice if there was a name on the van?'

'Yes, sir, it belonged to the Peregrine Transport Co.,' Fred replied. 'I noticed that particularly, for I used to have a chum who worked for them. Their place is somewhere Islington way.'

'What is their business?' Dr Priestley asked.

'Anything in the way of vans and lorries, sir. They'll pick up anything for you, no matter what it is, and haul it where you like. And a very good firm to work for, my chum always said.'

After thanking the chauffeurs for their information Dr Priestley left the mews, accompanied by Harold. As soon as they were in the street he issued his orders. 'Leave the keys at No. 3. Then fetch two taxis. I noticed as we drove up that there is a rank just round the corner.'

'Two taxis, sir?' said Harold inquiringly.

'Yes. One to enable me to return home and the other to take you to Islington. You should have no difficulty in finding the office of the Peregrine Transport Co. When you have done so, make inquiries about the van which is said to have visited the garage of No. 4. I am particularly anxious to know the nature of the load it carried on that occasion.'

Harold carried out his instructions to the letter. With the help of his taxi-driver he was successful in locating the premises of the Peregrine Transport Co., not very far from the Agricultural Hall. He entered the inquiry office, and announced that he wished to trace the movements of a van bearing the name of the firm, which had been seen in Cheveley Street on the previous Sunday morning.

The clerk looked at him a trifle suspiciously. 'You want to see Mr Gilson,' he replied. 'If you'll wait here a minute I'll go and speak to him.'

After a short interval, Harold was shown into an office and introduced to Mr Gilson.

'Sit down, Mr Merefield,' said the latter. 'I understand that you wish to make inquiries about one of our vans. Before we go any further, I must ask you if there is any allegation that it was involved in an accident?'

'Oh no,' Harold replied. 'There's no question of any

accident. I'll tell you what it is. My employer has taken a lease of No. 4 Cheveley Street, which has been standing empty for some weeks. On visiting it this morning he found that some packages of goods had been delivered there, apparently in error. The only clue to the ownership of these goods is the fact that one of your vans was seen to leave the premises early on Sunday morning last. He hoped that you might be able to help us in the matter.'

'What address did you say?' Mr Gilson asked opening the drawer of a filing cabinet beside him.

'No. 4, Cheveley Street, SW1. Not very far from Sloane Square.'

Mr Gilson consulted his files, then shook his head. 'I can't find a record of a van of ours having visited Cheveley Street on Sunday or at any other time,' he said. 'What makes you think that it was one of our vans?'

'We have been told that your name was on it,' Harold replied.

'Well, it may have been our van, but it certainly was not in charge of one of our drivers. You see, a large part of our business consists in hiring out lorries and vans to other firms, who as often as not supply their own drivers. And, of course, if this particular van was on hire under those conditions, we should have no record of its journeys.'

'This van was described to us as a thirty-hundred-weight Comet. Would that help you to trace it?'

'It might, for we have only six vans of that type, all of which were bought this year. Three of them have been on hire recently and, now I come to think of it, I remember that one of these was returned to us on Monday last. It had been on hire for three weeks to a firm in the North of England who provided their own driver. I saw him when he brought the van back on Monday, and a very decent young fellow he seemed.'

'I wonder if you could tell me the name of the firm?' Harold asked.

Mr Gilson made another reference to his files. 'Messrs. Ernest Willingdon & Sons, of Leeds,' he replied. 'They rang us up on the morning of July 26, and asked if we had a thirty-hundredweight van available immediately. They explained that they had several very valuable consignments of goods to be delivered in London during the following three weeks, and that they could not spare a van from their own fleet for the purpose. I said that we could help them out of their difficulty and told them what our terms were. They replied that as the matter was very urgent, they would send one of their men to London by the next train. The caller explained that he was Mr Francis Willingdon, one of the partners. "Our man will bring with him sufficient money to cover three weeks' hire of the van and also the usual deposit on its value," he said. And sure enough their man arrived that afternoon, collected the van, of which the number was ZOQ 1437, and drove it away. He brought it back last Monday afternoon, when I saw him. He told me that during the three weeks he'd done fifteen double journeys between Leeds and London. But we couldn't check the mileage he had covered, for the speedometer cable was broken. He told me that it had happened on his very first journey and that he hadn't had time to have it mended.'

Harold did his best to conceal his amazement. 'Willingdon & Sons!' he exclaimed. 'No doubt that accounts for it. My employer is very well acquainted with that firm. He will now be able to get in touch with them and find out the reason for the packages having been deposited. He will, I am sure, be most grateful for the information which you have given me.'

Having apologised to Mr Gilson for the trouble to which he had put him, Harold hurried back to Westbourne Terrace. Dr Priestley listened to his report with manifest signs of approval.

'You have done very well, my boy, very well indeed,' he said. 'I have no doubt that the van seen by the chauffeur in Cheveley Mews was indeed the van hired by Messrs. Willingdon.'

'It's most extraordinary that their name should have cropped up again, sir,' Harold replied. 'It was young Francis Willingdon, you remember, who took the cottage near Dr Thornborough's house at Adderminster. Shall I ring up the superintendent and tell him about this?'

Dr Priestley raised his eyebrows. 'The superintendent?' he replied. 'Certainly not. As recently as yesterday evening, in your presence, the superintendent gave me full permission to investigate for myself the matter of Sir Godfrey Branstock's death. I propose to take advantage of that permission. And I will begin by dictating certain particulars which we shall need for reference.'

Harold got out pen and writing pad and Dr Priestley continued:

'Particulars relating to a thirty-hundredweight Comet van, the property of the Peregrine Transport Company, and alleged to have been hired to Messrs. Willingdon & Sons of Leeds.

'Registered number of the van ZOQ 1437.

'July 26. The van was taken from the premises of the Peregrine Transport Company, by a driver whose identity is at present unknown.

'August 4. Sir Godfrey Branstock was found suffocated in his cellar at No. 3 Cheveley Street.

'August 15. The van was seen leaving the garage belonging to No. 4 Cheveley Street at 4 a.m.

'August 16. The van was returned to the premises of the Peregrine Transport Co.'

Dr Priestley made Harold read over these particulars. 'Very good,' he said. 'The first point to be established concerns the whereabouts of the van between July 26 and August 15. Can we accept the driver's statement to Mr Gilson that during that period it was engaged in travelling backwards and forwards between London and Leeds? The distance from London to Leeds is approximately 190 miles, and if the driver's statement is to be accepted, he must have covered 270 miles on each day of the three weeks, including Sundays. There is no means of checking this figure however, since, when the van was returned to its owners, the speedometer shaft was found to be broken.'

'I daresay that Willingdon & Sons would tell us how the van was employed, sir,' Harold suggested.

'It would, I think, be premature to trouble Willingdon & Sons at this stage of our investigations,' Dr Priestley replied. 'The next question is, when and why was the van deposited in the garage belonging to No. 4 Cheveley Street. The possibility exists that the van was never driven to Leeds at all, but spent the greater part of the three weeks unused in the garage.'

'But surely, sir, somebody would have seen it if it had been there all that time!' Harold exclaimed.

'Who would have seen it?' Dr Priestley replied. 'It seems to me that there was very little likelihood of the van being discovered during that period. We will suppose that the van was driven into the garage on July 26, or two or three days later. Sir Godfrey Branstock was then alive. Mr Mayland had made his preliminary survey of No. 4, and it was most unlikely that anyone would enter the house until he was ready to proceed with the alterations. On Sir Godfrey's death the question of the alterations fell perforce into abeyance until the ownership of the property could be determined. No. 4 was certainly entered by Mr Mayland and the Borough Surveyor on August 9, but their concern was solely with the cellar, and they did not inspect the garage.'

'The driver of the van must have been in possession of the key of the coach-house, sir,' Harold suggested.

'Exactly. But, as we observed this morning, that key was not in the lock on the occasion of our visit. Where was it at the time when Stowell handed over the other keys to Sir Godfrey? If you were to call upon Stowell you might be able to persuade him to answer that question for us.'

That afternoon Harold departed upon his errand and returned with the necessary information.

'I told Stowell that, with Mr Mayland's permission, we had inspected No. 4 this morning, sir,' he said. 'I went on to say that in the course of our inspection we had found that the garage key was missing and asked him if he knew what had become of it. He told me that in Mr Fransham's time the key was never kept in the lock, but when not in use was hung on a brass hook fixed just inside the area door.'

'I noticed that brass hook,' Dr Priestley remarked. 'But I am certain that no key was hanging upon it this morning.'

'Stowell told me that the last thing he did before shutting up the house was to take the garage key from its hook and go round to the mews. He told me that he didn't use the intercommunicating door, because the bolts were all rusted up and he didn't think it worth while to try and draw them. Having reached the mews he unlocked the garage door and went through into the harness room. He assured himself that the outer door there was safely locked and bolted, then went back into the mews, locking the door of the garage after him. He then hung the garage key on its accustomed hook and when he handed over the front door keys to Sir Godfrey reported that he had done so.'

'That seems a very straightforward statement,' said Dr Priestley. 'We may assume, then, that the driver of the van took the key from the hook. How did he obtain access to the house in order to do so?'

'I've been thinking about that, sir, ever since Stowell told me where the key was kept,' Harold replied. 'It occurred to me that we don't really know that those three keys for the front door are the only ones in existence. If one has a key of that kind in one's possession, it's the easiest thing in the world to have a duplicate cut. Any ironmonger will do so without asking questions. We have been told that Coates had one of these keys when he was in Mr Fransham's service. He might have had a duplicate cut, which he retained when he handed over the originals to Stowell.'

Dr Priestley nodded. 'Quite right, my boy,' he said. 'But at present we have no reason to believe that Coates was the driver of the van. Such slight evidence as we have suggests that he was not. I would therefore enlarge your argument to this extent. Anyone who had even temporary possession of one of the front door keys could have had a duplicate cut.

'We have now cleared the ground to this extent. We have

shown the possibility of the van having been left in the garage belonging to No. 4 for almost any period within the limit of the three weeks. We are naturally tempted to ask why it was left there during that period.'

'I can't imagine, sir,' Harold replied, feeling that he was expected to suggest an answer to this question. 'Everything had been taken out of the house some time previously, so the van cannot have been employed in removing furniture or anything like that. And it can't have brought anything, for the house, when we saw it this morning, was absolutely empty.'

'That does not preclude the possibility that it brought something when it came and took that something away again when it left. And this, I felt sure, is what actually happened. We must not lose sight of the possibility that the van was in the garage at the time of Sir Godfrey's death.'

Harold looked frankly puzzled. 'I'm afraid that I don't see the connection, sir,' he ventured.

'The connection is not apparent at first sight, I admit,' Dr Priestley replied. 'Take your pad again, my boy, while I dictate certain notes.'

When Harold was ready Dr Priestley dictated as follows:

'It is possible that a fourth key to No. 4 exists. The possessor of this key would have access, not only to the house, but through the communicating door to the stabling and garage as well.

'According to Stowell the bolts on the communicating door were so rusty that he made no attempt to draw them when he shut up the house. On August 21 the bolts and locks were found to work easily, and their appearance suggested that they had been oiled fairly recently.

'Again according to Stowell, the garage key was hung

by him on a brass hook inside the area door. It was not there on August 21. The van driver was observed on August 15 to lock the garage and put the key in his pocket.

'The Borough Surveyor, in his conversation with Superintendent Hanslet, expressed some surprise that foul gas should have been able to percolate through the debris which choked the gully in cellar No. 4.

'In the harness room belonging to No. 4 is a length of four inch stove pipe and a bend to fit it.

'Upon inspection of the cellar door of No. 4 on August 21, it was found that the lower panels could be pushed away from the framework.

'It seems probable that approximately an hour elapsed between the death of Sir Godfrey Branstock and Mrs Quinton's visit to the cellar in search of him. During this interval, the accumulation of gas in the cellar must have dispersed to some extent. Had it remained at its former concentration, Mrs Quinton would probably have been overcome when she bent over her master's body.

'In the course of her evidence at the inquest, Mrs Quinton mentioned a buzzing noise, which she imagined to be the sound of the motor of the refrigerator in the larder. When the presence of foul air had been established, it was assumed that this buzzing had had no actual existence, as such noises in the head are well-known symptoms consequent upon the inhalation of carbon dioxide. But Mrs Quinton heard the buzzing when she was standing in the basement before she descended into the cellar.

'Although the cellar of No. 4 is not wired for electric light, the basement of that house is wired extensively. A point exists in the ceiling of the passage just outside the cellar door.'

'That concludes my dictation for the present,' said Dr Priestley. 'Possibly if you consider those paragraphs, you may be able to deduce for yourself the true case of Sir Godfrey Branstock's death. We will institute certain inquiries of our own into that matter after the weekend. But your first duty on Monday morning will be to collect, from their respective makers, full details of the principal types of domestic refrigerator.'

CHAPTER VII

During the afternoon of Wednesday, August 25, Superintendent Hanslet received a telephone message from Harold Merefield.

'Dr Priestley will be very glad if you can make it convenient to dine with him this evening,' said Harold formally, in a tone which suggested that the professor himself was standing at his elbow. 'He would also like to know if Inspector Waghorn is available, and if so, whether he can accompany you?'

'I shall be delighted to come,' said Hanslet. 'And I'll bring Jimmy along with me. He happens to be in London at the moment and I'll see that he's free for dinner. Has the professor any fresh suggestions to make about the Adderminster affair?'

But Harold took no notice of this question. 'Dr Priestley will be very pleased,' he said. 'Dinner will be served at eight o'clock as usual.'

When Hanslet and Jimmy arrived at Westbourne Terrace they found that Dr Oldland had also been invited. In accordance with his usual custom, Dr Priestley would allow nothing but general conversation during dinner. But when they left the dining-room, instead of proceeding to the study for coffee as was the almost invariable rule of the house, Dr Priestley led his guests upstairs to the second floor. 'You are about to witness an experiment,' was the only explanation that he vouchsafed them.

He allowed them to proceed no further than the landing, from which extended a long corridor. This corridor was in darkness except for a single electric lamp hanging from the ceiling at the further end. Under this lamp stood a table and upon the table was a whitish object of unfamiliar shape. Oldland stared at this. 'What the devil have you got there, Priestley?' he asked.

'A calf's head, from which my cook has removed the meat,' Dr Priestley replied. 'Surely you must have noticed that our entrée this evening consisted of *tête de veau en tortue*? That head is to form the subject of our experiment. Ah, here is Harold with the remainder of the necessary apparatus.'

Harold appeared, holding a jug of water and a stout catapult with strings fashioned of powerful rubber. He walked down to the end of the corridor where he poured some water on to that part of the carpet surrounding the table, then he returned towards the landing, until he reached a piece of paper which had been tacked to the carpet. Upon this he took his stand, and then drew from his pocket an object, the nature of which the spectators were unable to make out. He fitted this object to the catapult, strained the instrument to its utmost and let go.

His first shot missed the head, but the missile, whatever it was, struck the wall behind with a reassuring thud. He took a second similar missile from his pocket and tried again. This time his aim was more accurate, and the missile struck the head with a splintering crash.

'A very good shot, my boy,' said Dr Priestley approvingly. 'We will now, with the exception of the inspector, adjourn to the study, where our coffee should be waiting for us. Harold will loosen the clamp by which the head was fixed to the table and bring it down for our examination. The inspector will remain on this landing, sitting in the chair which I have provided for the purpose, for a period of half an hour.'

They went downstairs, followed after a short interval by Harold bearing the head in his hand. He put this down in front of Oldland.

'Perhaps you will describe the injuries which the head has received?' said Dr Priestley.

'It is fractured, good and proper,' Oldland replied. 'If the beast to which this head belonged had been alive when Harold catapulted it, it would be dead now. A fracture like that could be relied upon to cause instantaneous death.'

'Does your examination of the fracture suggest the shape of the missile which caused it?'

'Yes, I think it does, to some extent' Oldland, replied. 'The missile wasn't round, to begin with. It seems to have been some hard object with several blunt edges. I'd make a guess that it was a roughly cubical object with a side of about one and a quarter inches.'

Hanslet laughed, a trifle scornfully. 'It's no good, professor,' he said. 'You've been trying to prove what we've known all along, that Mr Fransham might have been killed by some cubical object catapulted at him. But that couldn't have happened, for no missile was ever found. Both Jimmy and I are perfectly satisfied that no object could have been removed from the cloakroom without the knowledge of the police.'

Dr Priestley smiled tolerantly. 'If you are convinced of that there is no more to be said,' he replied. 'I trust you have not forgotten, superintendent, that you gave me full permission to investigate the death of Sir Godfrey Branstock?'

'No, I haven't forgotten that, Professor,' said Hanslet. 'I'm not interested in deaths where there can be no suspicion of foul play, and you remember what the doctor said in this very room directly after the inquest?'

Oldland nodded. 'There's no mystery about Branstock's death,' he said. 'What bee have you got in your bonnet now, I wonder, Priestley?'

'A bee which may perhaps produce the honey of wisdom,' Dr Priestley replied urbanely. 'On Saturday morning last, Harold and I paid a visit to No. 4 Cheveley Street on the pretext that I might be a potential purchaser. In the course of that visit we made several very interesting observations. Finally, we discovered that the garage belonging to No. 4 had been occupied by a motor-van as recently as the fifteenth of this month. I need not trouble you at this stage with the details of our investigations. It is sufficient to say that we have established the possibility that the van was in the garage at the time of Sir Godfrey's death on August 4.'

'But what connection can possibly exist between the motor-van and Sir Godfrey's death?' Hanslet demanded.

'That remains to be seen,' Dr Priestley replied. 'After our inspection of the premises, Harold made certain notes at my dictation. Perhaps you would like him to read them to you? The half hour which we appointed for the inspector's vigil has not yet expired.'

Harold produced his notes and read from them the paragraphs Dr Priestley had dictated on the previous Saturday evening. Hanslet and Oldland listened with polite attention, but when Harold had finished, the former shook his head.

'I can't see any possible connection between those facts of yours, professor,' he said. 'Nor do they seem to me to have any particular bearing upon Sir Godfrey's death.'

'I think I see what you're getting at, Priestley,' said Oldland. 'But I'm afraid it won't do. I was on the spot pretty early, you must remember, so I can claim to have some knowledge of this particular case. Your theory is that the van was left running in the garage and the exhaust fumes led into the cellar. It's quite true that the exhaust fumes of an internal combustion engine contain a large proportion of carbon dioxide. But they always contain a proportion of the much more poisonous carbon monoxide, and it is this gas which is responsible in cases of death from the inhalation of exhaust gases. As it happens, carbon monoxide produces definite changes in the blood and tissues, recognisable after death. In Branstock's case, no sign of these changes was visible, and I'm ready to stake my reputation that he died as the result of carbon dioxide and not carbon monoxide poisoning. That being the case, your theory of exhaust gases must be ruled out.'

'Did I say that it was my theory?' Dr Priestley asked mildly. 'In any case, I must of course bow to your superior medical knowledge. Ah, I see that the period of the inspector's vigil is now at an end. Perhaps, superintendent, you would now be good enough to go upstairs and, with the

241

help of the inspector, recover the missile which caused the injury to the call's head.'

As Hanslet left the room Oldland chuckled. 'What's the game you're playing with these two policemen?' he asked.

'It can hardly be described as a game,' Dr Priestley replied. 'It is a reconstruction of what I believe to have been the circumstances of Mr Fransham's death. Let us see whether our friends are now able to solve the mystery for themselves.'

Ten minutes elapsed before Hanslet and Jimmy returned. 'You and Mr Merefield have been up to some conjuring trick, professor,' exclaimed the former accusingly. 'We've searched that corridor from end to end and there's no sign of the object which Mr Merefield shot from his catapult. I don't believe—'

But Dr Priestley held up his hand. 'Disbelief is dangerous at times,' he said quietly. 'Will you tell us, inspector, exactly what happened during the half hour before the Superintendent joined you?'

'Nothing whatever happened, sir,' Jimmy replied. 'I didn't move out of my chair and nobody came near the corridor while I was sitting in it. I could see all the doors opening into the corridor and nobody could have entered it from the landing without actually pushing me aside.'

Dr Priestley nodded and turned to Hanslet. 'You are perfectly certain that your search was exhaustive, superintendent?' he asked.

'Of course it was,' Hanslet replied brusquely. 'There's nothing in the corridor under which the object could have been hidden. I even lifted the carpet, which is still wet in places from the water which Mr Merefield splashed on it just now. He must have picked up the object while he was undoing the clamp which fixed the head to the table.'

'Do you share that view, inspector?' Dr Priestley asked.

Jimmy shook his head. 'I don't altogether, sir,' he replied. 'I never took my eyes off him the whole time that he was unfixing the head.'

At a nod from Dr Priestley, Harold left the room, to return a few moments later with an object which he placed on the table beside the superintendent.

'That, I think, solves the mystery,' said Dr Priestley in a tone of satisfaction which he did not try to conceal.

Hanslet picked up the object and stared at it for a moment in stupefaction. 'Well, I'm damned!' he exclaimed.

'A lump of ice, taken from my own domestic refrigerator,' said Dr Priestley. 'I have demonstrated its power to inflict serious damage when projected with sufficient force. And your fruitless search has proved to us its power of disappearing after a short interval. Let us ask the inspector how far his experience of this evening throws light upon the death of Mr Fransham.'

'It makes it as clear as daylight, sir,' Jimmy replied promptly. 'I shall never forgive myself for being such an ass as not to think of a block of ice. The medical evidence that the wound had been caused by some cubical object ought to have put the idea into my head.'

'Can you now explain the technique of the murder?' Dr Priestley asked.

'Easily enough, sir. Somebody, the doctor, I suppose, took up his position in the field behind the wall and removed the loose brick. He watched through the hole until he saw Mr Fransham's head bent over the basin. Then he shot his block of ice through the cloakroom window. I decided at the time that if a missile had been used, it would in all probability have fallen into the basin, and that's just what happened. The basin was half full of warm water and the ice would have dissolved in this in a very few minutes. No wonder that Linton, Superintendent Yateley and I in turn failed to find it.'

'I feel sure that you have interpreted the facts correctly,' said Dr Priestley. 'I was anxious this evening to reconstruct the crime as closely as possible, but I was unable to contrive that the missile should fall into a basin of warm water. That was why I imposed a limit of half an hour before permitting the search for it. And that was why I instructed Harold to spill the water in your presence. Had you found moisture on the carpet where none had appeared before you might have unfairly guessed the secret.'

Hanslet laughed. 'Trust you not to forget anything professor,' he exclaimed. 'Well, thanks to you we've got the doctor laid by the heels at last. I'll see my chief first thing in the morning and I haven't a doubt that he'll decide upon an immediate arrest.'

But Dr Priestley shook his head. 'He will certainly not do so if he considers the facts in detail,' he replied. 'If Dr Thornborough was the criminal, whence did he procure the block of ice for his purpose?'

'Why, from his own refrigerator, of course. I see now what you were after when you asked me to make inquiries about those machines. I found out that there was one installed in the doctor's house but I didn't tumble to the significance of the fact.'

'Have you any information as to the doctor's movements that morning?'

'Yes, and pretty accurate information, too. He left his

244

house at nine o'clock and drove to his surgery in the town where he remained until nearly eleven. Then he started on his rounds, and didn't get back home until a few minutes after one.'

'Then he had no opportunity of extracting the ice from the refrigerator for at least four hours before the murder. In the absence of a properly contrived and insulated container, a small block of ice would not retain its cubical shape for anything like that time on a hot day. From our preliminary experiments Harold and I found that even if the blocks were wrapped in some non-conducting material, they would not retain their sharp edges for more than twenty minutes at the most. I feel convinced that in Mr Fransham's case the ice must have been removed from the refrigerator very shortly before the moment of the crime.'

'But where can it have come from?' Hanslet demanded.

'I do not think that the solution of that problem need present much difficulty,' Dr Priestley replied. 'You will remember that you left with Harold the paper upon which you had noted the location of certain refrigerators? At my request he has obtained particulars of the various types enumerated. These particulars include the size of the ice cubes made by each machine. Perhaps Harold you will repeat to us the results of your research.'

Harold took a piece of paper from his pocket. 'At No. 3 Cheveley Street, a "Storefresh" type AD is installed,' he read. 'This make and type produces ice cubes with a side of two inches. The Icicle type 15 which used to be installed at *Epidaurus* produces cubes with a side of two and a quarter inches. The "Snowflake" type Z7 installed at the cottage in Gunthorpe Road owned by Mr Whiteway produces cubes of a size of one and a half inches.'

'I may add that my own refrigerator, which is a "Cold Snap" produces cubes with a side of one and a quarter inches,' Dr Priestley remarked. 'Oldland just now correctly deduced the size and shape of the missile from his examination of the injury to the head. In the case of Mr Fransham the medical evidence suggested that the wound was caused by a cubical object of one and a half inches wide. And that, I think you will agree, points to the ice having been obtained from the refrigerator in the cottage nearby. Which at that time was occupied by Francis Willingdon.'

'But long ago we came to the conclusion that Willingdon could have had no possible motive for murdering Mr Fransham,' Hanslet objected. 'Why, it's most unlikely that the two men should ever have so much as heard of one another.'

'We will discuss the matter of motive later,' Dr Priestley replied. 'Let us first see whether the theory of Willingdon's guilt is tenable from the point of view of opportunity. We will begin with the letter received by Mr Fransham inviting him to lunch at *Epidaurus*. If that letter was not written by Dr Thornborough it must have been written by someone who had access to his stationery and to a sample of his signature which he could copy. We have been told that Willingdon visited the doctor in his consulting-room, where a supply of his stationery is kept in a rack. We have also been told that on this occasion the doctor gave him a prescription. The signature on this prescription would form an excellent model from which to copy the signature on the letter. Finally, there is the circumstance which to my mind, renders Willingdon's visit to the doctor extremely suspicious. Perhaps the inspector will remind us of the pretext he employed.'

'He had cut his hand chopping firewood,' Jimmy replied.

'Do people have occasion to cut firewood in June?' Dr Priestley inquired. 'Especially when the premises they occupy are heated throughout by gas or electricity, to the entire exclusion of all coal fires?'

'By jove, I never thought of that!' Hanslet exclaimed. 'You mean that he cut his hand deliberately so as to have an excuse for visiting the doctor?'

'So it would appear. In the course of his visit, he abstracted the copy of the *British Medical Journal*, the sheets of which the inspector found wrapped round the brick. He also discovered the internal arrangements of the doctor's house and the position of the cloakroom. We must now turn to his probable relations with Alfie Prince.

'I have no doubt that during Willingdon's periodic visits to Adderminster he had thoroughly observed his surroundings. He would thus have become aware of Alfie's appearance, and of his habits of spending his nights in the corner of the field. He perceived the use that could be made of Alfie's peculiarities. He himself could not enter or leave the field without exciting remark should he be seen. But Alfie's appearance in the neighbourhood would not surprise anyone.

'This I think explains Alfie's fantastic story of his encounter with the mysterious stranger. Willingdon required his coat, which in itself formed a most efficient disguise. Nobody in Adderminster seeing this famous coat would doubt that its wearer was Alfie, since it was inconceivable that anyone else should wear such a thing. Thus equipped it would only be necessary for Willingdon to imitate Alfie's gait in order to be mistaken for him. As, if my theory is correct, he actually was by Dr Thornborough. The coat having served his purpose, Willingdon deposited it in the corner of the field, in all probability early on Sunday morning, where it was subsequently found by the inspector. Willingdon strengthened his position by his description to the inspector of a wholly imaginary visit paid by Alfie to the cottage shortly after the crime.

'The incident of the cigarettes reveals the subtlety of Willingdon's mind. The superintendent has ascertained that these were ordered by postcard from the maker's shop in Knightsbridge. The postcard bore the Adderminster postmark and the date which showed that it had been posted on a Saturday. Since it was known that Mr Fransham was not in Adderminster on that date, it has been supposed that the postcard was written by Dr Thornborough, but it may equally have been written by Willingdon with the object of strengthening the case against the doctor. These cigarettes were of a most uncommon brand. If any of them were found in Alfie's possession the assumption would certainly be that they came from the box sent to Mrs Thornborough. But if Willingdon had this box sent, no doubt he purchased an additional supply of the same cigarettes from one of Black's other shops.'

Dr Priestley paused and Hanslet took the opportunity of putting in a question. 'But how on earth can Willingdon have known where Mr Fransham bought his tobacco?' he asked.

Dr Priestley smiled. 'Willingdon was remarkably well-informed on several unexpected subjects,' he replied. 'But let us consider the events which immediately preceded the murder. Willingdon had already loosened the brick, probably during the previous night, and provided himself with a powerful catapult. Willingdon knew that Mr Fransham would arrive at *Epidaurus* shortly before one o'clock, and he could safely assume that after his drive his first action would be to visit the cloakroom. A few minutes before one, therefore, he put on Alfie's coat and took two or three cubes of ice from the refrigerator. He had, I expect, lined one of his pockets with cotton wool or some similar substance in order to preserve the cubes as much as possible from the heat. Thus equipped, he took up his position behind the wall and awaited his opportunity. As soon as his object was achieved, he returned to the cottage and, while crossing the road, was observed by Dr Thornborough. He then took off the coat and was ready to answer any questions which might be put to him.'

'But what about the girl he had with him, sir?' Jimmy asked.

'The evidence of the lady's presence at the cottage on that particular Saturday fails to convince me,' Dr Priestley replied. 'There is no doubt that Willingdon wished to create the impression that he had taken the cottage for the entertainment of his lady friends. The subsequent discovery of feminine apparel supports this view. According to Mr Didcot, the house agent, a lady was seen with him in his car on the Friday afternoon. But there is no evidence to prove that he did not drive her back to London that night.'

'Well, I don't know what to make of all this, professor,' said Hanslet doubtfully. 'Unless Willingdon is a criminal lunatic, I utterly fail to see why he should have murdered Mr Fransham. But after what you've told me, I shall certainly send Jimmy up to Leeds to interview him.'

'A very sensible proceeding,' said Dr Priestley approvingly. 'I could suggest several questions which might be asked him. Why, for instance, his father's firm hired a motor-van from the Peregrine Transport Co., for a period of three weeks, during part of which time at least the van was accommodated in the garage belonging to No. 4 Cheveley Street. One moment, superintendent, before you make any comment. Harold, would you be good enough to repeat the conversation which you had with Mr Gilson last Saturday morning?'

Harold complied with this request, and the superintendent listened to his story with close attention. 'That's very extraordinary,' he said, 'and it certainly wants looking into. But I don't see that it connects young Willingdon in any way with Mr Fransham's death.'

'The connection is indirect, certainly,' Dr Priestley replied. 'But it seemed to me that the presence of this van in the garage belonging to No. 4 called for further investigation. The first and most obvious question was: How had the driver obtained access to the place? To that question there were many possible answers. If the van had been placed in the garage before Sir Godfrey Branstock's death, it might have been with his full knowledge and consent. He might have offered the use of the garage to the driver and given him the key. But if the proceedings had been as straightforward as this, why should the driver have found it necessary to make a false statement as to his movements to Mr Gilson?

'The alternative, and to my mind, the more likely answer to the question, was that some person had made use of the garage without authority. As I have already pointed out to Harold, there are several people who at one time or another could have provided themselves with a duplicate key to the front door of No. 4. Anyone of these people could have let himself into the house with such a key and abstracted the key of the garage from its hook.

'Bearing the possibility of unauthorised entry in mind, I could not fail to be struck by another curious circumstance. According to Stowell, the communicating door at the time he left the house had not been opened for years, and the bolts were so rusted that he made no attempt to move them. We have hitherto had no reason to doubt Stowell's statements. Yet when Harold and I visited the house on Saturday morning, we found that the bolts and locks of this door moved with remarkable ease. There is very little room for doubt that the door had been put in usable condition during the intervening period.

'Now, the sole purpose of that door is to form a passage between the house and the garage. If an unauthorised person had access to the house, it was only reasonable to suppose that it was he who had opened the door. But why had he done so? Certainly not to enable him to remove objects from the house to the van, for practically everything portable had already been taken away.

'I had better explain at this stage that I have never been altogether convinced that Sir Godfrey Branstock's death was accidental. I am perfectly ready to admit that accumulations of foul air in cellars due to escapes of sewer gas have occurred, and will probably occur again. But it seemed to me rather curious that Sir Godfrey's death should have taken place shortly after the vacation of No. 4. And with the incidents of the van and the communicating door in my mind, I began to seek for some alternative solution. With the help of a trade directory, I compiled a list of firms, and at my request Harold visited these in turn. Will you tell the superintendent what you discovered, my boy?'

'It wasn't until yesterday afternoon that I got on the track,' Harold replied. 'I had made inquiries at the offices of three or four firms, asking one particular question, and had received negative replies. My question was whether a cylinder or cylinders of carbon dioxide had been collected between July 26 and August 4 by a young man driving a thirty hundredweight Comet van, bearing the name of the Peregrine Transport Co.'

Oldland made a sudden movement in his chair, but said nothing.

'Eventually I found my way to a firm called Industrial Gases, Ltd.,' Harold continued. 'Their place is in Silvertown, and they deal in the various gases which are used for manufacturing purposes. I interviewed the manager and put my usual question to him. After some inquiry he told me that six cylinders of carbon dioxide had been collected from them on July 27 by a van which answered to my description. The empty cylinders had been returned on the morning of August 16.

'At my request the manager gave me further particulars; on July 23 he had received a telephone inquiry as to the current price of carbon dioxide. The caller asked for a quotation for six cylinders, and this was given him. He accepted this quotation, explaining that he had bought a small soda water factory in South London. He said that on the following Tuesday he would send a van to collect the cylinders, which would be paid for by the driver. On that day the driver appeared, paid for the cylinders in cash and signed a receipt in a book for them. The manager produced this book and showed me the signature, which appeared to be W. Coates. On August 16 the empty cylinders were brought back by the same van and driver. The deposit on the cylinders was returned to the driver, who gave a second signature similar to the first.'

'That's damned queer!' Hanslet exclaimed. 'But I'm blest if I can quite understand it now.'

'I will do my best to explain the theory that I have formed,' Dr Priestley replied. 'In the first place, Harold's investigations have established the possibility that a van containing six fully charged cylinders of carbon dioxide was standing in the garage belonging to No. 4 at the time of Sir Godfrey Branstock's death. The driver of that van had access to the house and could therefore open the communicating door and pass through at his pleasure.

'The distance from the back of the garage, through the harness room and the connecting door to the cellar door of No. 4, is approximately twenty feet. In the harness-room Harold and I observed a length of stove pipe and a bend which would fit on to the end of this. The cellar door is in such a dilapidated state that the stove pipe could be pushed through the gap in the panel. It would then reach to the bottom of the cellar, leaving the bend on a level with the basement floor.

'My theory is that the van driver drove into the garage very shortly after he had collected the cylinders, placed the stove pipe in the position which I have described, and then awaited his opportunity. It was known to several people that Sir Godfrey Branstock proposed to give a dinner party on his birthday, which occurred on Wednesday, August 4. Following his invariable custom, he would go down to the cellar that evening between seven and eight o'clock and select the wines he required. The man, whom we will continue to call the driver since we do not at present know his name, determined to take advantage of this.

'It was perfectly easy for him to fill the cellar of No. 3 with a lethal concentration of carbon dioxide. In order to avoid the necessity of moving the heavy cylinders, he probably led a piece of rubber tubing from the bend of the stove pipe to the nozzle of each cylinder in turn. He thus directed a stream of carbon dioxide into the cellar of No. 4. The gas rapidly found its own level in the cellar of No. 3 through the aperture in the dividing wall.

'I have no doubt that he was actually in the basement of No. 4 when Sir Godfrey entered the cellar of No. 3. If so, he could probably hear his victim's footsteps descending the stone stairs. When he failed to hear ascending footsteps, he would know that his plan had been successful.

'But he had a further point to consider. Sooner or later a search would be made for Sir Godfrey, and his body would be discovered. If the cellars were left full of gas, other victims would possibly succumb, and an immediate investigation would probably follow. That, I think, is the significance of the buzzing noise, which in my opinion was actually heard by Mrs Quinton. I observed an electric point in the basement of No. 4, close to the cellar door. I think it extremely probable that the driver had connected some sort of exhaust fan to this point. As soon as he was satisfied that Sir Godfrey was dead, he applied this fan to the end of the stove pipe and by this means drew the greater part of the gas out of the cellars. He then returned the stove pipe to the harness-room and closed the communicating door. Unless the garage of No. 4 were to be searched, no trace of his crime remained.'

There was a silence of a few seconds after Dr Priestley finished speaking. Then Oldland spoke. 'That's a damned ingenious theory,' he said. 'And I'm bound to say that it fits in with the facts as far as we know them. It gets over the difficulty of the gas finding its way from the sewer through the debris which choked the gully. And it also accounts for the dust on the floor on the cellar of No. 4 not having been disturbed for ages. There's only one possible criticism that I can make. When I went down into the cellar of No. 3 that evening I didn't detect any trace of sulphuretted hydrogen. Nor did the Home Office analyst next day. But the Borough Surveyor did when he inspected the cellar of No. 4 on the following Monday. How do you account for that?'

'By the fact that the inquest had been held on the Friday,' Dr Priestley replied quietly.

Oldland stared at him. 'What the devil has that got to do with it?' he demanded.

'Just this. The driver had not thought of sewer gas as a possible explanation until the coroner suggested it. But the idea having been put into his head, he saw the advantages of adopting it in its entirety. So, before the time of the Borough Surveyor's visit, he contrived that there should be a trace of sulphuretted hydrogen in the atmosphere of the cellars. Perhaps I had better explain for the benefit of the superintendent that the production of sulphuretted hydrogen is an exceedingly simple matter. If he will place some ferrous sulphide in a saucer and pour a little dilute sulphuric acid over it he will be rewarded by the characteristic aroma of the gas.'

'I'll take your word for it, professor,' said Hanslet. 'According to what I've been told, the stuff smells abominably. What I want to know is why this man you call the driver left the van in the garage for such a long time after Sir Godfrey's death?'

'For two reasons. First, because he had nowhere else to put it. He had hired the van for three weeks, not knowing, when he did so, exactly when his opportunity would occur. If he had returned it before that period had expired, questions might have been asked. Second, because he did not care to take the risk of removing the van until he was assured that all inquiries into Sir Godfrey's death were safely at an end.'

'That sounds reasonable enough,' Hanslet agreed. 'Now let me see if I've got this right, professor. According to your theory, this young chap Francis Willingdon murdered both Mr Fransham and Sir Godfrey Branstock.'

'I feel convinced that both murders were carried out by the same hand,' Dr Priestley replied.

'But what on earth was his object? I suppose it is possible that in some way we haven't yet discovered, he derives a benefit of some kind from one of these murders. But I utterly refuse to believe that he can have profited from both of them. All our investigations have failed to establish more than a mere acquaintance between the two men.'

'I hardly think that we are yet in a position to discuss the question of motive,' Dr Priestley replied, with a faint smile. 'But I think you will agree that circumstances warrant a further interrogation of Francis Willingdon.'

'Oh yes, we'll interrogate him right enough,' said Hanslet grimly. 'Since Jimmy knows him already he'd better have the job. He'll make it his business to go up to Leeds by the very first train in the morning.'

CHAPTER VIII

Jimmy reached Leeds shortly after eleven o'clock next morning and made his way at once to the police station. Here he explained his errand to the inspector on duty and asked his advice.

'Francis Willingdon?' the inspector replied. 'Oh yes, your people asked us some time ago to keep an eye on him. Our information is that he's kept his nose pretty hard to the grindstone since that little escapade of his two or three months ago. He's working in his father's office, and he hasn't left this town since he came back from London about the middle of June.'

'Are you quite sure of that?' Jimmy asked. 'We have very good reason to believe that he was in London on at least one day in July and two in August.'

The inspector laughed. 'I don't know what your reasons may be, but I fancy that our information's sound enough. One of our men is on particularly good terms with the cook at the Howdahs, where the family live. And you may be sure that he hasn't any difficulty in keeping himself abreast of the domestic arrangements.'

'Well, that's as may be,' said Jimmy doubtfully. 'Anyway I should like a few words with him if you've no objection. Where is this office you talk about?'

'Not more than a couple of hundred yards away. I'll ring up and find out if he's there, if you like. For the matter of that, I'll ask him to come round here and see me. I know him slightly and he won't think that there's anything unusual up.'

Jimmy agreed to this course. The inspector put a room at his disposal and went away to put through the necessary call. A few minutes later he returned, accompanied by a pale-faced and immaculately-dressed young man. 'Let me introduce you to Mr Francis Willingdon,' he said.

Jimmy stood up and looked searchingly at the new arrival. Several weeks had passed since his one and only short interview with Francis Willingdon in the cottage at Adderminster. During that period his duties had brought him into close contact with so many different types that he hardly remembered the details of Willingdon's appearance. Only the noticeable pallor of the young man's face aroused a chord of memory.

'Good-morning, Mr Willingdon,' Jimmy said briskly. 'I expect you remember our last meeting, don't you?'

Willingdon shook his head languidly. 'You'll forgive me, I know,' he replied. 'My mental processes refuse to react to the stimulus of your features. Didn't somebody once say that memory was a treacherous jade? I really can't locate your portrait in the gallery of my acquaintances. Perhaps upon some jovial occasion you were a boon companion of my cups?'

'Perhaps my name will recall me to your memory,' said Jimmy quietly. 'I am Inspector Waghorn from Scotland Yard.'

'Bless my soul!' Willingdon exclaimed, 'the very fact of meeting you in a police station might have made me suspect something of the kind. And what message has the guardian of the law for the humble transgressor?'

Jimmy frowned at this untimely levity. 'In the first place, Mr Willingdon, I have to warn you that any statement you may make may be used subsequently as evidence,' he said sharply.

Willingdon opened his eyes wide at this, but it seemed to Jimmy that his equanimity remained undisturbed. 'How too terribly thrilling!' he exclaimed. 'Evidence in support of what, may I ask?'

'Of murder,' Jimmy replied swiftly. 'Of the murder of Mr Robert Fransham in June last and of Sir Godfrey Branstock three weeks ago.'

Willingdon rubbed his nose thoughtfully with his forefinger. 'You've mistaken your environment, inspector,' he said. 'This is Leeds, not Delphos. There may be cells in this police station but I very much doubt that they're prophetic. And I'm certainly not the pale-eyed priest. As for the defunct gentlemen you mention, I never had the honour of their acquaintance. But I seem to remember the name of Fransham. Wasn't he the bloke who was knocked on the head in the cloakroom of his nephew's house in the country somewhere?'

Jimmy made a gesture of impatience. 'That won't do,' he said sternly. 'You know very well that you were living in Adderminster at the time of Mr Fransham's death, and that I interviewed you on the subject next day.'

'Living in Adderminster!' Willingdon exclaimed. 'You've got hold of the jammy end of the spoon this time, inspector. I assure you on my honour as a faithful beer-drinker that I never heard of the place in my life. Wait a minute, though. Yes, I have.'

'How did you come to hear of it?'

'Through a silly joke played on me by some facetious ass. Without rending the veil which covers my murky past, I may whisper into your sympathetic ear that a brief idyll of light-hearted dalliance led to my temporary banishment from this salubrious city. Shortly after my return I received a package, in which was enclosed a letter from a house agent in this place of yours. The package contained an article of lingerie to which clung a faint memory of all the scents of Araby. And the letter suggested that I—I mark you, the innocent blue-eyed boy—had left this flimsy but compromising garment in a residence which I was alleged to have inhabited.'

'What did you do when you received this package?'

'Burnt the lot,' replied Willingdon cheerfully. 'If my respected parents had seen it they might have indefinitely postponed the slaughter of the fatted calf. And as it happens I'm particularly partial to *Wiener shnitzel*.'

'Do you deny that during your absence from Leeds you took a cottage at Adderminster, which you occupied during the weekends?'

'Most emphatically I deny it. I never left London the whole time I was away from here. I dwelt, not in marble halls, but in stuffy rooms in Bloomsbury. To tell the shocking truth, I was by way of being the prodigal son just then, and my stern but just sire kept me uncomfortably short of cash. During the weekends I consumed not the husks that the swine did eat but the imported mutton that my landlady did boil. I don't suppose that there was much to choose between the two diets in the way of dryness.'

'Can you give me the address of these rooms?'

'Rather, I'm never likely to forget it. Does the released criminal ever forget the address of Dartmoor? 18, Limber Street. It's a turning off Gower Street. And the landlady's name is Mrs Peacock. Though why, I never could discover.'

'Where were you on Saturday and Sunday, 12th and 13th June?'

Willingdon flung out his hands in a deprecatory gesture. 'Search me!' he exclaimed. 'I'm not one of those people who can remember everything they did on every day of the year. While I was in London I was supposed to be employed in our London office, but, of course, that was closed during the weekends. And by the middle of June I was so dead broke that there was nothing for it but to stay put and twiddle my thumbs. Wait a minute. That must have been the last weekend I spent in London. Yes, I distinctly remember staying in those ghastly rooms all the time.'

'Why did you have your correspondence addressed to Harlow's Hotel?'

'Not guilty, my lud,' Willingdon replied. 'Never heard of the place. I'll admit that while funds lasted I did stagger round the town a bit in the evenings frequenting hotels and places where men drink. I made the acquaintance of several fellow sinners in the process.'

'Did you tell any of them the reason for your being in London?'

'Well, you know, one does get a bit confidential towards

the end of an evening. The ostensible reason for my absence from the paternal roof was that satisfying and comprehensive word, study. People like Mrs Peacock, no doubt, regarded me as an assiduous and promising student. What of, I don't know. But some of my merry comrades of the tankard got the truth out of me. Though it might have caused the eyebrows of the prudish to vibrate disapprovingly, it did not seem to offend their susceptibilities.'

'Did you meet a Miss Nancy Lanchester while you were in London?'

Willingdon shook his head slowly and deliberately. 'You may think it ungallant of me, inspector, but I studiously avoided the company of the female sex. Not the witching arms of Dido for this pious Æneas, thank you, just then. The fact is that I was in the process of being extricated from a particularly sticky spider's web, and I wasn't inclined to enter any more parlours.'

'Can you tell me the names of any of these acquaintances of yours?'

'Quite honestly, inspector, I can't. I could recite a string of Christian names as long as your arm, but that wouldn't help either of us. I didn't, so to speak, demand their visiting cards. All that concerned me was to learn the distinguishing label by which they were known to the girl behind the bar. Tom, Dick, Harry or even Absalom. So long as they answered to one or the other it was good enough for me. I wasn't likely to drift into the Orestes and Pylades business with any of them.'

Jimmy tried the effect of a sudden change of subject. 'Why did your firm hire a thirty-hundredweight van from the Peregrine Transport Company of Islington for three weeks from July 26 last?' he asked.

But Willingdon betrayed no uneasiness whatever at this question. 'We didn't,' he replied promptly. 'As it happens, the supervision of our firm's transport is my particular job. We have several lorries and vans of our own and it doesn't often happen that we have to hire. When we do, we call upon a transport company in this town.'

'Where were you on August 4, last, the Wednesday after Bank Holiday?'

'Here in the office. We opened again after the holiday that day. And I spent the whole evening at home, I remember, playing billiards with my guv'nor and a couple of his friends.'

'When were you last in London?'

'I left London on June 16, I do happen to remember that date. And I haven't been back there since. There must be a dozen people at least in this town who can prove the truth of that statement.'

Jimmy thanked Willingdon for his courtesy in coming to see him, and a few minutes later the young man left the police station. With the help of the local inspector, Jimmy spent the rest of the day in verifying his last statements. By the end of the evening he was fully convinced that he had had no opportunity of visiting London during the last couple of months.

However, there remained the question of Willingdon's whereabouts at the time of Mr Fransham's murder. Jimmy went back to London and on Friday morning made his way to Limber Street and interviewed Mrs Peacock. She remembered Mr Willingdon's visit perfectly well. He had been a little bit wild during the first week or two he had spent with her; stayed out disgracefully late at night and that sort of thing. But later he had settled down to more regular habits. She was emphatic in her assurance that he had never spent a whole night away from the rooms. And she was equally certain that he had hardly gone out of doors at all during the last weekend that he was with her, June 12 and 13. As for his correspondence, he had received about half a dozen letters a week, all addressed to Limber Street.

Feeling completely baffled, Jimmy felt that his only course was a further interview with Dr Priestley. Hanslet concurred in this view and they sought permission to visit the professor that evening. This was readily granted and shortly after nine o'clock they found themselves in the familiar study.

Dr Priestley seemed unusually affable. 'I am very glad to welcome you both again so soon,' he said. 'I assume that you have returned from Leeds, inspector? Were you successful in eliciting any information from Francis Willingdon?'

'I was sir, but it was nearly all negative. I'm quite satisfied that Willingdon was not on the spot when either Mr Fransham or Sir Godfrey were murdered. If he's guilty he must have had a confederate who impersonated him.'

'Have you any clue to the identity of this confederate?'

'Not the slightest, sir. But the Willingdon whom I saw yesterday can't have been the Willingdon who took the cottage at Adderminster. When I called at the cottage at the time of Mr Fransham's murder, I'm afraid I didn't observe the occupant very closely. I didn't for a moment think that he had any connection with the crime and I only called upon him on the off-chance that he had seen or heard something which would help me. Two things about him did impress me, however. The unusual paleness of his face and his ridiculous and rather affected manner of speaking.

'When I saw the man at Leeds I didn't recognise him. But it didn't seem to me that there was anything very extraordinary about that. I had only seen the man at the cottage for a few minutes in a comparatively dark room. He was then very carelessly dressed, and this man's appearance was unusually smart. The difference of light and clothes might have accounted for my failing to recognise him. But the two characteristics I remembered best—the pale face and the queer manner of speech—were there in both cases. On the evidence of appearance alone, I couldn't even now decide for certain whether or not it was the same man I interviewed on both occasions.'

'Then why are you convinced of the existence of a confederate?' Dr Priestley asked.

'Because, sir, if Willingdon was at Mrs Peacock's in Limber Street when Mr Fransham was murdered, he couldn't have been behind the wall at Adderminster at the same time. Nor, since he has never left Leeds during the past couple of months, could he have been in the cellar of No. 4 Cheveley Street at the time of Sir Godfrey's murder.'

'In other words, you believe in the existence of two Francis Willingdons—the false and the true? But why should you believe that they were in association?'

'They must have been, sir. Otherwise, how could the false Willingdon have passed himself off so successfully as the true?'

'Probably because they moved in entirely different circles,' Dr Priestley replied. 'But I should like to hear the details of your conversation with the true Willingdon.'

Jimmy described his interview in the Leeds Police Station

and the investigations which he had made subsequently. Dr Priestley listened to this and smiled when the inspector came to the end of his account.

'The true Willingdon displays the ingenuousness of youth,' he said. 'It requires very little stretch of the imagination to picture him during the first few days of his stay in London. He had left his home under something of a cloud. He probably felt very lonely among total strangers and was only too ready to pour his story into the first sympathetic ear.

'One of those in whom he confided decided to adopt his personality for his own ends. We may assume, I think, that the false Willingdon was in appearance not utterly unlike the true; he was at all events approximately of the same height, build and age. His first step was to establish himself at Harlow's Hotel, but nowhere else in London, in his identity as Francis Willingdon. The chances that the true Francis Willingdon would visit the same hotel were too remote for consideration. It would be simple enough for the false Willingdon to post letters to himself addressed to the hotel.

'That it was the false Willingdon who took the cottage in that name I have no doubt whatever. No one had any reason to question his identity. He endeavoured to disguise the real purpose for which he had taken it. His real object was the murder of Mr Fransham. We have already outlined in theory the method which he adopted.'

'But why did he want to murder him, professor?' Hanslet asked. 'It seems to me that, whether we are dealing with the true Willingdon or the false, we are still up against that question of motive.'

'Wait a minute,' Dr Priestley replied. 'Let us trace the

further career of the false Willingdon. He dropped this disguise, if such it can be called, immediately he left Adderminster for the last time. He ran the risk, of course, that you might some day meet the true Willingdon, inspector. But he must have thought that extremely unlikely, and in any case he had provided against it to the best of his ability. A little cosmetic carefully applied would simulate, sufficiently well to withstand scrutiny in a darkened room, the pallor which he had noticed in the original. And a trick of speech is very easily acquired by anyone possessing an attentive ear. His success in this matter is shown by your own confession, that on appearance alone you could not decide between the false and the true.

'He resumed the disguise, or possibly only the name, when it came to making preparations for the murder of Sir Godfrey. This I think was an error of judgment, though it must have seemed to him a very trifling one. It was most improbable that the death of Sir Godfrey would ever become the subject of investigation. Even if it did, the significance of the van in connection with it might easily have been overlooked. The man who hired the van had to pass himself off as the representative of some firm, and the name of Willingdon & Son occurred to him naturally. Since the expenses of hiring the van were paid in advance, it was highly improbable that the Peregrine Transport Co. would make any inquiries.

'And now, superintendent, we are in a position to explore the question of motive. Since it was evident from the first that Dr and Mrs Thornborough were the only people to benefit by the death of Mr Fransham, it was only logical to suppose as you did that one or other of them was guilty. Fortunately, I think, you were unable to supply the essential piece of evidence, the method in which the crime was committed. It did not take me very long to deduce the nature of the missile which had caused Mr Fransham's death. But had I revealed this to you before I did, you would, I feel certain, have arrested the doctor without further investigation. Even if no grave miscarriage of justice had ensued, needless agony would have been caused to innocent people.'

'I'm still not altogether convinced of the doctor's innocence,' Hanslet muttered.

'Because you are obsessed with the idea of a direct personal motive. I suggested to you some days ago that an investigation of Sir Godfrey's murder might throw light upon the death of Mr Fransham. Surely you must see now that the removal of Mr Fransham was an essential preliminary to the successful attempt upon Sir Godfrey's life.'

But Hanslet was not inclined to commit himself. 'I'd like you to make that quite clear, professor,' he replied.

'I will endeavour to do so. I begin with the assumption that the eventual aim of the false Willingdon was the death of Sir Godfrey. You have heard my theory of the means he took to achieve this end. But in order to carry out the scheme which he had formulated, he had to contrive that No. 4 Cheveley Street should be vacated.

'The situation regarding No. 4 was this: In the ordinary course of events, Mr Fransham's lease would have expired at Christmas this year. At the time of his death it was still doubtful whether or not he would renew it. He had, so far as we know, come to no final decision on the matter.

'But in any case I suspect the false Willingdon could not afford to wait until Christmas. It was essential to his purpose that Sir Godfrey should die by the middle of

August. He had, therefore, to dispose of Mr Fransham at least a couple of months before that date, in order that No. 4 should be vacated in time.

'This then was the true motive for Mr Fransham's murder. The false Willingdon felt no animosity towards him, nor had he any prospect of deriving pecuniary advantage from his death. If he could have seen any other way of securing the vacation of No. 4 he would probably have taken it. No man, even the most callous, commits a murder if it seems to him unnecessary. But I think we may conjecture that the false Willingdon was in such desperate straits that he dare not hesitate at a preliminary murder to achieve his end.

'He ran very little risk of detection, for his motive was completely hidden, and would have remained so had the true cause of Sir Godfrey's death not been discovered. It would be ridiculous to arrest, on a charge of murder, a man to whom no conceivable motive could be attributed. The fact that he had been sailing under false colours might have been revealed, but it is very doubtful whether his true identity would have transpired. The search would have been among those who had been associated with Mr Fransham, and not among those who had surrounded Sir Godfrey. Had we all been contented to accept the verdict of the coroner's jury in the case of Sir Godfrey the murderer of Mr Fransham would never have been found.'

'Hold on a minute, professor,' Hanslet exclaimed. 'So far as I know, he hasn't been detected now.'

'Surely there can be little doubt concerning the identity of the false Willingdon,' Dr Priestley replied. 'Let us briefly review what we already know about him.

'The fact that he rented the cottage in Gunthorpe Road

shows that he knew that Mr Fransham was a comparatively frequent visitor to *Epidaurus*. The forged letter shows that he was aware of the relationship between Mr Fransham and the Thornboroughs. He knew Mrs Thornborough's Christian name, but was not recognised by Dr Thornborough when he consulted him professionally. He knew that Mr Fransham kept a car, for the forged letter expressly suggests that he should drive from London to Adderminster. He knew where Mr Fransham was in the habit of purchasing his tobacco.

'Again, the false Willingdon possessed a fund of knowledge regarding Sir Godfrey Branstock. He knew of his habit of going down to the cellar in person before dinner, to select his wines. The date of his preparations suggests that he knew that Sir Godfrey would do so on August 4, when a dinner party was to be given at No. 3 Cheveley Street. In order to complete these preparations, he must have had the opportunity of securing a duplicate key to No. 4 at some time prior to July 27.

'These are the principal items of knowledge which we can attribute with some certainty to the false Willingdon. And I maintain that they are just the items of knowledge which we should expect one person and one person only to possess.'

Hanslet and Jimmy exchanged a swift glance before the former spoke. 'Anthony Mayland!' he exclaimed.

'Precisely,' Dr Priestley replied. 'I understand, superintendent, that you have never seen the man who called himself Francis Willingdon.'

'No, for he was supposed to be back in Leeds before I took over the case,' Hanslet replied. 'I didn't think him of sufficient importance to go up there to interview him, so I left him to the supervision of the Leeds Police.'

'Who, not unnaturally, concentrated their attention on the true Willingdon,' Dr Priestley remarked. 'And you, inspector, have never seen Anthony Mayland?'

'No, sir, I haven't,' Jimmy replied. 'When I was concerned with the case, there was nothing whatever to connect him with the murder of Mr Fransham.'

Dr Priestley smiled. 'Nor would there ever have been but for my incurably suspicious nature. Now let us endeavour to form a theory to account for this double crime on the assumption of Mayland's guilt.

'We have first to consider the relationship which existed between Mayland and Sir Godfrey Branstock. The latter had, to all intents and purposes, adopted Mayland as his own son, as is shown by the terms of the first will. I admit that at present we have only Mayland's statement as to the existence of this will, but it is unlikely that he would have misled us in a matter which could be verified by reference to Mr Emscott, Sir Godfrey's solicitor.

'After his mother's death, Mayland became Sir Godfrey's sole heir. He had no doubt grown accustomed to the situation, and had not taken into account the possibility of his stepfather marrying again.

'We shall probably never know what passed between Sir Godfrey and Mayland after the announcement of the former's engagement to Miss Nancy Lanchester. The terms of his second will suggest that Sir Godfrey thought that since Mayland had been established in a profession at his expense, he was amply provided for. In any case, Mayland must have guessed that on his stepfather's second marriage his own prospects as his sole heir would be at an end. He therefore decided to murder his stepfather before this event could take place.

'I need hardly point out how exactly Mayland fulfils the conditions of knowledge of which I spoke just now. He had at one time lived in Sir Godfrey's house, where he had met Mrs Thornborough before her marriage. He would, of course, have become aware of her husband's name and where they lived. He would also know that Mr Fransham was in the habit of visiting them. Although he was well acquainted with Mrs Thornborough, it is probable that he had never met her husband, for we have been told that the doctor very rarely visited No. 4 Cheveley Street. From his own observations or from Sir Godfrey's conversation, he would learn that Mr Fransham kept a car. Mayland himself told the superintendent that Sir Godfrey had been recommended to Black's shop in Knightsbridge by Mr Fransham, who therefore presumably bought his own tobacco there.

'Since Mayland for many years resided in his stepfather's house and was a frequent visitor there subsequently, there is no need to labour the matter of his knowledge of Sir Godfrey's habits. But we may profitably examine his opportunity of providing himself with a duplicate key by which to gain admission to No. 4. According to his own statement, which again is almost certainly true, Sir Godfrey gave him the original keys shortly after the house was vacated in order that he might inspect it with a view to modernisation. While the keys were thus in his possession no doubt he had a duplicate cut.

'A further point concerns the termination of the lease of No. 4 by agreement. To anybody but Mayland the murder of Mr Fransham might have proved ineffectual. Sir Godfrey might well have refused to terminate the lease before it expired in due course on Christmas day. In which case Mr

272

Fransham's executors might have occupied it until then, or sub-let it for the remainder of the period. But Mayland, as an architect, was in a position to represent to his stepfather the desirability of taking advantage of Mr Fransham's death, and of terminating the lease as soon as possible so that the proposed alterations could be carried out in time to secure a fresh tenant in the New Year.

'Finally, you will not fail to have realised that the method employed in the murder of Sir Godfrey Branstock depended entirely upon the existence of the aperture between the two cellars. And, surely, Mayland was more likely to be aware of this than anyone else. He had supervised the alterations to No. 3 and in all probability he made the discovery while the work was being carried out. It meant nothing to him then, but he remembered it later when he was seeking the means of taking his stepfather's life.'

Dr Priestley, having come to the end of his explanation, leant back in his chair and closed his eyes wearily. His interest in the matter was at an end. The problem had been solved to his own satisfaction; he had no concern in bringing the criminal to justice.

The two policemen rightly interpreted his silence as a sign of dismissal and quietly took their departure.

CHAPTER IX

On the following morning, Saturday, August 28, eleven weeks after Mr Fransham's murder, two taxis pulled up at the door of No. 3 Cheveley Street. Hanslet descended from the first and rang the bell. The door was opened by Grace, the parlourmaid, who immediately recognised her visitor.

'Is Mr Mayland at home?' the superintendent asked.

'Yes, sir, he's in the study,' Grace replied with a welcoming smile. 'If you'll come in, sir, I'll tell him you're here.'

A few moments later Hanslet was shown into the study and Mayland rose to greet him. 'Hullo, superintendent, back again?' he said. 'What can I do for you this time?'

'I want you to meet two friends of mine,' Hanslet replied. 'They're waiting in a taxi outside and I should like you to come and speak to them for a moment.'

Mayland glanced at him sharply. 'Not Nancy Lanchester or any of her friends, I hope?' he asked.

'So far as I know, my friends are not even acquainted with her,' Hanslet replied.

'In that case I'll certainly go out and speak to them,' said Mayland.

The two left the house by the front door, and Hanslet led the way to the second taxi. The blinds were pulled down, and Mayland could not see the occupants of the vehicle until Hanslet flung open the door.

'Miss Bayne, whom I think you have met before at Harlow's Hotel,' he said. 'And my colleague, Inspector Waghorn, whose visit to you at Adderminster you may possibly remember.'

Mayland recoiled swiftly but Hanslet's hand was already on his arm. As he did so, Miss Bayne's voice greeted him from the interior of the taxi. 'Why, Frank!' she exclaimed. 'I never expected to meet you. Why haven't you been to see me all this time?'

Mayland went deadly pale. 'There's some mistake here,' he stammered. 'My name isn't Frank.'

'But you told me yourself that it was, Mr Willingdon,' Jimmy replied quietly. 'Don't you remember, that day in the cottage in Gunthorpe Road?'

'I think you had better come with me, Mr Mayland,' said Hanslet.

Mayland allowed himself to be led unresistingly into the first taxi. Hanslet took his seat beside him and the taxi drove to the police station.

During the period of remand ordered by the magistrate, the case against Mayland was swiftly built up. He was confronted with the true Willingdon, who recognised him at once. During his stay in London, Willingdon had met him several times at a bar in Leicester Square, and had learnt that he was known there as Tony. They had had several conversations together, and Willingdon remembered that his new friend had been very sympathetic over the details of his misfortune. He had given him a full account of the circumstances, and Tony had told him that if ever he wanted a small loan to help eke out his meagre allowance, he had only to ask for it. But curiously enough, once Tony had received his confidences, he had never reappeared at their meeting place.

Dr Thornborough identified Mayland as the patient who had called upon him under the name of Willingdon. On being questioned by Hanslet he gave further particulars of the incident. The wound though not very serious had bled freely, and some of the blood had dried on the surrounding parts of the hand. The doctor had taken his patient into the cloakroom and washed his hand there before applying the dressing. After the dressing had been applied, Mayland had been left alone in the consulting-room for a few moments while the doctor went to look for his pen in order to write out the prescription. On the occasion of Mayland's call Mrs Thornborough was not in the house, having gone out to lunch with Colonel and Mrs Exbury.

Mr Didcot the house agent recognised in Mayland the tenant of the cottage in Gunthorpe Road.

The exertions of the police unearthed a lady who declared that her name was Gabrielle Sutherland. According to her she had, some time during April or May, made the acquaintance of a young gentleman whom she knew as Frank or Frankie. This acquaintance had rapidly ripened, and she had spent three weekends with him in a cottage at a place called Adderminster. On each occasion Frank had driven her down on Friday afternoon or evening and brought her back to London on Monday morning. A fourth weekend had been intended, and Frank had, as usual, driven her down to Adderminster. But on reaching the cottage he had found a letter waiting for him which announced that his mother was arriving on the morrow to spend the day. It was agreed between them that Miss Sutherland's presence might be somewhat difficult to explain, so she had returned to London by train that same evening. The date of this annoying occurrence was established as June 11. She had not seen Frank since, but she recognised him immediately when she set eyes upon Anthony Mayland.

Investigation threw a revealing light upon Mayland's circumstances. It was perfectly true that he was a qualified architect, and had an office in an imposing building in Kingsway. But the most painstaking inquiries failed to discover that he had any clients. He appeared to have lived entirely upon a generous allowance made to him by his stepfather. But this had not sufficed him, and he had run heavily into debt. His creditors had begun to press him and only Sir Godfrey Branstock's death had enabled him to stave them off. According to Mr Emscott, who confirmed Mayland's story of the two wills, Sir Godfrey during the last few months of his life had begun to suspect that his stepson was wasting his time, and not attending so assiduously to business as he made out.

In the course of a search of Mayland's office, a typewriter was found and handed over to the experts at Scotland Yard. According to them it was in all probability the machine on which had been typed the letter found in Mr Fransham's pocket, and also the postcard to Black's ordering the cigarettes. In the office were also found two plans, showing the basement and cellar of No. 3 and No. 4 respectively. On the plan relating to No. 3 the connection between the two cellars was clearly shown.

Mr Gilson, of the Peregrine Transport Co., attended an identification parade, in the course of which he picked out Mayland as the self-styled representative of Messrs. Ernest Willingdon & Sons. He recognised him as the man who had taken out the van on July 26 and returned it on August 16. The manager of Industrial Gases, Ltd., also attended this parade, and identified Mayland as the purchaser of the six cylinders of carbon dioxide.

A search of Mayland's rooms resulted in the discovery of the key of the garage belonging to No. 4 Cheveley Street.

Mayland was duly committed for trial, and in spite of the earnest contention of his counsel that the evidence against him was purely circumstantial, was found guilty and condemned to death.

THE END

By the same author

Death at Breakfast

'One always embarks on a John Rhode book with a great feeling of security. One knows that there will be a sound plot, a well-knit process of reasoning and a solidly satisfying solution with no loose ends or careless errors of fact.'
DOROTHY L. SAYERS in *THE SUNDAY TIMES*

Victor Harleston awoke with uncharacteristic optimism. Today he would be rich at last. Half an hour later, he gulped down his breakfast coffee and pitched to the floor, gasping and twitching. When the doctor arrived, he recognised instantly that it was a fatal case of poisoning and called in Scotland Yard.

Despite an almost complete absence of clues, the circumstances were so suspicious that Inspector Hanslet soon referred the evidence to his friend and mentor, Dr Lancelot Priestley, whose deductions revealed a diabolically ingenious murder that would require equally fiendish ingenuity to solve.

'*Death at Breakfast* is full of John Rhode's specialties: a new and excellently ingenious method of murder, a good story, and a strong chain of deduction.'
DAILY TELEGRAPH

By the same author

Mystery at Olympia

'*Readers know well what to expect from John Rhode, and in this story they will not be disappointed . . . The tale is neat and clear and logical, and there are no loose ends.*'
TIMES LITERARY SUPPLEMENT

The new Comet was fully expected to be the sensation of the annual Motor Show at Olympia. Suddenly, in the middle of the dense crowd of eager spectators, an elderly man lurched forward and collapsed in a dead faint. But Nahum Pershore had not fainted. He was dead, and it was his death that was to provide the real sensation of the show.

A post-mortem revealed no visible wound, no serious organic disorder, no evidence of poison. Doctors and detectives were equally baffled, and the more they investigated, the more insoluble the puzzle became. Even Dr Lancelot Priestley's un-rivalled powers of deduction were struggling to solve this case.

'Mystery at Olympia *is, of course, admirably pieced together. One expects that of Mr Rhode; but it also marks an advance in the psychological treatment of his characters.*'
ILLUSTRATED LONDON NEWS